Four exits to smoke

2015 Version

By the same author

Georges Vandine – a novel, revised edition 2011

Your Skyward Eyes – a poetry collection,
33 bird poems and others 2011

Openings and Endgame – a collection of
14 short stories, Vol 1 2013

My name is Max – a novel from 23 photographs, 2014

A number of poems have been set for piano and voice and performed in concerts.

Several stories from Vol 1 have been broadcast by the BBC.

Four Exits to Smolensk

A Novel by
Richard Cutler

*

Copyright © Richard Cutler

First published in 2015 on behalf of the author by

Scotforth Books (www.scotforthbooks.com)

ISBN 978-1-909817-20-3

Typesetting and design by Carnegie Book Production, Lancaster
Printed in the UK by Jellyfish Solutions Ltd

The parallel worlds

1 The beating

2 Alice

3 Brother Robert

4 Maria

The four exits from Euston Station

*

Prologue

November 16th 1987

"Will you come this way, please, Dr Liadev."

The low building was cold. A late Russian autumn shedding the warmth from earlier weeks. Liadev did not take off his overcoat.

"How was your drive from Gorky?"

"Long. But all right." He sensed the fear in the doctor's voice. "You have nothing to fear, Dr Limsky – yours was a better hospital."

The hospital doctor relaxed, his shoulders easing beneath his white coat.

"Thank you, Dr Liadev. I have always tried to keep things as humane as possible."

"We know that."

They entered a long corridor, turned sharply from it and entered a ward of 12 beds, two rows of six. All made, neat with hospital corners, uncrinkled green coverlets. The patients were standing to attention.

"Please relax your patients, Dr Limsky. Let them do what they usually do, except for the man I want to see."

A male nurse was called over. "This is my senior male nurse Anton Levin." They shook hands. The patients filed out, except for one – a thin-faced, grey-haired man with enquiring eyes. Liadev briefly examined the orange file. He introduced himself to the patient.

"I am Dr Liadev. I wish to apologize for your detention." The man said nothing. "Would you sit down, please ... on the bed." He turned to the ward doctor. "Would you bring me a chair please, Dr Limsky. And one for yourself."

"Do you wish to be alone with Yuri. I thought you would prefer that."

"No. But prepare a case extract for me, please. I shall be taking this man with me." Two chairs were brought over.

The doctor asked the visitor, "Would you excuse me for a few minutes please while I do that. And he will need discharge papers. My nurse will collect up a few things of his we have."

"Thank you. Is this patient on medication?"

"No. We use as little medication as possible."

When they were alone Liadev looked gently at the sitting man. He spoke quietly. "I have been given the task to see all falsely imprisoned artists are released and rehabilitated. Do you mind if I address you as Yuri? I understand you are suffering from amnesia – due to the beatings you received in camp 323. I am sorry. The shame of the past cannot be undone or forgotten ... but we are trying to do what we can. Unfortunately there is no record of your name."

The man looked at him through pale blue eyes – a gaze curious and at the same time touched with a bitter and ironic humour. Liadev was aware of a deep passivity. He had encountered it often, with long-stay prisoners. From an envelope he was carrying, Liadev passed the man a sheet of paper.

"What's this, Yuri?"

The man studied it slowly. Liadev noted a slight tremor. He saw tears enter the eyes. "It is a poem."

"Do you know who wrote it?" Only a stare. The doctor took it back. Nodded. "Pushkin." He then passed Yuri a print. "Do you know who painted this?"

"No." He shook his head.

"It is by Goncharova."

The man shrugged. No answer. Only the gesture. Liadev put away both sheets and drew out his last one.

"What is this, Yuri?"

Tears were now threading their way through the grey-black stubble on the man's face. "Bach."

Liadev placed a hand on his shoulder. "Good. Which piece?"

The man's face had aged with tears. He rubbed his cheeks with his fingers to dry them, sighed and said no more.

They left the hospital together. The large, black official car was driven fast – they had a long way to go. When they reached Smolensk darkness was enfolding the city. They were shown onto the rooms of the Holy Father, head of the cathedral school. Yuri Perm was enrolled into the music staff. The next day it snowed. Liadev's journey back to Gorky was stopped by drifts. He completed his return by train.

★

Thursday 29th June, 1995

A man, casually dressed in a thin, beige jacket, brown corduroy trousers and soft summer shoes, holding a black travel bag, walked up the ramp from the Manchester train into the hurrying panic and energy of the Euston concourse. A man not used to hurrying, inclined to observe things – a thoughtful man past his youth, hair receding at the temples and flecked here and there with grey. The air surrounding him was touched with distance as if he was unsure of his arrival – he might have been an artist or a mathematician; he was a writer of novels.

He eased the strap of his bag deeper into his shoulder, raised the sleeve of his jacket and looked at his watch – a gesture more to do with habit than a need for he had no plans for the evening. He felt for his mobile phone, a present from his ex-wife – not in his pocket. Strange that it had taken him so long to discover he had forgotten it – the way down his mind was elsewhere, outside the train. Sometimes inside it. A curious feeling to feel glad that something always with you was left behind. That perhaps it meant something not expressible in words. No one could ring him. Perhaps that was why he had left it there, a chance omission determined hours before that last minute scramble. Chance, and not chance. That was his feeling about his entire life. He paused at a chocolate stall to detach himself from the stream of people and took out his wallet, glanced at his two ten pound notes. Not enough.

Undecided now. Four exits from the station. He walked towards the one which had the cash point close by. Had he decided that the money was enough he would have left by the Euston Square exit – as it happened he turned his back on that direction. Hotels were cheaper in King's Cross and his account was overdrawn. He noticed that the light outside had become softer and welcomed the prospect of a coolness and quiet when he could escape from the station.

At the cash point he was aware of the presence of someone, near. The feeling went. The person had moved away. Yet there remained with him an uneasy sensation, that of being watched. The unease invaded him and he took the money quickly, folded it, pushing it deep down into his wallet. He looked up quickly – to his left. Two men were watching him. One took out a mobile phone and tapped in a number, turning away as he spoke into it. For an instant the man's eyes engaged his own. Cold eyes, weighing him up. The writer was irritated – and alarmed. He walked firmly and briskly to the Euston Road, turned away from a direction he might have gone on a different day and walked east, towards King's Cross and Argyle Square.

On a corner he saw them. The same two men. He was mystified how they had been able to get ahead of him. Should he cross and go up the other side – but the traffic was heavy. Moving fast. On another day he might have waited and threaded his way through the buses and cars, instead he turned off left. They didn't follow. By now he was nervous. Why were they there? Who were they waiting for? Why did they look at him during a phone call? He slowed as they didn't seem to be leaving the corner they were standing on and passed the grim, grey warehouses burrowing beneath St Pancras, past shadowy recesses for spent taxis, onwards towards the jaundiced desolate brick-faced Royal Northern Hotel. The sight of it added despair to his anxiety. Now he did regret not having a phone – he might have called Jack to pick him up. Such a simple mistake – or deliberate mistake to leave it on the table where he worked every day.

The road he found himself walking down passed under two broad railway bridges, throwing down a damp, airless darkness obliterating summer. Three men waited for him there. One with a telephone against his ear. The writer panicked. He raced back across the road and found a thin, pot-holed track leading to a grey Victorian block of flats. Everything now was stale – the flats, the bridges, the rough car park, and ahead – the canal. The men did not move; his pulse slowed. Not him they were after.

The neglected lane was lined along one side by a wire-mesh fence, broken down where it had been pulled and trampled on. The waste ground was studded with clumps of ragwort, marks and oil patches on the concrete squares – and everywhere Buddleia, its purple fronds drawing to it butterflies of all colours, a natural beauty within a wasteland with oil drums placed as goalposts, a single one as a cricket wicket. The pallor of emptiness, no children playing – deserted – only a long summer twilight reaching down and fading. The ground gave back to the incoming dusk some of its daytime heat.

The lane became a track, the track a footpath leading

to the canal. It dipped into a tunnel that reeked of urine – overhead, rails opposed in infinite junctions. When a train passed over him, it felt as if his head was being crushed, he was deafened, excoriated by the screeching. He was thankful to emerge beside the newer fencing of a city farm. On another day he would have paused to watch the ponies and look into the small paddocks with their enclosed sheep – perhaps gone in. But on this day he hurried on, his urgent desire was to get beyond it all, back to a road. He was unable to shake of the sinking feeling that he was being hunted. Like an animal.

He hurried on, a sweat arising on his forehead, a wetness under his arms. Leaving behind the farm, railways, sidings of silent trains and passive locomotives, he was overwhelmed with the sense that his life was futile – no purpose, no direction, a leaf blown about at random, anywhere and everywhere by the winds of chance. He did allow himself to pause before a group of ponies. He envied their closeness, the company they had from each other, the way they nuzzled and touched. Writing had divided his life, wrecked his marriage. All that remained was internal, a world populated by characters in books who loved him, but in the end they too had no further use for him. No way back – they were in print and no longer his, the property of others.

He did not hear the man coming up behind him. Things happening suddenly. Shock. A thickset man stepped out from behind a smashed shed and grabbed him. The fierce grip twisted his arm, wrenching it up behind his back. He screamed at the searing pain, the fear … the man in front thrust a long knife in his face.

"It screams, George … let's hear it again." He pushed the knife closer. The assailant with his arm winched it higher. Now the writer made no sound. The pain and thrust of it pushed him down, head down. A pain like fire. Unbearable. "Ah, it seems we've shut him up. We want your wallet, Manchester man."

A voice cruel and leering. The wallet was plucked from his pocket. The knife was taken from his eyes. The coins from his purse were flicked across the black waters like skimming pieces of slate, or cards flicked by a child. In that gesture the man's cruelty left him; he became a child at a seaside somewhere, on his own, watching a flat pebble skimming across a low sea, counting the number of times it jumped. Pain left the writer – he had become an observer.

The knife was stroked down his neck; the movement was soft and delicate, a surgical lightness of touch. He watched the dark red blood from his open vein splash down onto his shoe. It covered the toe-cap, soaked into the soft leather as if into a beige blotter. His blood ran across the towpath to trickle down and meet the water, where it spread out. The colour on the mirrored blackness of the surface seemed to him to be a sunset on a wet day. He fell to his knees. The man behind kicked his head. The writer fainted, and descended deeper into unconsciousness.

★

Euston Square Exit

He stood on the frantic station concourse uncertain. To give himself time to think which way to go, he stepped out of the throng to watch, gather his wits and used the moment to observe. He allowed his gaze to rest on the travelling multitude and grouped them by gesture, clothes, body language and carriage, urgency and rarely, like himself, a lack of it. Some were leaving the great metropolis alone, or with a companion, others arriving entering a new world, new life, old life, an arrival from a respite, or the drabness of return. He allowed his thoughts to delve deeper – what was the purpose of all this hurrying and urgency to leave one place and enter another after a long train journey and all the restlessness of change – hopes for a better life? Fears for a worse life, expectation or dread, pleasure or pain? Yet the journey itself was a world in which loneliness was shed and set aside for half a day.

An immediate problem – which way to leave the station? Brideswell lifted out his wallet, touched the two ten pound notes with his fingertips as if to reassure himself they there still there, a kind of comfort, confirmation of existence. He made a decision – did not need any more money from the cash machine, would go the other way ... Euston Square, the old way, a friendly, familiar way. Enough for a coffee and pasta, perhaps in that old café in Marchmont Street, Luigi's ... where they had always made him welcome in those student days ... if it was still there. Everything flows and nothing stays the same – and that was 2000 years ago. He pushed back the wallet, deep into the inside pocket of his jacket and walked across the wide hall, now beginning to thin out with the dispersion of the Manchester train's passengers.

He recognised her at once. His carriage in the train, across the aisle. She was standing by the automatic doors that led out into the world beyond, onto a wide pavement and the street. Their eyes met. A moment of recognition. He had helped her. He went up and stood close.

"My God! I cannot believe it!" She fingered the folds on the inner compartments of her bag. "I've been robbed. All gone – I cannot believe this it. How could this happen to me! Why me! Bloody hell – what scum they have in London!"

But not in London, he remembered. The strap was already cut on the train. He had seen it. Made a mental note. It was a fault his wife always chided him about, and very withering at the end – his making notes and not responding.

"Are you sure?" Her distress and agitation affected him. He felt sorry.

"Could you have put it in another pocket – one in your coat, or somewhere?"

She thrust her hand down despairingly into her summer coat. He knew there was no chance. A cut strap – no way back from that. She shook her head. Her eyes filled with tears. He wanted to comfort her. "It must have happened on the train. I did see that the strap was cut ... or broken." Definitely cut, but it seemed kinder to offer something less brutal.

"How could anybody do this to me! How vile people are!"

"I'm really sorry."

"What shall I do?"

"I don't know – maybe you need a coffee. For the shock."

She took out a small pack of tissues, snatched one out, wiped her eyes and blew her nose hard. "What a fool I am to be upset like this."

"I can help you. I'm in no hurry. Nothing in the diary."

"Oh." She took a deep breath. "I saw you on the train, didn't I? Well, I do feel hopeless ... you don't mind?"

"Of course not. I wasn't sure what to do anyway."

She touched his arm. "How lucky for me. Thanks."

Brideswell could hear in her voice an unusual accent – he listened to voices, it was his job – something of the north and underlying it something quite different, cadences and hard diphthongs of central Europe. Russia?

"The police have an office, I've passed it before – Transport Police. You'll need to report it. You'll have to anyway for the insurance, and take a slip from them."

"I do not need the police."

"Well – whatever – but you should phone in about credit cards. That sort of thing."

She shrugged. "I have no money for phoning. It's all gone. Everything!"

"I'll ring for you." He saw a phone booth. "Which bank?"

"Lloyds."

"That's lucky. Mine too. I have the number." She did not respond to his half-smile. Her face had become expressionless. "What name, please?"

She found something and closed her bag. "Here. The thief doesn't read. He's left me my library ticket."

He took it. The first name – Anya. Russian. No surprise there.

He bought coffee for them both and asked her where she was going.

"I was going to the hospital. Now I shall have to go home, back to Manchester."

Brideswell could have given her the fare, instead he said he would take her to the hospital – it was near. Ten minutes at the most. She said no.

"Please. I have a free day. I saw your name. I am Brideswell."

As they entered the hospital she stopped. "My friend's letter was in my bag. They have taken it, and I can't remember where to go. The ward number."

"We'll ask at reception."

"I shall do it." She left him and walked firmly to the desk. The name must have been difficult for the young clerk to grasp. She had to ask for it to be written down. Anya came back to him. "I must go to ward 2:1. Will you wait here. I can manage now."

"I'll come up with you – there'll be seats outside the ward."

They entered the lift with a cluster of people. She stood close to him. He was right – there were seats against a tiled wall. The smells had changed. A hospital smell – a smell he hated. Food and disinfectant. She left him and entered the ward behind two women from the lift. He had a book in his jacket pocket. Brideswell took it out with difficulty – wedged in to a space barely enough to take it – and he set it on his knees, looked at the cover but left it unopened. How strange to be sitting there waiting outside a hospital ward for a woman with a Russian name who had been robbed on his train. What whimsical fates to allow him to leave by that exit when there were at least three others he could have made for. Suddenly she was there beside him. He hadn't seen or heard her approach.

"He wants to see you."

"What …? See me – whatever for. Who does?"

"My friend has asked for you."

He stood up, astonished. "Whoever did you say I was? I have nothing … is there some problem?"

"I said you had pointed out University College where you'd been."

"Oh." He could not read the look in her eyes. "All right then. I'll have a go. Lead on. Why is he here?"

"He'll tell you himself."

The man he was asked to see, who had called him in, was old, and ill. He was propped up on pillows and an angled frame in a bed by the door. On either side of him stretching away to the far end were two lines of beds with sick men, drips and some half-pulled curtains. Around some there were visitors, others had no one, several slept, one or two stared ahead lost in worlds inaccessible except to them. As he came close he could see the man was younger than he had first thought, only aged by illness, eyes set deep into his face, watching him.

"Ah … Anya's friend. How kind of you to come and see me."

The formality of his grammar, the careful choice of words, the accent – was he also from the vast country re-becoming Russia? Brideswell sat on the bedside chair. He was unsure how to respond to the sick man's pleasure at seeing him. Anya left them.

"Anya says you were at my college."

"UCL ...? It was a long time ago."

"Also for me. And she says you are a writer. You must have been in the English Department ... or classics?"

"I had Professor Smith."

"Harry. A good man. What's your name? Anya told me but I've already forgotten."

"Brideswell."

"First name?"

"Michael."

"I don't remember that name. You were lucky to have Harry. He was gifted, most of the rest of us weren't – just good at the job. Don't be lured into academia, Michael. It is the death of genius."

"There's death outside as well."

"Yes. I am much closer to it than you. We haven't made friends yet – death and I." He moved his shoulders on the pillow to ease a point of pressure. "I asked Anya to send you in, in case you'd like to play chess."

"I'm not very good."

"Splendid. Then I shall have a chance. You will find the box in my locker. I have so longed to have a battle with someone, but no one in here wants to compete against my men. I find it such an interesting game – so revealing."

Brideswell leaned over towards the locker and lifted out a worn oblong box. He slipped back the clips and tipped the chessmen out, onto the pale green counterpane. The older man watched him.

"I am sorry it is not a full-sized board. Yes? This is an old travelling set that was my father's. I brought it out with me when we left the Soviet Union. Russia?" He stretched forward and gathered up two pawns, one of each colour. He placed his hands slowly under the sheet. In his eyes flickered a playfulness, and irony. The look puzzled Brideswell. The old man was teasing him. "Which hand?"

"Right. Your right."

He nodded. "Yes. You will be white, and take the advantage." With care he turned the board to face his young visitor with the white pieces facing him. "Your first move." A half-smile crossed his lips. "Chess is so beautiful. For me the first move is a pleasure to watch, like the opening of a gate to a journey which only one of us will survive. It has the tension of a duel without the violence. It is a hunt where one of us will be hunted. But it is far more subtle than that – more an entry into a world where the possibilities of action approach the infinite. Mostly in life our choices are much more narrow."

Brideswell moved his king's pawn forward. "So. You see. I already know you a bit better. You are not a reckless man, and wise to be cautious with a stranger." He countered the move by doing the same. "Forgive me for appearing boring, but I know so little about you. Thank you for your kindness to my Anya ... for bringing her to me."

Brideswell brought out his king's bishop onto the queen's side. The man nodded, a merest movement of the head, a gesture of approval.

"Yes, I like that move, too. I think we are going to get on very well. I am sorry – please ... your name again."

"Brideswell."

"Ah, so English – to give your surname only." He moved out his knight to threaten his opponent's piece. "In Russia it is one, two or three names. How many you offer on a meeting involves an awareness of many lifetimes. But mostly in life we are presented with only two choices – in my case it was either to stay or to leave."

Brideswell protected his bishop with a pawn. The man in the bed looked deeply into his eyes.

"I had a friend, a composer. A good man and brave – he asked me to take his daughter out with me. He had become unpopular, criticism in Pravda, questioned by Stalin's thugs. He was unsafe, He feared for his daughter. They were frightening times. Have you ever been to Smolensk, Mr Brideswell?"

"Once. Passing through."

"You will find it beautiful, as old as Rome, and a great river, the Dnepr, and several fine hills, perhaps not seven. When I defected they arrested my friend and took him out to some desolate place and did things to him of unspeakable cruelty. He may have died, or God may have found him and placed a guardian angel over him, at his side. Do you believe in angels, Mr Brideswell?"

"It is not a question I've thought much about."

"Think about it now."

"Yes. Something like that."

"Thank you. If I did not hope that my friend might still be alive, I would have killed myself." He leaned back into his pillow. "I would have saved my life and taken his from him." His eyes had moistened with the memory. He held out his hand. "Leave the pieces there, Michael. I shall think about my strategy when you have gone. If you have some moments to spare tomorrow, please, you will come in and make some more moves? It is such a beautiful and satisfying opening. It shows me you are a sensitive man."

Brideswell left the bedside and rejoined the woman. "Sorry to be so long. We started a game of chess."

"Good. That is what he wanted."

"I have to call back tomorrow, to carry on the game. He seems to think I will be going back to Smolensk."

"And will you?"

They walked down the wide staircase and out into a cool summer evening and a fading twilight. In the hotels around the hospital, in Gower Street, there were no vacancies. He shrugged.

"We can try the Exeter. My father used to stay there when he came down for his medical conferences. It's by the BMA, the doctor's place – but it might be more expensive than these."

"I have no money. What can I say except thank you, Michael."

They found it – large, square, solid and Victorian – as staid as an elderly doctor. The woman at reception was almost as old, and as neat.

"Yes, sir?"

"I hope you can help. We've been looking for a room for hours. Everywhere's full."

Anya had subsided into an armchair; she had closed her eyes. The clerk looked across at her with sympathy.

"Your poor wife looks all in. We've just had a cancellation. It's the only room we have left. Did you want twin beds? This one is a double."

He looked towards the Russian woman. No response. As if she had not heard.

"Fine. We'll take that. It's a great relief to have found something."

"It's Wimbledon fortnight, sir. I'm sorry we're so full but people book up for the tennis months in advance. It's a back room. It should be very quiet. I hope you have a good rest." She took a key from a panel. "Room 302, third floor. We do continental and full English breakfast from 7.30 to 9.30 am, and there is a room service if your wife is still very tired."

"Thank you. You've been very kind. I'm sure we'll be down. It has been a long and tiring day."

She moved a leather-backed ledger towards him. "Would you sign in please, sir." He took the pen and wrote across the page.

'Mr and Mrs M Brideswell, 14 Market Court, Queen Street, Chelford, Cheshire.' And moved the book back.

"Do you need a map of the area, sir. It has the Underground on the back."

"Thank you, but I do know the area. I lived near here once."

He did take the map and crossed to Anya. "We have a room on the 3rd floor. Very quiet – it's at the back."

They went up in the lift and walked down an airless corridor smelling of furniture polish and new carpets. He unlocked the room and pushed the door open. It rasped on the carpet pile. His first impression was of a clean freshness, a relief from the hot, staleness of the corridor outside. Before he turned on the light, he watched the array of colours playing across the wall opposite the window, a faint fingered spectrum, the withdrawing of the sun from a long and strange day. A day sent by an angel somewhere. When the lighting came on, it was subdued – from two lamps on each side of a wide bed covered by a blue bedspread. The coloured glass in their shades threw soft patterns blending and adding to the amber spectrum from the sun. A room to welcome two tired people. He stood to one side, touched

Anya's arm to allow her to enter the room first. She looked at the bed and then at him.

"A double bed?"

"Sorry. It was a cancellation. The only room left ... they're full up. I'm really sorry, but there was no other choice – and the night's coming on. I had to take it. I can sleep on the carpet – a pillow and a cover is all I'll need."

"Don't be silly." She opened the window wider and drew the curtains across in front of it. "That is quite ridiculous. I want you in the bed, not on the floor. Please be reasonable. Do it for me. Please, I'm asking you."

He took a deep breath. "Are you sure?"

"Very sure. I am sure."

"It's not necessary ..."

"Please. Will you stop! Which side of the bed do you like?"

He shrugged. "It's a long time since I slept in a double bed. I sleep alone. My wife and I divorced 5 years ago."

"I would prefer the side by the open window – I like to be cool in this weather. I have a son ... do you have any children, Michael?"

She used his name; it sounded right, it affected him. He was moved, that she wanted his company beside her after such a bad day. Robbed. "No. Perhaps it was just as well. She has two children now – with her other husband."

She looked into his eyes. A question, and a softness. "We are both rejects, Michael." She smiled and lay back on the bed. Anya raised her legs and smoothed down the dress. At that moment he felt her sadness was leaving her.

"Are you hungry, Anya? Shall I send down for something?"

"No, only very tired. I shall sleep." She closed her eyes.

"I'll go out for a while. A café I know. Can I bring you

something back – they would make up a roll?" She shook her head. "I'll be about an hour."

"Thank you for being so nice to me today. To go straight home without seeing Vladimir would have broken his heart – he was expecting me. You are a good man, Michael."

"I'm sorry he's so ill." Brideswell let himself out quietly.

Luigi remembered him.

"You have an astonishing memory, Luigi."

"How could I forget. You came to us so often. Like family, Michael."

"Thanks."

"What will you have, my friend?"

"Your pasta."

"Good. We make it special. The wine you do not pay for."

He opened the door to their room softly, slipping the key back into his jacket pocket. The room was in soft light, lit only by the bedside lamp on his side of the bed. Anya was in a deep sleep, her face, hair and shoulders relaxed, lifting in the even rhythm of a sleeper who leaves behind her identity until the following day. The light covers had slipped from her. The night-dress straps had come off her shoulder onto the upper arms, exposing the whiteness of the top of her breast. He went to the window and eased the curtain to allow some night breeze to cross her, showered, drew on his pyjama trousers and switched off the light.

Brideswell lifted the covers gently trying not to disturb her as he eased himself into the bed. The warmth of her body reached across. The fragrance of her skin enveloped him. In her sleep she sensed he was there and in the languorous manner of a sleeper rolled herself towards him, draping an arm across his chest. For a long time he remained like that, awake, bemused, and engulfed by the presence of a woman pressed against him, a stranger he knew nothing about, unknown when he had boarded the train at Stockport.

He fell at last into a light sleep.

As their sleep deepened, their embrace lost all remembrance of self. They entered a realm of oblivion and mystery, where all boundaries are grey, crossable, known or unknown. In the early hours she woke, reached down and found him in a state of urgency, moved herself up and guided him into her.

*

Dr Liadev;
return to Smolensk

For the second time Dr Liadev found himself back in the rooms of the seminary's Father Abbot. The last time he had brought to him a camp victim to be rehabilitated, Yuri Perm. Since then the whole edifice of state communism lay about in ruins, crashed and smashed. The death of it let in light, hopes, freedom on the one hand but on the other chaos, criminals and a nation-wide bewilderment. Bad, unspeakable things left behind, good things left behind, changed forever. The loss of the familiar shielding arms and bony finger of the state for an embrace of capitalist systems of profit, success or collapse would take a generation to swallow. Market forces ushering out love and a genuine concern to improve the life of her people, would bring into Russia new darknesses. Love had for that moment withdrawn, like snow melting before a growing flame. But love in Russia, for Russia, cannot be extinguished for long.

"Dr Liadev, come in please, I've been expecting you. Did you have a good journey … come and sit down."

The holy father took Liadev's outstretched hand in both of his — a blessing of arrival, and a welcome.

"Thank you, Father."

"Take the armchair and let me make you some tea – or coffee. I have been blessed with an electric kettle."

The older man smiled warmly and with sensitive concern for his visiting doctor. Liadev was a big man and sat himself down gratefully into the wide armchair in front of the study window. "Yes, a tiring journey, Father – they don't allow me a car any more. I go everywhere by train. It's tedious when I have to wait around at freezing stations – especially now … winter so close."

"May God protect you, Dr Liadev, and bless you in your work."

"Thank you, Father."

For a while nothing was said, each man moving away into his own thoughts – Liadev with his eyes on the thick, low snow clouds, wondering when the snow would begin to fall. The holy father stood at a Formica-topped table waiting for the kettle, watching the wisps of steam, listening to the noises within. He also was reminded of train journeys when he was still a young man, leaving once and for all his mother's house in the Orenburg Oblast for Kiev and the seminary.

"The rebirth of our school is a miracle, Dr Liadev. Who would have thought it possible, even only five years ago. Now we are training priests to fill all those empty gaps right across Russia. Even here in Smolensk we have so many churches that need our help. Our people have endured a spiritual starvation. Years of famine." The steam from the spout spiralled up into the room. The kettle clicked and switched itself off. Father Adrian poured the boiling water into the two mugs he had prepared. He waited for a comment from his visitor. None came. "We are re-opening churches everywhere, and they are full. For our older people it is like the rebirth of this school – a miracle. And the young people come in as well. It's astonishing – you cannot clamp a lid on Russia. In the end it is the lid that wears out. We can't take all the young people who apply to us to be trained for the priesthood. It breaks my heart to turn so many away – we don't have the room. I ask them to come back, another day. These are young years, and there will be plenty of time for them all. We are like new tea in a glass, we have to settle to grow stronger. It is the same for everyone." He stirred in the tea bags and pressed them flat with his spoon. "You see, Dr Liadev, no glasses for tea now – St Petersburg china mugs and tea bags. And, would you believe it, under this table is a fridge. Will you have milk in your tea ... the English way?"

Liadev shook his head. "Just some sugar, please, Father. I'm pleased for you – all these changes. This time it cannot stay the same. Losers and winners, though. But freedom is a force that can never be put out. It has taken longer in the past."

"You are in a philosophical mood, Doctor. The chill of your journey has made you thoughtful. Well, the man you brought to us two years ago, Yuri – we still call him that – he is also a thinker, philosopher, musician ... a man of many gifts. An artist so sensitive; we love him."

Father Adrian took the doctor his tea and a small bowl of sugar lumps.

"Have you discovered," asked Liadev, "who he is, Father? His real name? Does he ever talk about the past? Does he mention Camp 323 – his life before that?"

The priest brought his hands together, closed his eyes and sighed. "No. We don't ask him. He will tell us when he wants to – that is, if his memory comes back. Is that possible, Dr Liadev? Or can memory be beaten out of you never to return – no past, no childhood, no place?"

"There's no way of knowing. It may not be the head injuries which destroy your past, there are other traumas – to the mind, to the soul, all those indefinable things that make up a personality."

"What a savage crime, to beat a man's head until he loses everything. Our Yuri is encased in a shell. No, we don't know who he is, not yet – but he is a gifted man, composer, musician and is now the master of our choir. My bishop wants him to play at Mass in our church of the Archangel Michael. I have mentioned it to Yuri. So far he hasn't said either yes or no. But he is changing – he's calmer, more secure in himself, less sad, I think, and more accepting of everything. Being with us has changed him as much as he changes everyone here. So we thank you, Dr Liadev. It is a blessing to have such a kind and thoughtful doctor caring for him."

The doctor stirred in the sugar lumps, felt them soften and dissolve. He removed his outside coat, folded it and placed it behind him. From his jacket he drew out a folded letter. He neither opened it nor passed it to the Father Abbot, but hesitated.

"Has he ever mentioned to you a child, Father? A daughter?"

"No." Father Adrian was surprised. "His thoughts – the ones we're admitted to – only date from when he came to us. All the rest lies behind an impenetrable curtain. Why do you ask me about a child?"

"The doctor in his hospital sent me a photograph of a small girl. It was found behind his locker in the prison camp when the demolition gang were clearing everything out. The foreman of the crew, a good man, posted it to our doctor thinking Yuri might still be there."

"A daughter ... is that what you're thinking. It could have been anyone's photo concealed behind the locker. What does your doctor say in his letter – may I know? Is that all right?"

"He has no idea. Yuri never mentioned anyone. It may not be his child ... but I think it is."

"Why?"

"There is a likeness. In the face ... in the eyes."

The priest made the sign of the cross. "Let us pray she is. May God, in His mercy, find some way to forgive those who did this to Yuri."

"Afterwards, Father. The guards who beat and tortured him will first be found, and punished."

The holy father said nothing. Punishment, and a love for all God's people was a difficulty for him. They stood up and walked to the door. "You will be pleased with him, Doctor. Yuri is so much better, and a wonderful teacher. Come along and see for yourself."

They walked through the rebuilt chapel. The sounds from a piano reached them, faint at first, louder as they drew closer. Beyond in the next room, a young man was playing, watched over by a thin, grey-haired man. The music teacher glanced up at the creak of the door, saw them but allowed his pupil to continue. In a pause later, Yuri came to them. Father Adrian apologized for the interruption. "This is Dr Liadev ... do you remember him? Two years ago ... when he brought you to us? He's come back to see how you're getting on – and if we're being kind to you."

His voice was gentle. Liadev was aware of the Principal's affection for the gaunt man. He was also aware that Yuri had changed. He was not so dazed and bewildered. Father

Adrian Petrovich continued. "The doctor wants to talk to you. Find him a comfortable chair in the library annexe ... or you might prefer to take him to your room."

The man nodded. He glanced at his pupil. The music began again, quietly.

"My room is quiet. I'll show you, Dr Liadev."

They left together, just the two. The Principal returned to his room. They walked through long, cool corridors and came to a door in a side passage. The room was bare. Two beds. Around one bed had been placed several photographs and on its bedside locker a bible next to a neat stack of books and some sheet music. By the other bed – nothing. A table placed before the window separated the two beds. The window was like the room; narrow. Beyond it was a secondary window to be kept shut in winter – beyond that, shutters. The room was clean. It had the atmosphere of a cell. The older man was conscious of the size of his visitor and lifted towards him a simple chair.

"This is the best we have, Doctor, unless you'd rather sit on my bed."

"I don't mind a hard chair, Yuri, I was brought up on them. And I'm well padded." Liadev sat down. The man he had come to see sat on the edge of his bed. "Father Adrian thinks you're a lot better than you were. I can see how much he values your being here, you have a good effect on them – and there's your music skills." The man close to him made no response. He waited for the doctor to reveal the purpose of his visit, and listened. "Russia has lost so many fine, creative minds. No nation can afford to lose men and women of great talent and imagination. It is the lack of imagination that destroys everything, lets in stupidity and cruelty and everything we have been through. Now there are changes, a wind of change, new freedoms, Yuri, more open minds. We need voices to express the past and help us with the future. We have been like the foolish king who destroyed all the birds in his land – then there followed a plague of insects. If you could tell me who you are then I should do everything possible to recover things for you, the house where you lived, your family who must believe you died in that terrible camp – like so many other innocents. Perhaps we need you, Russia needs you, at some university or conservatoire. We are rebuilding. We need artists as well as buildings."

"My place is here, Dr Liadev."

"Have you any memories at all?"

"I remember a grey room. I was naked. The windows and doors were open and snow was blowing in. I was burned. Then I was beaten. They said I was cold."

"If we found these men, could you identify them?" A silence, deep as a Siberian forest, descended upon the man. Liadev reached forward, "I am sorry you have those memories, those unspeakable things done to you. We will track down and punish the guards. What about happier memories ... before Camp 323? Did you leave behind a family?"

"I may have done." His voice was flat. A past obliterated or locked away in places unreachable by the men of terror.

"May I show you something? A photo? It was found by workmen behind your locker when the camp was pulled down. I wanted to show it to you myself, not post it on here."

"You may show me."

Liadev felt inside his pocket. Within the folds of a letter he took out a small faded photograph of a child. He passed it. "Do you know who this is, Yuri?"

The man took it from him. A tremor entered his fingers. He studied the snapshot carefully. His eyes filled with tears. "Perhaps I know her. Perhaps I don't."

"There's a name written on the back. Turn it over."

He looked at the name. Whispered it. "Anya." His face had blanched. "Anya ... Smolensk ... 1967." He lowered his head and put the palms of his hands to his ears as if the sounds were unbearable. "May I keep it?"

"Of course. It is yours. Do you know who the child is, Yuri?"

"I recognize her, but I don't know who she is. But I heard her say my name."

"And what was the name you heard?" asked the doctor gently.

"She called me Andrei." He wept.

Liadev left.

★

From the canal

Not for the first time. He had seen them before, but not with the clawing nausea in his throat urging him to vomit. Rapid, dropping images. Falling like an old film slipping. Frames racing, blurred – and inside them a jangle of voices. He had heavy arms. One was weighted, something on it like a leech sucking and pulling, gripping, grasping and stinging. He tried to move his head to see what it was. A fierce pain leapt up from his neck into his eyes, making his eyes wash with tears. Someone beside the bed he was in.

The visitor had been contacted by the hospital from the telephone number found in the victim's diary before he went up to theatre – the stabbing case from the canal. A voice. A command.

"Don't pull on your arm, there's a drip up."

He moved his fingers away. The pulsing images slowed. He reached up to touch his neck.

"I wouldn't touch your neck – it has a long plaster on it."

So he pressed his eyes, trying to impose upon the figure speaking a sharper outline, a form, a shape. "Who are you?" His words set up a repeated cough and he felt the darkness coming back towards him. He could have screamed or entered the offer of darkness but a sweet gas was thrust into his face from a mask. Voices different. Clearer, female – not addressing him now.

"It's too soon for him to speak. He's lost so much blood. His neck has a severe gash. It was very deep. He's a lucky man ... a few more minutes."

"They've stitched him up?"

"Mr Wilkins did the operation himself. Fortunately the knife didn't cut the artery – but a big vein. Maybe you should come back tomorrow."

"Yes, nurse. Maybe I should. What are his chances – will he survive?"

"Mr Wilkins is our senior vascular surgeon. I think your friend has every chance."

"He'll be in for some time?"

"I would think so."

"Should I cancel his hotel booking. He wanted me to reserve a room in his father's hotel in case he couldn't find anywhere cheaper."

"Of course."

"Is there a telephone?"

"On the landing outside the ward. You'll see it."

"Thanks." The man left the bedside and found the public telephone. He put in the coin and dialled out. A woman answered.

"Yes, can I help?"

"I booked a room for my friend, a double room – I'm sorry to ring so late in the day but he won't need it now. He's had an accident and has been taken to hospital. In fact he's had an operation."

"Oh, I am sorry. Your poor friend. How unlucky. What was the room number, please?"

"It was booked in my name – Coldstream. The room number was 302."

"Thank you, that is kind of you to ring in. We are so full and there's someone here in reception who is desperate for a room. His wife will be so pleased. But I am so sorry about your friend."

"Thanks. I think he'll be OK." The phone became dead. The receptionist turned to the man at her desk.

"Your wife looks all in. We've just had a cancellation come in, it's the only room we've got. Did you want twin beds? This one is a double."

The man looked at his wife but she had already closed her eyes. He said:

"We'll take it. Thanks. It's a relief to have found something."

She explained to him that it was Wimbledon fortnight and people book up for that months in advance. She lifted down the key from her panel.

"302, sir ... third floor. We do continental and full English breakfasts from 7.30 to 9.30 am, and a room service if your wife is still tired ..."

*

Breakfast in the Exeter Hotel

Alice woke – the sun had found its way through a chink in the curtains and was resting its beam across her face, a thin wedge of bright sunlight like a loving hand, the fingers of a bridegroom. Deep within her she still felt the love she had received and given to a man she barely knew. The place beside her was empty, cool, but despite his absence it still contained something of the man. She moved over into his impression and felt a tightness grip her thighs. Slowly it ebbed away. Alice rolled back to her own side and reached for the telephone. She asked the switchboard for an outside line and dialled out. A woman answered.

"Hallo, Carol? This is Alice. I'm ringing from London. How's Kenny?" The reply cold – underlaid with annoyance and irritation.

"He's all right, Alice."

"How did he sleep? Did he have his dreams?"

"I don't know. He didn't say. I think he slept well."

"Where is he now?"

"Frank has taken him in the car for a ride, and a haircut." Alice's anger surged up. "A what!"

"We both thought his hair was far too long. He's nearly eight, Alice. What do you imagine his friends think? They all have short hair. Boys do. Frank has promised to take him afterwards to a rugby match."

"That's monstrous! How dare he take my son for a haircut!"

"Frank is his father, Alice. He saw at once Kenny's hair was too long. He'll be teased – a mother's boy. Frank knows – he was a boy. He knows what it's like to be bullied if you're any way odd … I mean – anyway different from your peers."

She felt like screaming. Or weeping. "My son is not odd! He doesn't like rugby. He goes to football – Altrincham – Frank knows that perfectly well!"

"Please don't worry so much. Frank is his father after all, Alice – you must see that – and for goodness sake … the boy should see much more of his father, much more. Be reasonable – it's not good for a boy to have input only from the mother."

Alice was stunned. Speechless. That pious moralising bitch. "I haven't rung up for your advice, Carol. Will you just give him a message when you've finished grooming him."

"Yes." Said with a sigh and wearisome tone. "All right."

"I shall be catching the 3.15 pm from Euston and will be home about seven. I'll come over for him then."

"Whatever."

Alice thrust down the phone, throat choked with rage. Her eyes filled with fury at what was being done to her son. She threw on the hotel dressing gown and stormed into the shower.

At breakfast she felt better, calmer, sitting opposite Michael. "I missed you when I woke up."

His smile was tender. "I'm sorry. You were so fast asleep.

I went for a walk. I used to live around here – everywhere is so full of memories."

She looked away from him at the other couples in the dining room. At that instant she was one of them, a wife and a loved woman. "I don't want to lose you, Michael, now I've found you."

He answered with his eyes. "Then should I call you Alice or Anya?" He poured the coffee out for her. So simple a gesture, but years since anyone had done that for her. Because it was so natural, his movement, his hands, tears came up into her eyes.

"I'm Alice. It was a long time ago I was Anya. It would be a shock to be called that again – days, years, places I've left behind. I don't mind it from Vladimir, he has called me nothing else."

"Then I shall call you Alice – like all the others."

She sensed his unspoken enquiry. Later. She just wanted to see him, feel his nearness, accept and receive love which for so long had been absent in her life. "Will you be coming back to the hospital this afternoon for the chess game? Vladimir would be so disappointed if you didn't. He'll have been working out his moves all night."

"Of course. I promised. I'll come along after seeing my new editor. I was supposed to be seeing him yesterday but I wasn't in the mood. He doesn't like my book. I've left a message that I'll come today after lunch. I don't like him. Our business won't take long."

Alice made no answer. A sadness invaded her mood. They might miss each other. "I have to catch the 3.15 pm from Euston. My son is expecting me – he's unhappy. I had to leave him with my husband and the woman he lives with."

"I'm sorry. He won't like that much. His father with someone else."

"It's not just that. Much worse – they've dragged the boy off to have his hair cut. I'm so angry – I could punch her. What a spiteful thing to do. It's so cruel! I always cut his hair."

Brideswell reached forward and touched her hand. "Don't worry. A boy's hair grows back very quickly."

"That woman is a cow – how I hate her! Of course, she insists that it is his father who wanted it. Frank has marked him down as a junior for his rugby club. Kenny simply hates rugby – I shall never send him to a school that plays that horrible game! It's so violent. Children are always getting injured. Sometimes really badly."

He nodded and thought. "I shall cancel George Lev again – we'll spend the day together. The man will have to wait. The book took me a year to write. I'm not ready for it to be dismissed in half an hour on a Saturday afternoon."

"He won't be pleased with you, Michael."

"I wasn't pleased when he summoned me down on Thursday."

"What will you say."

"That I'm playing chess with a Russian friend in hospital."

Alice watched him leave and cross the room. All anger was leaving her, being replaced by a warm feeling that a man cared enough about her to cancel an appointment with his publisher. When he came back, a wry smile on his face, she asked, "Did you get through?"

"No. Too early for them. I left a message on their answerphone. Another one!" He touched her shoulder. "Let's spend the morning in a beautiful park I know, and we could have our lunch there."

"I'd really like that, Michael." Using his name drew him closer to her. The feeling she had last night was rising up. "Have you written a lot of novels?"

"Ten I admit to." He gave a short laugh and shrugged.

"So many?"

"It keeps me sane. A diversion from melancholy." As they left the dining room she linked her arm through his, pressing her warmth into his side.

"There must be easier ways to lose a black dog that doesn't take so long."

In the room she lay on the bed and pulled him down beside her.

*

Way out
with Brother Robert

Brother Robert was feeling hot in his cassock, the suitcase was too heavy and he regretted bitterly having packed so much into it. So much easier and more sensible to have gone to Chester. But Stockport it was; the porter there had helped him and he thanked God for sending one of his angels to him dressed in British Rail livery. Here at Euston no one, no angels, no porters, not even an abandoned trolley. He stopped, took out his inhaler, turned his back on the exodus of determined Mancunians and took two puffs. He then did offer up a prayer; he thanked God in His mercy and compassion for His human children for allowing a doctor to discover not only the life-giving spray but also the jet to deliver it – and for its smallness and neatness. He believed in a caring God who did intervene in his life, in ways obscure and mysterious. A voice, a man, startled him.

"Can I help you, that's a big case and it looks pretty heavy."

He swung around, surprised and embarrassed. Caught in the act of inhaling. He thrust away the inhaler and tightened his waist cord. "Well ... I was going to try and find a trolley.

So silly of me to bring such a large case. You'd have thought a man of my age would have had more sense."

"I'll find you one. Leave it to me. You wait here."

"I won't say no. My asthma is a devil if I get hot and flustered. This heat, I'm not used to it. And arriving in London doesn't help. I never was any good with large, busy stations. They don't do me any favours." He smiled apologetically at the man. "I'm afraid I'm not as fit as I was."

"Fine. I won't be a minute. There'll be some on the concourse – usually are."

Brother Robert watched the young man disappear at a jog, marvelling at his youth, ease of movement and good nature. Sent by God in his hour of need – just like Stockport. This was a day of revelations. He smiled at the Samaritan when he came back pulling a luggage trolley. "Well done – you've found one … what a blessing. I do hope I haven't held you up."

"I'm not in a hurry, Father."

"I hope there's no one waiting for you. I wouldn't want that." He could see now that his helper was not as young as he had first supposed – youthful in movement and manner, older around the eyes. His case was taken from his hand and hoisted aboard the rather extraordinary wheeled contraption.

"No one waiting for me, Father. I'm on my own, and the rest of my day is free. Just down from Cheshire for a few days."

"What part. My monastic house is in Cheshire."

"Do you know Holmes Chapel – not far from there. Chelford. We are lucky – there's still a station. Long may that last. Some people on the west side of Macclesfield use it – and there are some big offices not far away. Apart from the station you'd pass us by without noticing." He stopped several times as the pull up from the platform made the elderly friar short of breath.

At one pause Brother Robert said, "Yes. But I do know it. Quite close to Knutsford. Our house is in Mobberly. That also has a station. I imagine about the same size as yours. I could have taken the train the other way, to Chester. But I'm glad I didn't. I would not have met such a kind person as yourself.

It is very nice of you to call me 'Father' but I'm only a lay brother with a silly case far too large for my needs. I am Robert ... Brother Robert at home. We are the Lexikon Brothers." He felt for his inhaler but decided he was calmer and didn't need it. "Please tell me your name. I should like to offer up a prayer for all this help you're giving me. Not aloud, don't worry."

"Brideswell. Michael – I can do with all the prayers I can get. I've been low recently. Like yourself – not as strong as I was."

"Sorry to be so slow. These ramps and this London heat! I'll gather speed at the top. My brothers should have warned me and told me to wear a back-pack. But they are so sheltered and don't travel much any more – whatever they knew about London probably dates from the war. We're all getting on a bit. I don't blame them, we all do what comes easiest to us. Except those with ambition and want to overcome everything. Fortunately I was born without it. Just pleased to be in a beautiful world and able to appreciate it."

"That seems to be a good way of looking at things."

"I'll be able to manage now, Michael. You've been a wonderful help. Without you I'd still be down there in the underworld of arrival." He reached forward and touched the younger man's arm. "Thank you. Don't be low, you have the nature of a Samaritan and there are many roads to Jericho, some are smoother than others, but you're a good walker and a born traveller. All will be well."

"Thank you. I shall have to look around for somewhere to stay, but let me help you push this to a taxi."

Brother Robert looked out into a late afternoon settling a quiet hour upon the vast, restless city. He sensed that the man beside him wanted to remain with him longer. He made no further protest – glad to have an assistant sent by God.

Brideswell hesitated, uncertain which exit they should leave by – a number of choices, but only one by a taxi rank. His cassocked companion paused, folded his arms and rubbed his elbows. "You're a thoughtful man, Michael. In many ways."

"Sorry ... a moment of hesitation. We're going to need the Eversholt Street exit."

"Would you be a writer?"

"How did you know that? Ink on my fingers?" Brideswell laughed, at ease for the first time. He was glad to be next to this perceptive and philosophical monk. "I write novels. They're mostly pretty weak, but my publisher likes them and they sell. One day I'll write something worthwhile. If I didn't think that, I wouldn't bother with all of it."

"Only God creates in 7 days – most of us take a lot longer – and a novelist needs lots of time, and space."

"Yes. That is exactly what I need. I am also the lucky one – to have met you, Brother Robert."

They left the station and joined a small queue for the taxis. The monk pursed his lips.

"Is it all right to bring this trolley outside the station, do you think? I mean, where do we leave it when our taxi comes in?"

"I'll push it back in."

"Thanks. I've been worrying about that. Tightens my chest. All worries do. The inhaler is a godsend, I'd be lost without it."

"I think I'll come into the taxi with you – where are you going?"

"Clerkenwell."

"I know that area. Well, more on the Holborn side – Grays Inn Road."

"We have a guest room in Church House ... is that any good to you?"

"Really? I'm not sure if I'd be the right sort of person in a holy space. Far from perfect. Rather imperfect, in fact."

"That makes two of us, Michael. The Carthusians are very generous. I don't think we should worry."

A red cab pulled up for them. The driver leaned across and opened his window.

"Where to, Gents?"

Brother Robert took a diary from an inside pocket and opened it. "Clerkenwell Green please, driver. We are staying at Church House. It is on the main road at the junction with St John's Square."

"I know it, mate. I take monks there every day." He gave Brideswell a wink, raised his eyebrows then stepped out. He lifted the case into the recess beside him as if it were no heavier than a holdall. The taxi accelerated into a U-turn then jerked to a stop at the Euston Road lights.

"I'd be glad to stay in your guest room, Brother Robert, if they'll have me."

"Splendid. Excellent. Then I shall have time to tell you something about as – as we are almost neighbours. We are a small unit with what you might call our monastic base in Mobberly. There's a larger priory in South London.

We have a Victorian sort of villa, rather cold in winter, and quite close to the station. I do like to hear the trains – I find them a comfort." He paused and allowed himself to sink deeper into the softness of the back seat, relaxed by the thought the journey was almost over, Euston done, and with a new companion he had liked from the first, sent down by a benevolent God. "We are only six. Six brothers, an outpost of our Order."

Brideswell pondered on that. "It has Greek name?"

"In some ways you are right. Our spiritual home is in Smolensk."

"In Smolensk?"

"Why ... does that surprise you?"

"It seems to be somewhere important for me, but I'm not sure why. I didn't think so yesterday – but the place is in my last novel. I have described it. But hardly been there, only passing through."

"Then perhaps you'll go and stay there. If you do I may ask a favour from you."

His new friend shook his head. "When I have the ticket I'll give you a ring." He laughed quietly, but thoughtfully.

They travelled the remainder of the journey in silence. For the night he was given a strangely cool, un-aired and remote room. Brideswell slept badly. His dreams were disturbing. In one he was being mugged and left bleeding by a canal-side. In another near morning, he dreamt he was drawn to an enigmatic Russian woman. On waking at dawn he dreamed Brother Robert had set a task for him in Russia but he didn't say where. Smolensk was printed on the large ticket he was handed. He fell back into a light, restless sleep.

He woke in the morning with a warm sun streaming into his room. Brother Robert had opened the curtains and placed beside him a mug of hot tea.

"Sleep well, Michael?"

"Not really. Some bad dreams, and some odd ones. I dreamt you had sent me to Russia to search for someone. My ticket was for Smolensk."

"Hmm. You were thinking of what I said in the taxi."

"Something odd is going on. I do feel someone is calling me."

"Perhaps it is God?"

"I don't think so. I have always been prone to odd feelings. I haven't had an epileptic fit for years. I thought all that nonsense was over."

★

From George Lev to Maria

A novelist arrived at Euston on a day in late June, towards the end of a long afternoon. The heat of the day was diminishing although it still remained hot – the sun was strong and the platform air stale. His mind was everywhere and nowhere. The phone-call the night before still rang in his head.

"Mr Brideswell?"

The voice had disturbed him. "Yes?"

"This is Angela speaking from Mannings."

"Really ... so late? What hours do you keep down there in London?"

"We've come back to the office after a book-launch. I have Mr Lev for you." A pause, then a man's voice, assertive. Oxford vowels.

"Michael Brideswell, this is George Lev."

"I'm sorry but I don't know who you are. I see Richard when I have a book ready."

"I'm the new editor. Richard has asked me to read through your latest book, 'House at Spissikoye', because I have a Russian background."

"Oh? Did he read it first?"

"Of course – you are one of his authors. He likes your work."

"So why are you ringing me at this time of day. Or any time?"

"Sorry, we had to come back to the office – unfinished business. I needed to speak to you. You see, I've just finished it. I quite liked it – beautiful in places. Tell me, have you ever been to that part of Russia?"

He felt a mounting hatred for this new editor. Why the hell had Richard sent his book to this man. Never done anything remotely like that before.

"Of course I've been to Russia. How else could I write about it?"

"How well do you know Smolensk?"

"I stayed a few nights."

"Smolensk is a place people only pass through like that – it's a sad city. A victim of violence and war and much else. Did you find it so?"

"I can't say I did. What's all this about, Mr Lev?"

"But you saw enough to be able to write about it – pick up a mood ... something affected you?"

"I went to the cathedral. Look – I don't like this phone call. I don't know you. Richard hasn't needed some secondary editor before. We always work together to sort things out. Are you telling me my book's not accurate. Is that it?" His anger was rising.

"My dear Brideswell, don't upset yourself – your novel is quite accurate. We would expect that from you, your work has always been careful. It's not the factual side. There are some sections we need to go over, together. You see, my family are from Smolensk. We are also rather like your character Davidov, square pegs in round holes. I am free tomorrow

– why not come down … say about 6 pm. You won't need to take an early train. Just a chat about a few things. Good book – just some creases to iron out."

"Will Richard be there?"

"Unfortunately not. He's away in North Carolina – we've opened up an office in Chapel Hill. He's getting that up and running … so you see – I'm afraid it's me who will be guiding this book into print."

That had rocked him. Shocked him. "He didn't tell me. I've always worked with him, for years."

"I know. It was sudden. Our man in the US had to pull out. Heart attack. Richard flew out two weeks ago. We shall get on fine – he's told me all about your other books, and about you, and his feelings about this one. I am glad to pick it up – it's my country … that was. I have exchanged my city for London. The fact is, we can't take your book any further as it stands – that's why I need to see you, very soon. Like tomorrow."

"All right."

He didn't sleep well. The call shook him badly, and made him angry. Brideswell boarded the afternoon train the next day, the 2.11 pm Stockport, platform 3. The many passengers hurried down to the first carriage they could enter – standard class, including a monk in a brown cassock, flushed and short of breath and a fair haired woman with a shoulder bag. The three entered by the same door. He might have helped the old monk – the case was too heavy for him, but a porter had carried it down the platform and passed it up into the boarding bay. The woman took her reserved seat diagonally across the aisle from him. He noticed her – it was his trade as a novelist to notice things, and that a strap on her bag was loose. He was surprised, she did not give the appearance of being a careless person. The monk settled first, by the door. They both had to squeeze past him as he edged down into his place.

*

The train gathered speed and left behind the sprawling towns of Greater Manchester. The woman, once called Anya but who now had adopted a closer English version –Alice – loosened her coat and took from her a side pocket in the bag a letter, a letter asking her to come to London, to a teaching hospital. Vladimir was in hospital there, ill.

She had been plunged into a journey not of her choosing – she had to go. It meant leaving behind Kenny. He was a sensitive boy, they had no secrets, she explained why – but it was no solace. Her son was upset.

For Kenny there were moments in each day which were touched by the divinity he heard and felt on Sundays.

One of the revelations into the mystery of God, His endless powers to surprise, His unfathomable mystery, was the arrival of the morning post. His mother had made it his job to gather it up, sort it, study each stamp and postmark and to re-address his father's letters to that woman in Wilmslow, her house in Chapter Road. Letters were laid on the soft blue-white of the breakfast table. He would place them so as not to cover up the language of the cloth's embroidery, strange messages woven within which, as yet he, had not cracked the code. The letters were so arranged that the stamps, postmark and handwriting were showing

– a rare joy when he placed there a letter to himself. A boy who believed in signs, omens, mystery and the hand of God – chance had no part in his understanding of the world. He had always believed that the reason for no mail on a Monday – always a severe disappointment – was because no one in their right mind writes boring letters on a Saturday, never on Sunday.

On the morning that had been left behind before Stockport, the previous day, he had arranged the three letters and went into the kitchen to tell Alice. He loved her for the smells which surrounded her, bacon, fried bread, and mushrooms, the smell of her hands when she touched his forehead, her perfume which reached him when she was going to a party after a concert. And he loved her for the beautiful tunes she played on her violin, the strange Russian songs she sang to him when he couldn't sleep – and when he woke from the dream crying. One day he would find a way of rubbing out that dream, or leave it on his pillow while he walked away.

"Alice, there are three letters."

"Three ... well we are doing well for a Monday, dear."

"Will you come in and look at them?"

"Are the stamps all English?"

"Of course they are."

"But I do get letters from abroad."

Not for ages. He entered it in his diary when a letter came from a foreign country. Alice lifted out his bacon – crisp as he liked it – and placed it on the fried bread.

"What are the postmarks?"

"Manchester, the Isle of Wight and London. That one's personal."

She passed him his breakfast and they walked together

into the back room. Alice brought with her a mug of coffee. "Which one shall we look at first?"

He removed the postcard from the small pile and handed it to her. For a moment she wanted to kiss his fingers, but Kenny was embarrassed by shows of affection. Instead she touched his cheek.

"Who do you think this is from? Will you read it to me?"

He took it back and answered reluctantly. "All right, but it's boring."

"Not boring, dear – it's kind for someone to be thinking of us when they're on holiday."

"It's from Graham – he's not kind. Just showing off because he's missing school." He read out the message coolly without enthusiasm. "'Dear Kenny and your family, how are you getting on. The weather here is bad. It is raining. Please save this card for me because I want it back. Graham.'" Kenny looked up and screwed up his lips. "There, didn't I say so. Who wants a card about that sort of thing."

"Doesn't he say anything else, dear? Where is he, in all that rain?"

He turned over the card. "Torquay. He says something else stupid."

"Well read it out. It may seem different."

"'Ps. This is the most boring place in the world and in the northern hemisphere. City won again. Altrincham are so pathetic.'" He looked away and held out the card not wanting to ever see it again.

Alice took. "He spells pathetic very well. He'll be glad to get home after all that rain." She placed it back down on the table. "Let's try something else. A bit more cheerful."

"This letter is from Manchester."

"Who will that be from, darling?"

"I don't know. It might be your orchestra."

She had opened it – and sighed. Extra rehearsals for the Mahler. How could they expect her do those with so much to do, and Kenny needing her all the time. And she had asked for the third. "You were right about that one, darling. From Alec – extra work. Find me something nicer in the last one."

Her mind returned to the train racing through a station. People standing back. A child looking in catching her eye for an instant. She noticed that she had folded the letter in her hand several times. Alice stood up, squeezed the letter back into her bag and set it on the rack a little distance from the large cases above her. Yet the memory of opening that letter would not leave her mind. They had looked at the envelope together, the tall sloping handwriting, the crossed 7 and the central London postmark. A wave of unease.

"This is a mysterious letter. I'm not sure I like it." She had said.

"What does WC1 mean, Alice?"

"West Central – the middle of London. Bloomsbury, Holborn, King's Cross, that sort of area. Literary and newspapers."

"And the foreign 7?"

"So it is." Her voice was flat. Kenny heard the foreboding and saw it in her face, in her fingers as she opened it. Not a good letter. Monday was a bad day for all mail. "It's from Uncle Vladimir, darling, he's had to go into hospital in London near where he lives. He wants me to go down."

A hateful Monday. Alice would go and who would protect him from the dream. "Can you go for the day?" He asked the question knowing in his heart there was worse to come.

Much worse. Breakfast had lost its wonder. Now it had no taste. Alice put her arms across his shoulders. "But it's such a long way, dear, and I might have to see Uncle Vladimir twice. I know this sounds horrible but please ... could you stay just one night with Daddy and Carol? Please ...?" He grimaced and moved his shoulder away from her arm.

"I hate Carol. She is horrible. She is the worst woman I know. Worst, worst, worst in the whole world."

"Only for the one night, Kenny. Please ... for Uncle Vladimir. He's not well and he's calling for me. There must be something he's really worried about. Graham's away. Where else can you go?"

"I'm old enough to stay here on my own."

"Darling, you know you're not. I couldn't ever do that." She brushed the hair back from her face. Life could be impossible. The worries endless.

"Uncle Vladimir is a very special man, he's part of our family, and he was very kind to me when I was your age – younger. He is very ill and that's why I have to go down and see him. He has asked and I can't say 'no'. He's never asked me to do anything like this before. Please ... just for the one night."

"What if I have that dream again, Alice?"

"Daddy's there."

"Frank might not hear."

"I'll give you my mobile and you can ring me if you wake up. As soon as I get to London I'll ring you from where I'm staying to say where it is and what my number is. I shall choose somewhere so close to the station that if you need me I can just jump on a train and come back home."

"I suppose I've got to do it." He sighed. The day was a bad one, just like Mondays always were.

"Next Saturday we'll go and see Altrincham. Isn't it a summer friendly against Stockport County?"

"Graham says they're pathetic."

"We know they're not. He's just showing off."

"All right. Just one night. No more."

She hugged him. "One night. It's a promise."

Alice did not realise she was weeping. She opened her handbag, wiped her face with a tissue and blew her nose. A flat countryside, fields green, hay cut and rolled into circular bales. The calm beauty of it pointed to her, a finger, that her own life was drab and loveless apart from Kenny. And far too busy. No time to look from a window to watch and stare. Only two islands emerging from a sea of restless waves and coldness – Kenny, and her violin. She looked back into the train. Her eyes rested upon a man she had seen before, on boarding, steadying the arm of the old monk. She admired his concentration as he read, not sensing that her gaze was on him, not raising his head from the book to see who was examining him, not looking up as the train slowed at signals. She was glad their eyes had not met, it would have broken into her thoughts, invaded her private world, an outreach from the man's existence, an insertion she did not want.

Yet she did already know things about him, the way he had looked at the monk struggling to board the train with a big case – whether he should leave him to the porter or take over. A man of sensitivity, of compassion. She wondered why he had such a new travelling bag, was it his or his wife's, why was it still on his shoulder and not, like hers, up on the rack. He was alone and had a smart bag because he was coming down to London on business and had to impress someone. Perhaps he would get out at Rugby or

Milton Keynes – she hoped not. Nor did she think he was travelling back to London – something about him made her think he was travelling towards someone, something, not leaving behind finished business. As the train slowed before Crewe she looked away. The world outside depressed her; the station even in summer was bedraggled and drab, litter on the lines, paint peeling from the platform canopies. A station for waiting on endlessly on wet days, a town of vast railway workshops – a town familiar with waiting.

Several people boarded, entered their carriage. A young woman with a back-pack sat down beside the brown-gowned monk. She was thankful no one came to sit down beside her, or beside the reading man. She didn't want him being talked at and interrupted – certainly not by any of the three tall young men who seemed to be in an argument beneath her bag, arms thrusting up and down in all directions. The train left Crewe far behind, a fading memory. They had entered a wild, hilly district, the empty sprawling uplands of Cannock Chase. Her eyes returned to her book man. She decided she liked his face, the shape of his hands and fingers, the gentle way he turned a page as if reluctant to leave behind what he had just read. A writer, she thought, and she noticed for the first time flecks of grey in his hair. Suddenly he set down his book, stood up, looked about him in a bewildered way, then holding the tops of the seats to steady himself in the sway and rock of the train, passed by her.

Alice also stood up. She took her handbag, left her silk scarf, book and paper on the seat and went the other way, towards the buffet car. As she passed his seat the book on it had slipped off onto the floor. She bent down, picked it up, and the green bookmark. Alice smoothed down the creased pages and replaced the marker. Her eyes lingered on the cover, blue and white – a woman in a nightdress looking wistfully out of a window. She hesitated a moment longer, a slight wave of anxiety reaching into her in case the reading man was on his way back – the title. It surprised her. 'First love and other stories by Ivan S Turgenev.' How extraordinary that he should be reading a Russian classic and get so deeply immersed in it that the world beyond did not exist. And that the man she was going to visit in hospital was also from Russia. The USSR when he had left. With her.

Brideswell came back from the toilet. He had not hurried back but spent some time in the space at the carriage end looking out to see where they were. Pine forests and hills, just like Turgenev had been describing, only this was the English Midlands – Cannock. Near his seat he stopped to allow a woman to pass him. She was carrying a carton of coffee and a packet of sandwiches. She smiled at him.

"Thank you."

He saw her look at the scarf and things on her seat, unable to sit down, uncertain whether to risk setting down her coffee onto the table because of the swaying and jerking of the train.

"Can I lift those up for you so you can sit down ... you've got your hands full."

"Oh ..." She looked at him – an enquiry and something searching in her gaze, a relief at an unexpected offer of help. "Would you ... it would be such a help. I should have thought of it before going for these, but I didn't want to lose my place."

He was surprised at her voice, the sadness in it. He bent down and lifted up the book, scarf and paper. "It's hard to put anything down when the train is rocking like this, especially a full cup of boiling hot coffee." He looked up and saw the two large cases above her. She had boarded with a handbag and shoulder bag – no sign of that. "Your bag?"

"I've had to push it in down there near you. I don't need it till Euston."

He took the coffee from her while she eased herself back into the seat.

"Thanks for helping. Actually your book fell on the floor. I picked it up."

"Ah, well there you are then. My turn this time. It's a pity they don't have a trolley on the train with this sort of thing. Who wants to stagger about with hot coffee, stepping over legs and bags."

"I shan't open it up until we slow down a bit."

She has an accent, he mused as he returned to his seat. He looked up for her bag. It had a small, dangling strap. Had it finally come undone?

Alice watched him return to his seat. He did not look back at her but picked up his book. She would have liked him to come back. To sit across the table from her and say he was reading Ivan Turgenev, a book that was so locked into her Russian childhood. A book that was always on the small table beside her father's chair, the deep wicker one in his study with the pale, embroidered cushion covers her mother had worked on throughout that last endless winter.

And the words that she could still hear. "What would people say, the students, if they came into the study of Andrei Andreyevich and found old ragged cushions?"

At Euston Brideswell hesitated on the platform. He saw again the woman he had helped on the train in the jostling hurrying crowd ascending the ramp to the concourse. He was disappointed she hadn't seen him and in a curious way missed her – a brief meeting of two people travelling alone and pitched into a humid, remote city that cared for no one. Perhaps he was the lonely one and she wasn't. He lost sight of her in the crowd of streaming out people.

On the concourse he checked his wallet, £20 pounds, probably enough without having to cross over to the cash-point. He left the station by the entrance to the Underground but decided against the tube and came out the other side, crossed the Euston Road and entered his past. A bed and breakfast near his old flat, the place his parents had stayed in whenever they came up from Somerset – when they came up for the wedding. It wasn't far. The promise of a cooler evening hadn't come. The day's heat lingered everywhere, rising from the pavements, in the still air, even higher where the building tops touched the sky. He walked slowly along Judd Street hoping a cool breeze might blow in from the east, from the river.

When he crossed the entrance to Mecklenburg Square he was surprised to see the guest-house had its blinds down, the upstairs curtains drawn. He knocked. An elderly woman answered, dressed all over in black. She placed her fingertips beneath her eyes and slowly drew them down her cheeks as if fingering away a wetness. Her voice dull and distant.

"Yes?"

"Sorry ... I'm looking for a room. For the night, possibly two."

She said nothing but continued to look at him, or past him, or through him. Or not seeing him at all.

"I apologise, Maria. I did see the curtains and shutters. It's been a long time. I wouldn't expect you to remember me ... Michael Brideswell. The flat on the corner over the off-licence. My parents stayed with you when they came up for my wedding."

She sighed and shook her head. "I can't take you. This house is in mourning."

"Ah ... forgive me. Of course. I should have known."

"Where have you come from?"

"Manchester ... quite near it."

"So far? On such a hot day?"

"I apologize for barging in like this, when you're so sad. I'll walk back to Argyle Square."

"You can't go there. Is not a good place now. Please, come in."

He entered a dim hallway lit only by candles. "I shouldn't be here, Maria, breaking into your mourning. I shall be quiet and respectful."

She sighed deeply and touched his arm. "Maybe it is good. I am on my own. Maybe you have been sent by my Holy Mary, Mother of Christ." She pointed to a chair and drew one forward for herself. "I am glad you remembered me, Michael. I do need someone here tonight. Do you also remember my husband?"

"I remember him well, Maria ... a good man, very kind, always smiling."

"He is dead. The funeral is tomorrow in an English Protestant church. It is very hard for me, but he wasn't a Catholic."

"But surely your family should be here? This of all nights?"

"You don't know? It was a second marriage. I have fallen out with his daughter. I said he wanted to be cremated, after a service in his own church by his own priest, the vicar. It is all arranged now – it was his wish. His daughter is not coming. She does not believe, not in anything, not in saying goodbye to her father."

Brideswell nodded and remained silent for some time. "Do I remember… wasn't there a son?"

"He is mine. He lives in Italy."

"No family at the funeral – that's very hard, Maria."

"There will be some of Boris's friends, that's all."

"I shall come with you. You need someone."

"You haven't come to London, Michael, to go to Boris's funeral."

"I am a writer. No one is in a hurry to read what I say. I'd be happy to come."

"You're a good boy. Your wife is a lucky woman."

"I'll tell you about that, not now."

"Let us go through to the kitchen. I make you some supper. Maybe we have both lost someone."

"I think so. Thank you.

*

After a canal knifing

Brideswell signed the sheet of paper the ward sister handed to him. Taking his own discharge against medical advice. The woman leaning across him was cold, angry and upset.

"You're a very silly man, Mr Brideswell. Yesterday you nearly died. We had to give you four pints of blood and you were two hours in theatre. How can you possibly want to go now, so soon … it's so stupid! And quite wrong. We fought to save your life, now you just walk out, walk away. The folly of it I find quite callous … have we all been wasting our time? Should we have been operating on someone else who might be more appreciative?"

"Sister, I am appreciative. I know you saved my life, but now I feel normal – just a bit of neck-ache. I shall be grateful to you and all the surgical team for the rest of my life. I want to give this bed to someone else."

The sister watched him sign, riven with misgivings. "We have no powers to detain you. You must come back up here, to me, if you feel faint. I shall forgive you because you are a silly, stubborn man who does not value his life."

She walked away abruptly. He was sorry he had brought

tears to her eyes. Brideswell packed his travel bag and carefully drew on his polo-neck jumper. It covered up the plaster, would stop looks and questions. A cooling breeze reached him from an open window – an east wind. He liked that.

He walked slowly along Gower Street somewhat lightheaded and with a neck even more sore with the roll-neck of his pullover pressing against it. He ran his finger round and pulled it down, sighed and breathed in the coolness of the fresh wind. Another ache disturbed him – it ran up from his wrist to his shoulder – the arm where the drip had been. Yet apart from that, as he had told Sister Elliston – he felt well, his life had been saved, but for what purpose? Something unanswerable, a life of questionable value. Yet he would not have lived if nothing now was wanted from him. A new view of everything had been ushered in – no depression, no futility and feelings of worthlessness, simply pains. No place remained for philosophy and endless self examination. A brush with death had evaporated all that. He now felt new feelings, elation and a waiting. Waiting to receive further orders. Yes. Simply that. Not saved by God, but saved by kindness, caring and a surgeon's skill. That was full of meaning. Words were absent. Handed a second chance.

The heat of the day before had gone. In his face blew a cooling easterly breeze which had brushed him on the ward, a wind from the North Sea funnelling up the Thames Estuary and setting a normality once more on a sweating city. He rested on a bench in a quiet part of Bedford Square, away from the hurrying students and less-driven tourists, overcome by the beauty of the morning and aware of a new calmness within himself. He watched the trees leaning away from the breeze, turning their leaves this way and that – dark green, light green, touched with a dazzle when mirrored by a filtering sun.

Brideswell rang a bell beside a blue door on the east side of the square. The entry phone remained silent but a buzzing told him he could go in. He found to his dismay that after three stairs he was dizzy, the light seemed too bright and a coldness entered his forehead from his neck. He stopped, held on to the banister and bent over, lowering his head towards his knees. The attack of nausea and faintness passed. No smells – he praised his guardian angel for not sending down a fit. Up, on, climbing slowly the airless stairwell he came to and pushed open a door – a door of thick frosted glass, a door to keep people out not to welcome them in. It moved easily under the pressure of his palm. A young woman sat at a desk, a mug beside her. The room smelled of her perfume, and coffee. His mood had become light and detached. He nodded with a half-smile, avoiding but the barest movement of his neck. In an instant the wave of faintness flashed light in his eyes. His face became over cold. His knees uncertain.

"Mr Brideswell …? Are you all right – you look so white!"

"Just a passing thing."

"Are you sure. We didn't think you were coming."

He looked around the reception room. "Oh … why was that?" He touched the edge of the desk. "Would you mind if I sat down?"

He crossed the room to a green chair and sat down thankfully, resting his hands on his arms and stared down at the floor until it stopped moving.

"We had two messages." She was concerned for him, and alarmed. "You don't look at all well, Mr Brideswell. Please let me get you something ... a glass of water. A hot cup of sweet coffee?"

"Yes, now that does sound good. Thank you. Two spoons of sugar." A kind woman in a cold place with an unbreakable door. "I don't think I left any messages, did I?"

"Oh yes. One about playing chess with a friend in hospital and then another about having to go to a funeral."

"A wrong number. Not me. I've been in hospital. I was mugged behind King's Cross."

"Oh dear! I am sorry. You poor man. How good of you to come on here after all that. Perhaps you were confused ... something so horrible."

"Could be. I don't remember anything."

She brought him the hot coffee, stirring in the extra sugar. "I never go to King's Cross – it's such a bad place. I always walk down from Euston Square underground. I've never had any trouble that way. Never." She gently handed him the mug. "Mr Lev is here ... I'm sure he'll see you soon, I know he wants to. Please don't get up till you've had your coffee and feel a bit better. I shall ring him and tell him you're out here waiting, but you need a few moments."

She lifted her telephone and pressed the extension. "Mr Lev? Your appointment has arrived after all. Mr Brideswell is here. He's not very well and is relaxing for a moment with some coffee." A pause while she nodded and looked in his direction. "Yes. I know it's him. He was confused with those messages – or a wrong number. He was mugged and has come here straight from the hospital."

She listened for a few moments longer then replaced the receiver. "You won't mind waiting a little – I'm afraid he's with one of our other authors. We gave him your appointment. Mr Lev thinks he'll be ready to see you in about 20 minutes."

"Ah ... then I'll finish this and go back outside. It's a beautiful day. So much cooler and nicer out there in the square. I'll feel better then."

George Lev was free when he returned.

"I'm sorry, old chap, you're not feeling so good. I must say you look as pale as a sheet. So what's been happening?"

Brideswell moved his chair further from Lev's desk, setting it at some distance, near the window where he could see trees and sky. "Some hooligans robbed me. I've been in hospital."

"Really sorry to hear that. Angela did say. I'm glad she made you some coffee and sent you outside." He paused, looked down to file cupboard and lifted up a manuscript. "We were a bit thrown by your messages. Very courageous of you to come out – put everything off – brave the day, and me."

Brideswell's dislike of the man increased – not what he said but the tone of his voice, the superiority. He had no energy to take up random phone messages or why they assumed he had left them.

"What's wrong with my book."

"Ah, but wait a minute. Before business, how are you fixed? Have you still got a ticket back to er ..."

"I came down from Manchester."

"Of course. Did those thieves leave you with any money? Let me advance you some cash on your book. Because we like it, and you've had a bad time."

Brideswell remained silent. He detested game-playing. It bored him. "You're a cautious man, Mr Brideswell. Take it – a loan – it won't break Mannings. Let Angela fix you up with £50 pounds. We don't want you leaving us a penniless ghost.

Stay down another night. Better than being shaken up for hours in a stuffy train."

"What's wrong with my book?"

Lev flinched. He took up the telephone brusquely. "Angela. Give Mr Brideswell £50 out of petty cash. Those bastards left him with nothing." He moved the manuscript in front of him, turned several pages, not to read or even see them – a gesture. Editor to author. "Beautifully written, as all your books are." He stopped. "I won't keep you long – you've been through enough already. Bad luck to be picked out by criminals. They hang around Euston waiting for victims."

He stood up and crossed to the window, closer to Brideswell but on the other side of him. "You write very well about London – like a Londoner. Like an Englishman. I observe it because I once wasn't English. I may have said. When you move your book to Manchester you write with all those places in your blood, from your past – all those nuances from people who lived there before, part of you, the roots of your family." He leaned forward, pushed open the top window some more, then engaged Brideswell with a more distant look. "There is a flaw. Many people would miss it. A tear in a valuable stamp that makes it worthless for a collector. When you write about Smolensk, you write like a tourist. You'll convince many people, your admiring public who love your words, your prose, your images, those poetic descriptions, but it won't convince a single Russian.

They will see you as you would an Eskimo, writing home about a Test Match. Sorry. That's how it is."

The door opened after a light knock. The receptionist brought in Lev's lemon tea and passed his visitor a buff envelope. When she had gone he continued.

"Brideswell ... you're a good writer, but we want it better, much better. Richard has suggested you go to Smolensk for a month or so, get yourself a room somewhere. Live like a Russian, the bars, the cathedral, go to the old churches and stay for the service, see the factories, stand on the building sites ... get yourself a woman and see what she says. How she says it. Then when you come back, send me chapters six, seven and eight. Rewritten."

He stopped, returned to his desk and from a drawer lifted up a second envelope. "Richard has bought you an open ticket. Return to Smolensk. He's even put in some roubles. He likes you, Brideswell. We both know you've written a good book. Good we don't want. Only an outstanding novel. Nothing less."

For the first time Brideswell spoke, quietly – deeply hurt. "I am to re-write three chapters."

"Yes. We will take your book, but not as it is."

"Supposing I don't agree."

"We'd be sorry to lose you, and your work. Someone else may take it as it stands. We are aiming higher than that, Brideswell. Much higher."

"Are you a writer, Mr Lev?"

"George. Let's leave all that 'Mr' stuff behind. I can't write. I don't have your imagination. I am an editor and a Russian *émigré.* I understand your anger." He pushed the manuscript across the desk and placed the two envelopes on top of it. "A holiday will do you good, Michael. We are not interested in a piece that will ring the cash tills. We are past all that with you. Two beatings ... thugs and your editor. I want a fine novel. Nothing else is worth the candle. You owe it, because you have the gift. We pedestrians don't."

Outside, Brideswell signed for the cash. He walked out into a summer's day where the light was unusually and abnormally bright. He returned to the bench in the square where he had watched the tree move in a cooler morning breeze. The sun had become hot. A stillness was invading the heat.

He was in no hurry to walk to Euston for the train home. Strangely, he liked George Lev better. The pain the man had inflicted wasn't made any less because Brideswell knew deep down he was right. The chapters could be better. The book would be strengthened. He would go there.

He placed his novel and the envelopes into his jacket pocket, thanked God for giving him back his life, for the skill of the surgeon who had saved him, for publishers who believed he was capable of writing something of value. For ten minutes he closed his eyes, felt the heat of the sun on his neck assuage the pain, felt it's balm on his arm and shoulder, its power to evaporate the after-image of George Lev. He fell asleep. Much later he left the square, the light around him had returned to normal. Brideswell ran his finger again around the inside of his jumper. In the train he would take off the pullover, ease the pressure on the plaster, upon the wound beneath. Diminish the fire.

*

With Maria: Boris's funeral

Later Maria asked him if he would like to see Boris.

The lid had been left off the coffin. Though he was a Russian protestant, the Orthodox practice of open coffin and valediction was being observed. Brideswell went into the front room, an airless oppressive space too small for so long and sombre an object. The sun had beaten down all afternoon against the drawn shutters but the heat had not been kept out. He smelled incense more Eastern than Anglican, burnt to replace the smell of death – a joss-stick from a market in Soho. Two candles had been lit on either side of the coffin which threw a flickering light across the face of the dead man. White flowers had been carefully placed on small tables giving off strong scents of summer, orange blossom, lilies and iris. He bent over, kissed the man on the forehead and remembered a Russian prayer.

"Lord, let me lie down like a stone and rise up like new bread."

Maria at his side bent low and made the sign of the cross over his chest.

"Jesus have mercy, Holy Mary have mercy, God show His mercy to a good man." Brideswell placed his hand on her shoulder as they withdrew. She began to weep.

Maria led him into the kitchen where she had prepared supper, spreading a white tablecloth as she would for any guest, following an instinct for kindness, tradition and order implanted deep within her by her mother. She was glad to have a man's company and offered up a silent prayer to the Virgin Mother for sending Michael to her on her day of deepest need. She would not have been afraid to be alone all night with her husband lying downstairs – a husband who is a friend in life does not suddenly become a stranger in death. Nor was she superstitious; but sadness would have finally overwhelmed her, laying upon her a paralysis against what she must do the next day. She would not have slept.

Maria served spaghetti bolognaise into two wide bowls – Italian china that once had been her mother's and only brought out when she ate pasta with her husband. She warmed through some Italian bread, set the pieces into a basket and brought in with it a carafe of red wine. She wiped her hands on a cloth in her apron pocket and sat down.

"How many people have been in, Maria, to pay their respects?"

"Some of my neighbours … the two girls next door in the top flat. My nephew Lorenzo has been. Yesterday, in his lunch hour … he stayed as long as he could."

"Then he'll be coming tomorrow to the funeral."

"I don't know. He doesn't think he can get away from work. Friday is a busy day for him."

"Surely … for his uncle's funeral."

"He works at Mount Pleasant. The big sorting office. They're short of staff all the time."

They ate the meal in silence while it was hot. "If Lorenzo doesn't come, who will be there, Maria?"

"How should I know. Maybe from his work."

"Family?"

"No."

"There are not many Protestants in Russia."

"He was from Kaliningrad, Michael. It was German once. The churches are not like ours in Italy."

"Was Boris born there, then?"

"No. In Smolensk. You like the wine? Is from near my village."

"I do. Very much."

At the entrance archway to the church the coffin was transferred to the care of three strong men, market traders in Smithfield – a Russian, a Lithuanian and a Pole. Brideswell offered to take the fourth corner. They nodded. The sexton tolled the bell. Maria walked behind them with Lorenzo, the nephew, a tall, thin man who peered about him as if he were still sorting letters. A strange and lonely cortege. The vicar came in behind the chief mourners, dressed in a white surplice and dark coloured sash. Beside him walked his curate. There was only one other man there – he sat at the back in the shadows, a friend of the visiting organist. He had come down from Manchester and had helped his friend who had asthma with a large case, a monk. The man had been invited to stay the night in a guest-room of the monastic house nearby.

The cortege entered the high south aisle with its Norman fan vaulting and darkness, both remaining since the time it had been a priory. They swung to the left. In front of them a square of marble mosaic pavement. The four men lowered the coffin onto its beamed frame. The ancient church became filled with Mozart's tender music. Four people wept – the organist Brother Robert, the widow Maria, her unexpected visitor who remembered her in her need, and the organist's friend deep in the shadows of the east window. He wept because he believed himself to be a second-rate novelist and the music of Mozart, its tenderness, moved his heart. He felt a voice telling him that he did have it within him to produce something the world might value, that he possessed the gift to do it, that there was a way, not in England. He would find it in Smolensk.

The service was Anglican, the music Catholic, the church Augustinian – a priory founded by a jester after a vision. The rector prayed for the soul of Boris Madewski, for rest in eternal peace. The dead man's forehead was kissed for the last time. The priest blessed the spirit leaving the body. He touched lightly the face and drew upon it the sign of the cross.

"Boris, who came into this world with nothing, travelled a long journey from Russia to England to become a loving husband to Maria, the father of two daughters, a friend to many, a colleague to trust at work, a good man. God protect his family and give them comfort. Let Boris find in God's mercy, and the love of Jesus Christ, eternal peace." The lid was slowly lifted up and placed on the coffin. Maria sobbed, coughing in her crying. The men on each side of her took her arm. The pall-bearers came back to the coffin, lifted it high onto their shoulders. They left the church slowly to music of utmost sorrow and compassion – the Lacrimosa.

Later, after a long silence, as they drew up to the crematorium, Brideswell asked Maria something that was troubling him. "Two daughters, Maria? Who is this second one?"

"Ivana."

"Where is she? Why is she not here with us?"

"She lives in Smolensk."

"Ah ... then when I go I shall find her for you. Does she know her father has died?"

"She is a mystery, Michael. No one has ever told her about her father's marriage in England – to me. He never once mentioned her. They had lost touch. Maybe a reason. I never knew."

"She should know."

"Yes, you find her for your Maria. Tell her to come. There are things she should have. Her sister in England is bitter. There is no love, no memory. Only rejection. Both of us. Ivana and her father's wife from Italy."

When the organist finished the Lacrimosa, he came down from the console platform into the nave, now empty and silent, dark and enigmatic, embracing its deep past and the centuries of prayer and holiness. He walked down the south aisle to meet the man at the back, a funeral visitor who had remained half-hidden in the shadows, who had not moved throughout the service for the dead.

Yet the man had been deeply affected, shaken and at times the tears in his eyes spilled onto his face. He had listened to one funeral, heard the voice of all funerals in Mozart's music, wept for the transience of human life, the sorrows at its ending, the joys at its unfolding – funerals great, funerals unattended. He had also been shaken by the appearance of one of the pall- bearers. For one instant a beam of light had fallen across the man's face. It was as if he was seeing himself, that he, Michael Brideswell, was assisting in transforming the dead man into the enigma of eternity.

They left the church together. A web was settling across and around him, like a vast garden cobweb containing a leaf from some other unknown tree, in some other forest – a web secured at four points. Two strands of which had been revealed in the dimness of a priory founded in 1100.

"The man, Boris, he had two daughters. Neither came."

The organist nodded and looked up into the sky which had clouded over, shielding the full heat of a midsummer sun, softening the colours in the churchyard, setting a half-shade over a parched ground.

"The nephew was there, and a few friends. The widow has a son of her own in Italy. The London daughter almost never existed after the marriage. She rejected them completely. She did not come, and will live to regret that unkindness."

"The other one?"

His friend shook his head. "I have heard she is known in Smolensk."

"Yes? For what?"

"My brothers there know of her. She is a cleaner in the great cathedral. The Cathedral of Our Lady of the Assumption."

"Has no one tried to find her, to tell her that her father has died."

"Perhaps you will do that, Michael."

"Yes. Perhaps I might."

*

Guest of Brother Robert

He decided to leave the window open – the room needed airing. A damp staleness still clung to it from the weeks of being unoccupied. He washed, shaved and came downstairs. Brideswell found a ground floor room and a window table covered with a white cloth, laid for one and sat down. A long room, a central glass partition drawn back – at the far end were two more windows, tall and old-fashioned with sash cords and traditional wooden frames, seen always once in older, spacious houses. He felt the smooth white cloth of his table then allowed his gaze to take in the scene beyond the windows – a wide area of gardens and ancient buildings. A room within a city far from crowds, a room of no urgency, unknown to hurry, haste, a space which served many purposes other than breakfasts. The smells reaching him were not those of any holy order – only coffee and frying bacon. He became aware of movement and turning saw the smiling presence of his new friend. The monk was not any longer dressed in a cassock but grey flannels and a blue open-necked shirt.

"You've found where we have breakfast – guided by my bacon? I hope you're hungry, Michael."

"Thank you. Yes, I certainly am. Shall I come through and get something?"

"No, just sit here. It's the work of a moment – all ready. I'll join you with my coffee." He soon returned with a tray and took his own mug from it.

"I'm sorry you had all those strange dreams – it comes from being a writer with an endless wheel of imaginary pictures. I never have interesting dreams."

"Thanks for all this." Brideswell took his plate of breakfast from the tray. "I didn't expect you to cook for me."

"We all had the same – the other brothers and I."

"Where are they?"

"This is an open order, a working house – just like our little unit in Mobberley. Here they are more gifted … we are from a different tradition – crafts, gardens, hives. We sell our honey and carpentry, smaller items of furniture, in the Knutsford market once a month."

"I know the market. I must look out for your stall. What is different about this place, Charterhouse?" He cut into his bacon. "Their talents can't be any greater than yours, only a different kind."

The older man smiled. "I don't know about that – but our honey is very popular, and our little stools and tables sell well. Here they are more scholarly – a monastic house at this site for centuries, scarred but not destroyed by Henry the Vandal. They moved sideways somewhat, schooling. They have a very good school now resited in Surrey. They also have musicians, some – and I have been invited to play in an old abbey church in Smithfield, for a funeral today."

"You are an organist, Robert?"

He nodded. "I am glad to do it. One of the brothers was down to play but he has an infection in one of his fingers. It will be a pleasure to play in such an ancient church – though sad, of course: parts of the Mozart Requiem."

"Which church would that be?"

"St Bartholomew the Great."

"I know it well."

Brother Robert drank some coffee. "Tell me some more about your dreams."

"Are you sure you want to hear?"

"I'm interested in dreams – as someone who never has them."

He did not say at once but finished his breakfast, drank the glass of orange juice and looked out of the window across the lawns. He could feel the sun's warmth beginning to enter the room – a cloudless sky. Another hot day.

"They were very odd … sort of happening around people in our carriage – and you were there, too."

"Yes …how very strange… you mentioned it when I came up. Something about Smolensk. I have something to tell you about that later. But why was that Russian city in your dream?"

"I had to go there to find someone."

"Was it revealed, who this lost person was?"

"No. It wasn't."

His monastic friend stood up. "Come out into the day. Leave the night behind. Let me show you the lovely gardens and lawns. But … you have things to do? Business you came down for?"

"I came down to see my publisher. They have a new and rather pushy new editor who doesn't seem impressed with my latest book. I am to be quizzed about it."

"Let's forget him on such a lovely day. Come with me to a church. I shall be playing Mozart for a soul who has moved on from a life that wasn't easy."

"I should be in the way."

"Not at all. The man was from Smolensk. That great ancient city is also a home to our order. You see – it does seem you are wanted there."

After walking for some time in silence, they rested at a bench. Brother Robert took out his inhaler and eased his breathing.

"Who is this Russian man? How come he's having a funeral in central London?"

"Listen to this story. It concerns you, of that I am quite sure. His name is Boris, born in Kalingrad – and a protestant. You remember it was once a Lutheran province of Prussia. He worked and married in Smolensk, and when his wife died he brought one daughter to England, the other, an older girl refused to leave. Boris married an Italian woman; she ran the guest house he was living in. The daughter was outraged, a Catholic wife, her mother forgotten – she left. They were never reconciled, nor is she coming to the funeral."

"There's an Italian district around Rosebury Avenue. I know about the Italian Church and the Italian Hospital…"

"The guest house is not there … in the Gray's Inn Road."

"Really? How strange. I might even know her. My flat was on the corner – over an off-licence. Maria …?" He did know her.

"So you see, my friend, you have to come. God is asking you to."

"Ah … but I don't have your faith, Robert."

Brideswell remained at the back of the ancient church within its shadows. The music played by Brother Robert reached into all his uncertainties and sadness. Tears tracked down his face. A fourth man at the coffin corner, a pall-bearer seemed lost also. So like himself. In fact, he could have been his double. So much so, it was chilling.

*

Ward round for a Russian chess player

Mr Gill went onto the ward early so as to be quite ready, informed and unflustered at his consultant's ward round at 11 am. The sister handed him the notes of the sallow, ill man in the first bed. He read the A & E report and lifted his gaze to the patient.

"Good morning. I am Mr Wilkins' registrar, my name is Gill. I see you live quite near us, Mr Andreanov."

"Yes, thankfully."

"The Gray's Inn Road."

"Yes."

"You have quite a severe anaemia, I'm afraid. It means you are losing blood from somewhere."

"Is that bad, doctor?"

"Of course it is. See for yourself. You're very pale. We could correct it with some blood, but Mr Wilkins won't want to do that yet. We need to find out what's wrong – where it's coming from."

"I can wait. Do what you have to do."

"I shall need to ask you some direct questions."

"Ask away."

"How long have you felt ill?"

"I can't say. I've been tired for a long time – not exactly ill."

"Then I shall have to go back a long time, Mr Andreanov. You came to England in 1967?"

"Yes. I did."

"From Russia?"

"The USSR ... Smolensk."

"Did you have any health worries there – a tendency to anything ... any bleeding problems in your family?"

The doctor was surprised at the man's English, almost faultless and no accent – yet some sounds were over emphasised. The man in the bed raised himself, sighed and eased his points of pressure.

"I was a university teacher, Mr Gill – heavy smoker, and drank too much. The Communist Party had no time for me – I wouldn't join them. Maybe I loved Shakespeare too much. I was on the hit list, they came for me one night and pulled my flat apart. Next time I knew they would take me. I had a conference in England. Due to fly out. I managed it."

"You came in with a delegation?"

"On my own, but with a girl of 10. Not a niece really, but like that. She was the daughter of a composer. He wanted me to bring her to England for safety. He was right. They took him a few weeks after I got out. I feel bad about that. He had become the friend of a defector."

The surgical registrar wrote in the notes: "No family history of bleeding, smokes and drinks heavily." As he liked music he asked, "Who was this composer?"

"Kutsov. Andrei Andreyevich Kutsov. Those camps were horrific. Cruel. So many died."

"Your friend?"

"How can anyone know? I had sent him to a death camp, but saved his daughter."

The doctor nodded. After several moments he continued. "Over here ... did you carry on drinking hard and smoking?"

"Guilt is a bad thing to carry around, Doctor. I brought up his daughter – that gave me some comfort. Then one day she married an Englishman. Our ward sister has seen her – Anya came to see me yesterday with a young friend from my college."

"Ah yes. Which college was that?"

"UCL. I was in the Russian Department. I have a pension from them."

"Who looks after you now?"

"I haven't needed looking after. I have a small flat – my needs are just as small."

"Do you cook?"

"Not much. There's an electric oven, but everything takes so long. I'm impatient, so I go out – to an Italian café. They all know me there, and are like family. They like me. I give them all presents. Birthdays and Christmas."

"What do you eat there?"

"Pasta. It's good and cheap."

"Vodka?"

"Not there. Sometimes at home when I think too much about Russia. But I like the pub too. You have made me into a Englishman, and I prefer a few pints."

"How many in a week?"

"Varies. Sometimes only 6, sometimes twice as much."

Dr Gill was aware that the ward sister beside him was becoming restless and wanted him to move on. But he had already noticed an empty bed. He wanted an explanation. A man they had operated on. A main vein in his neck.

"Nearly finished, Mr Andreanov. Two things. Mr Wilkins will be come round to you this morning. We will have to run quite a few tests on you before we decide how to fix you up." He gave the sister the notes and moved down to the empty bed. "Where the hell has this chap gone?"

The sister flushed, bit her lip and gripped her hands together.

"Mr Brideswell took his own discharge, Mr Gill."

"What! I can't believe it. Is the man mad? We only had him in theatre yesterday. He had blood all night. How many pints did you give him?"

"Four."

"I am stunned. Would you believe it! Why wasn't I informed. I would have stopped him in his tracks."

"You were off duty. I couldn't stop him, Mr Gill. I did everything I could, but he was determined to go. He said he wanted to give his bed to someone else, more deserving. He signed his own discharge, against medical advice."

"Sister ... How could you! You should have sent for someone higher. The matron if you couldn't get me. My houseman was on all night."

"I don't think he would have listened to anyone, not even Mr Wilkins. He had made up his mind. He had somewhere he had to go."

"The man's an utter fool! Have we all been wasting our time saving his precious life? What's his job?"

"A writer."

"A writer! I suppose that's what you'd expect from someone who doesn't live in the real world. Maybe his firm will next publish his death notice!"

Andreanov heard no more of the angry exchange. The doctor and sister moved on to the next patient. He lifted out his chess set, smoothed the covers across his knees and surveyed the pieces with pleasure – a pleasure derived from a sense of order, precision, imagination and the mysticism surrounding choice, choice of move, choices which became narrowed down as bonds were wrapped around the pieces. A halter reining in the horses, hesitation weighting down the front line, the pawns. Unlike the foolish man whose name he did not catch and who had fled from the surgeons that had saved him, his opponent in this encounter was fully engaged. He had been challenged, a duel, by a battle-hardened man, worthy and intelligent.

*

With Maria after the funeral

The wake, the funeral reception, back at Maria's Guildford Street Guest House was a subdued affair. The Smithfield men – the Polish porter, the Lithuanian and Russian traders talked among themselves in low voices. They spoke a language they all understood and discussed prices and people, only when politics inserted itself did their voices rise up. They drank tea from mugs. It did not seem right to remember and mark the loss of their friend Boris in vodka, not then – he had not been a drinking man. Brideswell stood with them for a while, though he found their dialects hard to follow. His knowledge of Russian was limited to two terms in the City Literary Institute before he went to Smolensk, St Petersburg and Kiev two years before. He rejoined Maria.

"It's going to be hard for you, Maria, on your own now. You'll miss Boris so much."

"Hard – it is always hard to a woman left. I loved him. He was a good man. I was lucky to have two husbands. Some women never find one." They sat together at the table where, the night before, she had given him supper, where he had drunk the sharp Italian village wine with Boris lying in the next room in an open coffin. She reached forward and touched his hand. "I am sorry, Michael, you've had to be part of all this, but I am pleased very much you remembered your Maria and came to me. An angel must have spoken into your ears. Do you believe in angels?"

The question seared into him as if he had heard it before, somewhere. He nodded. "You miss your publisher man, too," she added in a concerned tone.

He did not answer that. George Lev was not part of this world.

"I'm sorry your daughter and son couldn't come."

"They could, but they don't. My son stays in Italy – he did not like a step-father from Russia. My step-daughter, she doesn't come to see her father's coffin – from Ilford. It is as far away as Italy ... do you think?" He nodded and felt her sadness, the bitterness of her words. "But you come from Manchester and do not go to see your publisher."

"He won't miss me, Maria – already we don't like each other. And he thinks my new book is not good enough for him. A new man, making his mark before the partners. He is also like Boris, a Russian become English. Mr Lev. Next time I shall see him. Why should I hurry? My friend Richard who always takes my books and sees them into print has gone to America. I have been passed like a parcel. It is like going to the dentist and finding you have been transferred to someone else."

"You must stay with me, Michael, whenever you come to London to see this man. I give you proper food, clean sheets and my best room." She looked at him with tenderness and gave a smile. "I remember your wife. Such a pretty girl. I feel bad you still not together. Sad for you. Sad for her."

"We are divorced, Maria."

"That is so painful. It is not our way."

"I know." He looked away. "So much of what happens to us is governed by chance. Sometimes it's good, sometimes it ushers in a load of trouble and bad things."

"Tell me. What was her name? I forget."

"Katherine. Everyone called her Kit, even her family. It was bad luck for all of us ... she met a man at a party and fell in love with him. Now they have two children. With me it did not happen."

"Who can understand the heart of a woman. I was not sad to lose my first husband. He never liked me – maybe that's why he gambled. I said 'no' – you don't touch my money, Georgio, it is from my family. He hated me for that. In his village in Umbria the woman do everything the husband say, even money. Not me. My mother, her mother – all the women are strong. Family yes, husband no. He would have taken everything from me and left me poor. No. No way. Then one day, very sudden, he died. It was a shock. Very big shock. Then after, I meet Boris. He loved me. We are so happy. Now it is all over. No men, only a Guest House my father put money into. He also love me very much. I have a step-daughter who stays away and a son who makes his life in Italy."

"But there is another one. Boris's Russian daughter. She may be quite different. You still have a family."

"Ivana. Please ... when you go there, you find her for Maria. Say I understand. She does not know her father is dead." She stood up and went to the kitchen – a space she lived in and where she felt at ease. From the fridge she lifted out a white wine in a broad carafe. Beside it, an Italian cake, the sort made by women in her family for every funeral of their loved ones.

The men stepped forward. They must go. Each kissed Maria. They left. She sat quietly for some time then went to the table, cut Brideswell a slice of cake and handed it to him with the white wine. "Michael, I have a photo of Ivana. It will help you. It is in our bedroom. Wait." She left him and brought it down, a small faded photograph in a dark frame. "She is a big girl like her father. Who knows what she may look like now."

He took it and studied the portrait for a while, saying nothing. His mind returning to Smolensk where he knew Lev would be sending him. Why else would he ring. Why else had Richard passed him over to a Russian *émigré*. The young woman had the rounded face of northern Europe, clear features and physical strength. The hair was coiled onto the back of her head in the old-fashioned way, secure and neat for working. She was standing at the entrance to a church and perhaps it was that, the place and her pose, that transmitted a sensitivity and shyness. "Yes," he said at last, "she looks a nice woman. A little shy, I think."

"Boris was like that. Big men are often shy."

"I don't think she's standing by the cathedral, not as I remember it. Maybe she goes to a different place of worship." He turned over the photograph. "Ah ... something here. In Cyrillic script. It says 'Ivana'."

"Of course. But there are other letters? Boris never spoke about that photo. He always moved it to my side of the bed."

"Smolensk. A date. I can make out the name of the Church ... the Church of the Archangel Michael, and a date. 1989. The date it was re-opened, perhaps?" He paused and thought. "May I take this with me, Maria? I should like to have a copy made. I shall bring it to you when I come back down. It will be safe with me. I may need it. Before very long."

He left her after embracing, anxious for her to spend some time alone, reassured that the nephew Lorenzo was coming in later to have supper with her. He walked away and turned at the corner to wave back. She was there. Watching.

Brideswell turned into Mecklenburg Square and walked through the entrance to St George's Gardens. The afternoon was cooling under a freshening easterly breeze blowing in a normality across a sweating city, a sharpness from the North Sea and the Thames estuary – a wind which had its origins in the Baltic and beyond. He looked at his watch and quickened his step. He might be in time for the 3.15 pm, if he hurried.

★

Alice, and Kenny

Alice ached with love for the man beside her. For the first time in her life she had loved in this way, with such tenderness and with a desire overwhelming, lingering, ready if he wanted her.

"We hope you enjoyed your stay, Mrs Brideswell. You were so tired last night!" The receptionist, the same one, spoke warmly to her and took a small square card from the room board, handing it to her. "Please come and stay with us again, our number is on the back, I'm Angela – ask for me."

Alice watched Brideswell take back his credit card. His hands – he had the most sensitive hands she had ever seen on a man, his long fingers, smooth skin with thin veins showing through, fine hair at the wrist she wanted to kiss. He thanked Angela and they left, walking away slowly arm in arm. They approached a garden with tall trees. A much cooler morning; she had lost all sense of direction, but it had to be a breeze coming in from the east. It blew the sweating of yesterday into a memory. She was feeling a rare sense of peace, a calmness with Michael by her side, his arm linked through hers as if they were man and wife. Yet this man had told her nothing about himself, nor had she invaded their closeness with facts of her own – their touch and contact was more eloquent and sensitive than words. She allowed the erotic desire encircling her legs to spread downwards, into her feet, her toes, and to disappear. A feeling of such rarity and pleasure she was reluctant to let it go, but she was glad the tension in her breast remained. It linked her to him. One touch and she would be alight again. They sat closely on a bench on the western side of the gardens, feeling the growing heat of the sun upon their faces. Alice closed her eyes and kept at bay the anguish she would feel when he left her. She rested her head on his shoulder and felt like crying.

"I shall miss you so much when you have to leave me to go to your publisher." She straightened herself. Alice would have liked to kiss him everywhere, on his face, his eyes, his lips, his fingers, the wrist and the soft hairs on them – instead she lifted his hand and held it against her cheek.

"I'm not going to see them, Alice."

Then she did cry – for all her loveless past, for the sadness in her son, for a father she was taken from when only 10 who was tortured and died alone in a Soviet prison camp for intellectual non-believers. He put his arm, around her shoulders and held her into him. He did not know the reason for the tears.

"Tell me about Kenny, Alice. What sort of little boy is he?"

She opened her handbag and dried her face with a tissue. "Poor Kenny. He says he cannot understand why his father lives with another woman and not at home like other fathers. The woman is called Carol – and I detest her. I hoped that Kenny could have gone to his friend Graham's house, but no chance. Just my luck – Graham is on holiday. Now Carol and

Frank have dragged my son to have his hair cut … so stupid, and so cruel!"

"I'm sorry about that. Tell me what Kenny likes doing."

"He loves letters and stamps … and he supports Altrincham. We'll go to a match tomorrow. I promised him that."

"I used to be thrilled with stamps. Do you think I might come along with you to the match? Would Kenny mind?"

She looked into his eyes with a searching, smiling look. "I would have to ask him, Michael."

Because they had specially come down from Manchester to visit him, the ward sister allowed them to come into the ward when Mr Wilkins had finished his round. They could stay with Mr Andreanov for half an hour, then the lunch trolleys would be coming in. Alice went through first but soon was back.

"How is he?"

"He wants to see you, Michael." She sat on the bench next to him. "Will you be coming back with me on the 3.15 – or a later train?"

He touched her hand. "Alice, what a silly question. Of course I'm coming with you on that train."

When he approached the bed, the Russian man's gaze was elsewhere, misted in a distant world of memories. When he saw Brideswell, he brightened.

"Ah. Here comes my opponent, Mr Brideswell. I've been thinking of your chess opening all night. Would you mind lifting it out – it's just as we left it. I had to shoo away a woman who wanted to clean up my locker. I said 'Come back when my chess match is over,' She thought I was mad, but left me to my bacteria."

Brideswell smiled and carefully lifted out the small board

with its array of ivory pieces. The man's eyes were alive. The dry humour was back.

"Good. Nice steady hand, not like my stupid shakes."

"That'll go," said Brideswell, "when you're stronger."

The pallid man did not answer. He smoothed down the covers and eased the board around. "So, there they are again, itching to get on with it after a night out of the action, waiting and thinking, just like an old Russian duel – important not to fire the pistol too soon. I believe you moved up your pawn to protect your bishop. I have been thinking about that – it's far too hot in here to sleep. What a way to approach the dawn, planning the downfall of a king. But then, I was born into a revolution. My move?"

"Yes. Your move."

"You're not distracted if I talk as I play? Some people would find it very irritating – bad form."

"It doesn't bother me."

"Good. Then I shall move up my knight. Watch out – he's a bit of a devil. There – and I shall turn his head around so he can see where he's going."

Brideswell moved his queen to the far side of the board. Andreanov began to laugh softly.

"Such an impetuous queen! Who is she – running out like that. What a cheeky woman – quite shameless!" He looked up at Brideswell. "What a bold man you are, Mr Brideswell. The man for me, sent by God and St Chrysostom." He leaned forward leaving behind on his pillow the concave imprint of his back. "You see, chess tells us everything. To play chess with an Englishman is like going out in the rain – you cannot tell at the outset if you will enjoy it, or be drowned. Now I shall have to stop this headstrong woman of yours." He moved to block her. Brideswell brought out his bishop.

"Ah. I see ...a Holy War." He raised his eyebrows. "You have a sharpness beneath all that quietness, my friend ... not a man to be trifled with – good as an ally, but dangerous as an enemy. Let's leave it there. I need another night of thought to get myself out of this. Would you please lift them back into my locker, then listen. I have a task for you."

"A task, Mr Andreanov?"

"Yes." He waited until he had the young man's full attention. "Kutsov ... Anya's father. I must know what happened to him before I die. He is on my conscience. When I think of him I want to cry out with pain. Is he dead ... did he live? Will you do it? Please – for the three of us. I know you have it in you to find out, if you take this up."

"Where should I start?"

"In Smolensk." He turned away from Brideswell and allowed his gaze to leave the hospital bed, the ward, for a space eastwards and north. Suddenly he returned. "There was a poor man in here a few beds down ... he had his throat cut. Take care, my friend."

Alice's son Kenny did not question God's hand in all things that happened to him. He accepted it as a fact – the result of two large hands, hands ten times the size of any human hand, lifting and placing him like dust in a sunbeam, or like a grain of rice which fell to the floor when his mother made a rice pudding. When these hands pulled in opposite directions, he was stretched, widened, but nothing would happen. A dull day. Like yesterday. The bad day – when Alice drove him to stay with Frank and Carol, and left him there like Robinson Crusoe, on an island with no hope of escape. If he were a prisoner in a cell with barbed wire all over the windows and doors, he would mark off each day with his penknife, cutting into a piece of wood every passing hour, every endless night.

They put him into a pretty room with children's wallpaper. When the Hands of God were uppermost, drawing him along so fast his feet did not touch the ground, all was wonder, excitement and joy. That would not be until Alice came back, or the time when she had bought him his mountain bike, when she let him sit in the front row for her concert and they came all the way home by taxi at midnight. The time Alice took him to watch Altrincham when they had a player on free transfer from Wrexham and the new goalkeeper on loan from Preston. God's hands lifting him and offering him a postcard with a foreign stamp on it, a card he wouldn't have to give back. The time when God held him up and said when he grew up to be a man he would be needed, to be a priest. A messenger of God, with His request written in the clouds. At night he knelt by his bed, longer on special days, and thanked God for having such big hands.

But there were other hands, smaller, sharper, and with claws. The Hands of Dog. They had stretched out of the black shadows today, grasping him by his hair as it was being shorn away by a cruel scissors-man who smelled of smoke, had brown teeth and who had deeply humiliated him – placed him up on a baby's board across the chair arms.

"Better up here – I can reach him without bending. He's a small boy for his age ... seven, is it?" Snip, snip. Hair falling onto his shoulders. Onto the floor. The Hands of Dog, with the terrible woman-witch watching him through the mirror, smiling and enjoying his torture. Carol – he never sang Christmas carols, not even before she threw her net around his father. He apologized to God at Christmas, saying he did not intend any offence, only that the word carol made him feel sick. "The lad's hair is far too long, Missus, unless he's hoping to become another Beatles boy. Mind you – they would have him in Old Trafford. Man United." The barber laughed and cut deeper. He was a Cardiff supporter.

"You're right, Mr Evans," said the woman in the mirror, "his father has been saying so for months, but it's not easy to get him along to see you. All his school friends have short hair – it's just that Kenneth has to be different."

In another 15 minutes he was shorn – a stubble only on his scalp. Kenny looked down at the heap of soft hair and sighed. His eyes pricked with tears. No use crying when the Hands of Dog were at work, they would only laugh and fit him with an ear stud. Frank came over and lifted him off.

"That's more like it, Kenny – much more the man. Now we shall have to get you to eat more. No use to my rugby club as a peg-man." He paid the barber and left a good tip in his hand, as if to apologize for the length of his son's hair. He stood his son on the linoleum and brushed him down with his hand. "There – not so bad, Kenny, was it. You look the real deal now – a solid chap." He smiled and raised his fist. The mirror-woman linked her arm through Frank's. She rubbed Kenny's head.

"He's quite the little man now, Frank."

The boy, eight not seven, had a vision – the woman Carol strapped to a baby-seat by a hundred ropes, the man cutting off her hair chunks at a time until she was completely bald. Then Kenny would say, "Quite the woman now, Frank." He was placed in the back seat of the car.

"You won't mind being in the back, Kenneth. I always sit next to your father in the front, he likes me there." She opened the glove box and passed back to him a paper bag. Kenny did not open it; tears were falling down his face. He hurriedly looked away, out of the window, sighed and wished he were at the dentist.

"Open it, Kenneth. See what your father has bought you."

A woollen hat and scarf – both striped.

"Sale colours, lad … you'll find them a lot faster than your Altrincham – and they win games."

He sat on the scarf and pushed the hat to the other end of the seat. If he had a sharp knife and a stick, like Robinson Crusoe, he would make a fire and notch the stick, one cut for every minute until Alice came back to take him away.

★

Liadev.
Third visit to Smolensk

Before arriving at Smolensk, the Moscow to Warsaw express follows for some miles the north bank of the great Dnepr River. Dr Liadev watched its endless flow, brown from recent November rains, level high, clawing its way up the reinforced banks searching for a weakness to spill out and become free. Two years had passed, a nothing to the river but a long time for the city he was approaching, a momentous time for old Russia and the new Russia. The nearness of the city, the swirling brown current, the endless grey sky, all combined to place upon him a sad and heavy mood. The USSR was no more – Communism had left through a small shabby door retreating before the cold power of capitalism, the ruthlessness of market forces – a world system with as little mercy as the one it had driven out. Yet communism had not begun that way.

Liadev had been a believer – that the Soviet way was better, a better life for his people, for hospitals, schools, jobs, houses which were warm and dry – the rebuilding after the Patriotic War and the devastation by the German armies. New planned estates, 5 stories high and provided with clinics, creches, meeting halls – everything new, positive, optimistic and a renewal. One flaw arose, one man. Slowly, bit by bit, he lost his faith in the face of naked power and greed, repressions and cruelties, the ever unchallengeable dogma that had become a religion never to be questioned. He was too intelligent to accept that – the iron rules of despotism. He knew that any organism which cannot change and adapt is on the downward path to extinction. The suddenness of the collapse had stunned him. When it arrived he had no other thought than to rescue artists from detention and torture – to apologize, and to try and give something back. To say sorry. So much human suffering. The train slowed. The river became less important – buildings, cranes, repairs and renewal. How many times had Russia repaired Smolensk. Not from the flooding river but from the hands of man, savage wars, wars within and without.

The doctor opened his old briefcase and placed gently back inside the book he had taken out – the sonnets of Shakespeare. The train brakes hissed and set up a grinding, grating noise as they bit into the steel wheels. A thin vibration was set up – the long express shook as it crossed webs of points. He held on till the moments passed then lifted down his greatcoat. His mood of sadness had become overlaid with shame and guilt, that he had made no contact with his patient for two years. In that time he had travelled from the Baltic to Sakhalin, from the north to south, Murmansk to Chekhov's Taganrog and Rostov. And he knew his patient's name was a fiction.

The sun broke through and suddenly light swept in with an uplifting radiance. A warmth was set upon the ground for the first time that day, but in the shade the deep frost was unmoved. Liadev climbed down the steps from the train and joined a throng of people making their way along the platform to the exit.

At the old archway leading into the entrance hall, he was surrounded, compressed and bumped into by the good-natured crowd. He was a big man, people couldn't avoid him – mothers grasping children, women with cases, men with vast bags stuffed as if by laundry … some looked up and apologised, others laughed. The excitement of arrival. The doctor was not only large but tall. He looked over the bobbing, restless heads towards the timeless river and its bridge into the city. He detached himself from the stream of people heading for buses, walked a short distance down a busy road then turned into a side street. He passed new blocks of flats rising beneath their swinging cranes, their jibs describing purposeful, geometric patterns across a blue-grey November sky – like giant clocks with pendulums from the clouds.

He found himself on the northern promenade looking out over the river to the old city walls, at the eternal flow of life in every direction along the road on the far bank, the Ulitsa Soboleva – trucks, buses and all manner of hurrying people. He was in no hurry to join them. The late morning sun that had forced and burned its way through the cloud cover still had warmth. The doctor took off his overcoat and draped it over his arm, holding his briefcase in the other hand – he had come over too warm and to his annoyance a sweat had broken out across his forehead. On a bench he sat down heavily, conscious of his quickening pulse, aware that he had no longer a young heart. He smiled at a woman passing in front of him with a white dog.

"Good morning."

The woman returned his smile. "It's still warm, isn't it. My dog likes this weather."

"I'm sure he does. He looks in fine form."

She bent down to touch the dog's head, the animal aware he had become a source of interest and was being talked about. "He's spoiled. He won't come out in the rain and he hates snow. Come along, Gaga."

"Gaga? He's not a sensible dog?"

"Gagarin." She walked away from him. Liadev was saddened. He would have liked to talk to her some more, ask her about her life in this city, how she was coping with all the changes. A lady with a white dog stepping straight out from a page within Russia's great literary past, undamaged and untouched by revolution and repression, a hidden place which always remains whatever men think up to change it.

Several yards on, the dog Gaga lingered at a shrub. The woman waited patiently, touched her scarf, adjusted her hat as if she had a mirror or had not forgotten she had been talking with a man, a tall large man with a clear, engaging voice. As she called to the dog, their eyes met. Liadev raised his hat in her direction, a gesture of sympathy and amusement. He was pleased she smiled back. So unlike Moscow. Her smile warmed him – and saddened, reminding him that he had no wife who would smile at him like that. He wondered who she was, her name, why she was not at work, had she been ill – or on holiday from somewhere? A visit to a relation? Absurd questions, for which there could never be an answer. Gaga ... a sense of humour. Perhaps she would turn around and walk back his way. He hoped so.

Liadev snapped open his briefcase. From a banded pocket beneath the top, he took out his mother's letter. He opened it absently, his thoughts still lingering with the lady and her dog, and her image from a more certain, more tender past.

Gorky 1.11.91

'My dearest Maxie,

I hope you will find time and a quiet place to read this long letter. It will be long because I have a lot to tell you, important things. I never know if my letters get to you. I know your secretary Sasha keeps the ones I send you, she has told Irina Bloch that when I've asked her to check, but I hope she doesn't put them in a drawer for months.

I am writing to you with some very special news. First let me say that I couldn't ask you first because your cousin didn't arrive until two weeks after you left me for Moscow. What I am saying in my silly roundabout way is that Natalya has come to live with us. Now don't be cross and upset yourself. You know you have always liked her and she does think the world of you.'

Liadev was aware of the sun's warmth on his face. He raised his eyes from the letter and watched the columns of water-dazzle trace across the river towards him, only broken from their lines by the swirls and eddies of the tumbling water. He looked away, the light too bright and watched a file of ducks swimming through the slack water – a drake with two females. He read

'Of course you remember, but I am trying to remind you so that you can understand. Natalya was married to Martin, a big Swedish man who repaired buses at a works depot in Central Moscow. You couldn't go to the funeral, you had just started your new job and were travelling to all your hospitals. That was four years ago when he suddenly died. His body was too big for his heart. They used to have a small flat from the Transport Directive, but then finally she had to move out. So Natalya was without a home again. I'm sorry about this rigmarole, the fact is she caught a train to Gorky with all her possessions in a single bag, and there she was, on our doorstep.

'Aunty, can you put me up for a bit while I try and get a job ... please?' What could I say? My sister's only daughter and her arriving like a blessing after so many years of living on my own. I know you can't be with me all the time, that's not what I'm saying and whatever you're thinking, it is lovely to have her with me, such a nice kind woman, so friendly and careful, and company for me in the long winter nights coming.

Now listen. I have told her she must be very quiet when you come home because you have very important government papers to read, that she must keep the TV turned down and not sing or laugh.

When you come home, Natalya will sleep in my room. Now she is in your bedroom, but I have warned her that she must on no account touch anything.

Dearest, I do hope you're not cross with me, taking in your cousin.

She has found a job at GAZ and the rent money she gives me is useful. I do love having her here, she is like a daughter. Somehow your father and I could only bring one child into the world, and we loved you so much. If only Papa could see you now, rescuing all those poor artists so wrongfully and shamefully shut away in those awful days. Whatever happens to us now, I thank God none of that can ever come back. If only Auntie Ada her mother could see us, Natalya and I, laughing and being so happy with each other she would be at peace. If I should die, which one day I will but with God's love and mercy not for a long time, your cousin will be here to look after you. She has had a big husband and knows all about men.

I'm sorry this has been such a long, rambling letter, but I felt I had to tell you everything. How shocked you would have been to come home and discover Natalya was sleeping in your room, in your bed.

With all my tender thoughts, may God always bless and protect you,

Your loving Mama, always.' XXX

p.s. Don't wear the thick socks I sent you too soon because you know how easily your feet sweat and it will bring back your athlete's foot. For a man who walks so much, you don't want that. And it can become infected if you can't always wash.

At first he left the letter on his knees.

It seemed to him the day was lighter, the sun stronger, that winter was being held at bay. Far from being annoyed with his mother, he felt a deep sense of relief that his cousin was there and she was no longer on her own. Of all his relatives, Natalya was his favourite. He was smiling now and did not mind so much if the lady with the dog returned home another way. Natalya was a good woman with a tender heart. He admired the way she had loved that giant Swede and gently kept him in his place – never a woman to be dominated, either by size or mind. He found himself laughing at no one – the company in front of him was only three ducks come up for bread.

The doctor made his way slowly along the promenade half-hoping to encounter Gaga and his mistress again. She had gone. He climbed the steps onto the bridge, noting how short of breath he was getting when he had to exert himself more than usual. Near the top he stopped and stared down at the brown water as it boiled and tumbled around the bridge pillars. A calmness had invaded his heart. He looked down at the great river almost with affection – the river was so Russian; he was so Russian. They shared a common beginning and a long journey from the source. His own journey was through a life that often disturbed and upset him. The river's course took it to Kiev and the sea; it had no age, embracing an eternity he was familiar with and drew him into a spirituality where some part of him might last after his body released him. Liadev had no fear of death, he neither welcomed or rejected it. Today he felt good. Glad to be alive.

When up on the bridge he saw something else that pleased him. Though the central span had been renewed, the rest of the bridge kept its original steelwork, not yet painted to match the new arch. So often that which is destroyed is not smashed completely, like a spider's web holed by a gale or a falling twig. Man's powers of recovery were as firm and as hopeful as the garden spider. He made his way to the cathedral school, the seminary, and found himself for the third time in the office of the principal, Father Adrian. He was welcomed warmly by the soft-spoken priest, greeted by a firm embrace.

"My dear doctor, what a faithful man you are!"

"It's two years, Father ... that's not faithfulness, more a weakness and negligence."

"Of course it isn't. You're here, aren't you?" Father Adrian paused and surveyed his large visitor. "As far as I can remember," he shook his finger at the visiting doctor, "you have two spoons of sugar in your coffee?"

"What a memory! And not for the best thing."

The Elder made two cups of coffee. The coldness in the room showed as spirals of steam rose from them. He passed one over to Liadev, and a porcelain bowl of sugar lumps. "Your friend still calls himself by the old name. He is blocking out his past."

"He knows his name is Andrei. Perhaps the name is too painful to use."

"You must have discovered something, Doctor, I can see it in your eyes."

"I wouldn't like to have any secrets with you looking into me, Father. Yes – a composer, as we all knew – first name Andrei …"

"Go on, don't hold me in suspense. The rest?"

"I believe him to be Andrei Andeyevich Kutsov."

"Great Heavens … Kutsov! It can't be. We are told he is dead."

"And he has a daughter."

"You astonish me, Liadev! Is it possible. Kutsov was one of ours, a Smolensk man. He disappeared – with so many others!" Father Adrian shook his head in wonderment. "Lazarus raised from the dead and returned to his birthplace! You are a gifted man, Doctor, with your insights and an ear for God's wishes – His message. I am astonished. Kutsov was a composer on the threshold of greatness – it is a name known and honoured all over this city, but he was too modern for our masters. He is found … thanks be to God!"

"We have new masters now. Wiser ones. Less cruel."

"Wasn't there a friend. It is coming back to me from so long ago – someone who taught at our university, who defected. That's right, with the daughter."

"You are still using the old words, Father. It is true the

friend saved himself – but the child in the photograph ... what allegiance had she to a state which was intent on killing her father?"

"I'm sorry. I didn't mean to use that old Soviet word. I never met Kutsov. He was brought in by OGPU, like so many of our creative talents, composers, artist, writers ... but the friend, I did meet. Wait a minute – I think I have the name ... it's near, hanging in the air."

"I shall help you. We know – Andreanov. Vladimir Kazimirovich Andreanov. He took the child, Anya, to England."

"I remember. Everyone talked about it. The child's disappearance and Kutsov's arrest soon afterwards."

"Supposing, Father, Kutsov had asked the photographer for a copy of that portrait for the child to take with her. It was done just before she left, when the secret police were closing in?"

"It's possible. Maybe it's likely. One photo the father kept and concealed, the other he gave to his friend?"

"We have the KGB file. No child was mentioned in that arrest, nor afterwards." The doctor let his eyes return to the window, one he was coming to know, the sky beyond and the swaying tops of the silver birches. The sun had gone in and the greyness which it parted in the morning was closing back over. "The wife shot at the time of the dawn raid. 'Resisting arrest.'"

"I'm sorry. The dark night of the soul. Those were evil times, Doctor, cruel, stupid and barbaric – and all for what? My dear Liadev, you are a kind and wonderful friend to Yuri ... do you want to remind him of all this?"

"I don't know. I am not wise enough to answer that."

"It is better to walk slowly than fall on the ice."

Liadev nodded and rubbed his hands together, "That's right. I shall have to take my time."

"You may not know, he is to leave us. My bishop wants him to build up a choir across the river at the church we've re-opened near the station. He is thinking of a male voice choir, unaccompanied like our brothers have in St Petersburg ... and perhaps one for mixed voices. The Church of the Archangel Michael."

"That is a challenge for anyone. Will he go?"

"He hasn't said yet."

"Then this is definitely not the time to bring back the past, not when he's leaving – you have been his family, given him a place of normality, a resting place for a trouble mind."

They stood up. The Holy Father touched Liadev on the shoulder.

"You are a good man, Doctor. You have more wisdom than you know."

Dr Liadev left the seminary and re-entered the striving energy of the day and the city beyond its wall. He felt in a mood where time was of no importance. The great city seemed to be welcoming him and in the four years he had been its visitor and admirer it had changed more than he had – more churches open, new shops, fast food, businesses springing up. All reminded him that Smolensk was a city founded upon the intersection of two great trade routes, Balkans to Baltic, Moscow to Europe. He decided at that moment he would visit the art gallery, to see their collection of Goncharova and Popova – two women artists of the 'mighty six'. The day had become cold and a wind had got up with the chill of winter in its fingers. He lifted up his overcoat collar and tightened the soft English scarf, a memento from a dockside shop in Kaliningrad. He paused for a while at the monument to General Kutusov and the defenders of Smolensk against the Napoleonic war machine. He read the inscription and wondered – could it be that Andrei Andeyevich Kutsov was a descendant, the name marginally altered?

After the art galley he walked through to the cathedral. Dusk was coming in early beneath the cloud. A woman was on her knees scrubbing the stone steps at the cathedral entrance, a woman, large like himself. Her hair was tied up beneath a headscarf. She scrubbed with an old brush, its bristles flattened and splayed out, and a bar of red soap. For a moment the doctor watched her, his mind seeing her and not seeing her, all over the place – images from the gallery and similar women, in the train, on the bridge ... she became aware of him and stopped.

"That's kind of you," he said, "leaving a dry path up so we don't slip. You've got a cold job there ... hands in the water ..."

She sat back on her heels, glad to pause, to say something after the silent work. "I do it summer and winter. I don't notice. It's a warmer job than you'd think." The hair pushing forward from under the headscarf was streaked with grey. Liadev saw her northern blue eyes, red fingers from scrubbing, years of immersion and irritation by her carbolic soap.

"Have you been scrubbing these steps for years? I'm a doctor – I notice your fingers."

She studied her hands and bent her fingertips in towards herself. "My nails are not much either. Twenty years ... could be more. Doesn't do much for my fingers, no man would put a ring on them."

Liadev smiled. "You must love this old cathedral."

"It's all I have, all I need."

He was moved by the simplicity of her remark. Could he have said that about his own work.

"You can go in now, Doctor. There's no Mass till 7pm."

He saw she wanted to continue. "Thank you. It's good to speak to someone who loves this cathedral so much. Tell me – what is your name?"

She hesitated. A name is private. Memories of the past. Police and the KGB. A name was very private. She crossed herself. He was a doctor and understood about her fingers.

"Ivana …. Ivana Madiewska."

"Thank you. I am Maxim Liadev. Did you ever hear mentioned, Ivana, the name Kutsov? A composer … he lived in this city. It's possible his music was sung in there once. In the cathedral."

She began again to scrub. "I know of General Kutusov."

"No. Not him. Andrei Andreyevich Kutsov. He had a daughter. I suppose she'd be about 35 now – called Anya."

"So many Anyas, Dr Liadev. No Kutsovs. No one here has that name. Perhaps he was from the north, Kaliningrad – that way. Not a Smolensk name."

"His daughter was taken to England when she was ten."

The cleaner drew her brush across the bar of red soap. She made some circular movements than looked up at him. Her voice was firmer.

"To England?"

"Yes, I believe so."

"My father lives in England, Doctor. Should I ask him? Is the composer in some kind of trouble?"

"Not at all. The bad days are over, Ivana. We are trying to help him."

"I might write to my father but I'm not sure where he is. He keeps changing his address. I know he's married to an

Italian woman. I think they have a hotel in London. We've lost touch. I suppose I could find out, there can't be many Madiewskis living in central London. A phone book."

" Would he know Smolensk people?"

"Of course. He was a glass blower."

"Really? Such a skill."

She shook her head and rinsed out a cloth. "Perhaps. Fumes ruined his chest. Are you from Smolensk, Doctor?"

"No ... Gorky."

"Ah. So far away. Then I wouldn't be able to tell you about your friend and his daughter, if my father wrote back to me."

"I'll be back. Smolensk seems to draw me to her ... as if she wants me."

She laughed for the first time. The soft humour in her face was meant for him, and for all her past. "Yes, that's Smolensk."

"I'll speak to you again," he said, "now I need to go into your beautiful cathedral."

He entered the quietness and space, breathed in its calm and allowed the spirituality all around him to enter his heart and mind. To move him. He stopped before a block of tiered candles, took one and lit it. Liadev placed it among the others – he said a prayer for the love his mother had given him, he prayed for health and happiness for her, and for the blessing of his cousin's arrival. He thanked God for all the love and help sent down to him. The doctor placed coins from his purse into an offertory casket and took two more candles – one for Ivana, one for the daughter of Andrei Kutsov, a woman living in England called Anya.

The hotel was cold. It smelled of paint. Next morning he found Kutsov reading in the seminary garden. He wore a frayed overcoat in anticipation of winter. The colours of the coat had faded, leached out by wind and rain, bleached upon a hook in the summer sun. The musician did not look up to watch his visitor approach.

"Good morning, Yuri."

The overcoated man seemed dazed, drawn out of his book, eyes blank with no recognition. Then a smile crossed his eyes and he stood up. They embraced with feeling. "Dr Liadev. I heard you were still here."

"I'm sorry, I didn't come back yesterday. I wanted to see the cathedral and the collection of Goncharovas … it became rather late."

"Provincial Landscape, Moscow in Winter … yes."

"You know them then?"

He did not say. "Shall we go in, Doctor, it's getting a bit cold out here now the sun's gone in."

"I'm all right. In a bit of a sweat after the walk up. How are you?" They sat down on the bench. "Everything going well?"

"Yes. Quite good. They keep me busy. How are you, Doctor?"

"Still travelling everywhere." Liadev shrugged, spread his hands and gave a wry smile. "No one can have seen as much of Russia as I have, or the inside of so many trains. Not even Dr Zhivago."

The older man returned his smile. "Zhivago travels well."

"I spend half my life in railway carriages and a quarter of it on platforms waiting. But, I do meet interesting people, from everywhere, doing everything. Yesterday I talked for half an hour with a woman scrubbing the cathedral steps.

"And composers – are you still discovering them?"

The man's voice was touched with an irony directed inward, against himself.

"Not so many now. Artists, writers, poets ... what was done to them was a crime against Russia, against humanity. I help the ones we have brought back. Creativity is a frail and tenuous thing, Yuri, it switches off easily and doesn't always return." He touched the arm of the man beside him. "Father Adrian tells me you are composing again."

"They are small things, Doctor, for my choir. There is something larger inside me. One day I shall write it down, if I am spared."

The visiting doctor hesitated. "In the old days ... before the arrest, what do you remember? Your compositions ... your family?"

The man heaved up his greatcoat higher and closed several buttons. He breathed deeply and audibly, as if the cooler air of the morning might reach into his past, free it, like it loosened and sent spiralling the last leaves from the silver birches at the far end of the garden. He made no answer. A wind eddy brought leaves around their shoes. Kutsov bent down and lifted up a leaf. He held it in his palm. "Some things fall, Dr Liadev, and leave no trace of where they have come from. Tell me about your family."

"My family, Yuri?"

"Yes. Were they also doctors?"

"No. My grandfather was a sea-pilot on the Black Sea. We had a small house provided by the Soviet Navy. It had been a private house once – I remember it well – once it belonged to a high-up customs officer. His job was dangerous and difficult, the entrance to his port narrow with rocks and cross-currents. A gale across the harbour mouth could wreck a ship, pound it against the breakwater. My grandfather was a cautious man, he would rather ride out a storm than take his ship in when the weather was bad."

The picture of that seemed to lay a silence on Kutsov. "I often look at the photograph you brought me."

"I'm glad – she is a pretty little girl. You think she knows you ... you told me she did once say your name."

"Yes. I am used to Yuri, but my name is not that."

The doctor drew his English scarf tighter in the freshening wind. He had been hot, now a chill was entering him. "I am Maxim, but how many people ever call me that – only my mother. I am used to 'Liadev'. I call my mother 'Mama', though I am a man of fifty. It would be strange to call her by her name."

"I am to leave, Doctor. They want me to live across the river in a church there. Am I ready to go? Tell me what your advice is – am I able to cope with being alone again?"

Liadev thought. He allowed the uncertainty in Yuri's voice to affect him. The solitude of Siberia was still able to reach out, bring back a more recent past, its terrors, torture and trauma. "I don't think you're ready for that yet. We'll talk about it next time."

"In two years?" The man's irony was softened by his smile. He liked the large, sweating doctor who had found him a place where his life could begin again. He saw in Liadev a caution and carefulness of his grandfather – not a pilot of great ships, but a pilot of people.

"What are you reading, Yuri?"

The old musician lifted up his book. The doctor nodded.

"Ah ... Ivan Sergeevich Turgenev. You like his work."

"Yes. Always."

"Since a boy?"

"Yes. How do I know that – but I do."

Liadev continued, not with a question but a comment which might widen the window of memory fractionally opened. "I have been reading too, on the train coming here. It's a long ride but I enjoy it. I like to bring a book of poetry with me on long journeys ... it seems the right time and place to read poetry. I have some poems by Shakespeare."

"Ah. So English, and yet so everywhere. King Lear of the Steppes. The story is in my book." Was it deliberate, unconscious or intuitive that the doctor posed the next question using the right name?

"Andrei ... who do you know in England?"

"Do I know someone there? So far away? That is a strange question, Doctor."

"The woman I talked to yesterday, the one I met on the cathedral steps – she was scrubbing them with a hand-brush and a bar of red soap. She was telling me about her father in England. You see – not so very far away. He was a Smolensk man, a glass-blower. The fumes from the factory got into his lungs and he had to stop. His voyage of departure took him to England and he began a new life there. I liked his daughter – she is a brave woman with a deep faith. She scrubs the steps not for wages, but out of love."

"What are you telling me, Doctor? Is there someone I should know about in England? Would they scrub me for love?"

Liadev smiled. "Not exactly."

"Why do you fill my mind with England."

"You tell me, Andrei."

"The child in the photo ... did she go to England?"

★

Brideswell's father

Dr Brideswell did not know why he had never loved his son. It had nothing to do with his fits, which had long since disappeared. Childhood ones. The simple thing was that he had always found Michael irritating. But not his daughter – he had loved her deeply from the start, and it had always been fiercely returned. Perhaps it was the bitterness that racked him, her death, which changed his irritation with Michael to an actual dislike. And its usual fellow travellers – criticism, sometimes contempt. He knew it was unkind, unfair and irrational, but he couldn't help himself. They had never got on, he had never understood his son's love of shadows or why he had always to retreat into an imaginary world, with imaginary people – inaccessible to anyone except his mother.

He missed his daughter with an un-diminishing rage. The death of his wife he bore more easily, almost with a philosophical and equal mind. Michael had never come back after that, and why should he – they were strangers. His friend sitting opposite drew him back into the present, into the match.

"Harold, are you sure you want to leave your knight there?"

"Sorry, Ralph ... not concentrating. Let's leave this game till next week – things on my mind." His chess partner stood up and took his jacket from the back of the chair.

"It's getting late anyway ... I should be going. Mary will be looking at the clock."

"Don't go for a minute. Sit back down – a moment more, let me get you a beer."

The doctor stood up, went to the fridge and brought back a bottle of lager and two glasses. He tilted the glass as he poured. "Have you seen Michael recently, Ralph?"

"At the funeral. We had a few words. Mary likes his books. We were talking about that."

"Yes. Books. Well, he takes after his mother. Very timid boy, always reading, nose in a book. He doesn't think a lot of me."

"Different interests, Harold."

"I've not been sleeping too well. The boy's on my mind. Never comes down ... doesn't ring. I am his father – no one else left. There's a problem."

"There often is. Father and son." His gardening friend put his hands to his beard. "That's children for you. Sometimes they like us, sometimes not – you can't do much about it. Take my daughter Emily – I see her once a year when she comes down to us for Christmas." He drew his fingers down the beard. "Michael was always the quiet one. Have you two fallen out over something?"

Dr Brideswell gave out a deep sigh, "Fallen out? Did we ever fall in, Ralph?

No ... we've never got on. I'm to blame. I loved his sister too much and Michael not enough. You can't repair that, only say sorry." He shrugged. "Penny protected him too much – that always annoyed me. She thought he was delicate. Some scares when he was little. Maybe I was the wrong father for him. You'd have done a lot better, Ralph ... he loved gardens, anything to do with nature. I've been wondering ... these last few weeks ..."

"Wondering what?"

"If I was to ask him down – Michael lives on his own up in Cheshire – you might show him your allotments, and the roses. Maybe you could tell him."

"What should I tell him?"

"That his father is very sorry and wants to be a friend. As it should be."

His friend drank down the glass of lager, stood up and set his cycling clips onto his trouser bottoms. "Would he want to come and see my allotments? Michael's a busy man, a well-known writer. Maybe the roses – they're very good this year. He might remember coming up there as a lad ... a useful helper. But saying sorry you'd have to do yourself, Harold. Can't see me doing that. Wouldn't make any sense."

"I wouldn't know how to begin."

"Have you read any of his books?"

"No. Not a thing."

"Read one. I can't see how you can become his friend if you won't read any of his work. They're in the library. He puts a lot of himself into his writing, might tell you a lot ... and they're an easy read. You could finish one before he comes down."

They walked to the door together. It seemed there was no more to say. Ralph straddled his bicycle. "You might phone Mary for me, Harold – tell her I'm on my way."

He kept to the middle of the drive, out of the reach of the overhanging bushes and branches. At the road he stopped, stretched a hand back to set the dynamo onto his rear wheel.

But the cone of light had no brightness, no distance, no penetration, because night had not descended. In midsummer it wore no darkness.

The doctor's phone was in the hall. He rang Mary as asked and apologized for keeping Ralph so late. After replacing the receiver he sat at his desk, at first doing nothing, his mind aimless and without direction, roaming through Michael's childhood and being diverted with other images – Penny, Josie, Ralph and the chess game. He reached forward and snapped on the standard lamp, opened the desk and drew out a writing pad. No words for it – the sadness that surged up so unexpectedly, not frameable in words, images or issues. Simply down-pressing sadness. He placed his pen on the pad then slipped beneath it his blotter. Dr Brideswell began slowly, his address and the date. The movement of the pen carried him beyond the curtain of invading sadness.

> Church House, Trent
> Sherborne, Dorset. DT9 6ZP
> 28. 06. 95

My dear Michael,

              It seems so long since you came down to see me. Such a large house, so empty with just me in it. It seems wrong and selfish for one man, an old man, to have this big place just to himself when so many people have to live cramped in small flats on vast and troubling estates. I can't change all that, only comment and regret. I've been playing chess tonight with Ralph but don't feel like going to bed yet – it's warm and I'm sure I won't sleep. I've not been a good sleeper recently, and awake alone in this old house full of ghosts and memories, isn't always good for me.

I'm well, and I have got used to living on my own, though I miss your mother, and you know how much I miss Josie. Ralph is a good friend – he comes to me on Thursdays for chess – we didn't finish it today, rather got into talking. I wasn't concentrating. We talked about you. His wife – do you remember Mary who used to make all our jams and marmalades – she reads your books and likes them. Quite the fan. Ralph says that I must read them now, and I will. Tomorrow, I'll find one at the library. He says the Yeovil Library has them all. I'm not a natural novel reader as you know, too many other things to have to read, all those medical papers and keeping up with the latest changes.

Well, all that's gone. Time I opened up my mind, the long summer evenings. I'm pretty hopeless in the garden and not a pub man, it's the right time to read your work. I'm sorry it's taken me so long. Ralph says he'll show you his roses, the best ever. I like to read outside. It's better there than in the house, and at the quiet end of the day I love being on the patio – a different view of time. You would appreciate that – as a child you always wanted to be out whatever the weather, summer or winter.

What about coming down next week if you're free? I'm sorry that we haven't always got on. I hope that my old age has injected a bit more sense and caring into me. I have been a bit of a pig sometimes. I have an excuse, it was the job, dealing with patients, all their traumas – and mine. Then losing your mother and then our dear Josie so young, with her whole life in front of her. I shall never get over that. So cruel and so unfair. You have suffered too, I know.

Long walks here would do you good and your bike is still in the garage. I pump up the tyres from time to time and ride it to the post office to keep it oiled up. I was never much of a psychologist but exercise, fresh air and seeing the countryside are good when you're feeling low. We have now our new vicar and he often comes for walks with me, a good companion, doesn't feel he has to talk – he spends enough time in the week talking to people, and in his sermons. I've started to go over there on a Sunday from time to time. John speaks a lot of sense and occasionally I hear and feel the mystery.

When you come, I've a number of your mother's things I'd like you to have – those miniature seascapes. They would look good in your flat and remind you of the days when we were more together as a family. We had some good holidays in Wales – remember Munt? I was the only one who dared to have the farm's black pudding for breakfast. The Prescelly Hills – and the Carmarthen Creamery – good times. I suspect that up there in Cheshire you don't get back to Wales and the coast very much, or go out walking – so arable – and busy with Manchester breathing down your neck. Come home for a break. I'd like to see you. They do a decent pint at our Red Lion, and it would be nice if you got to know the people down here again – lots of changes. One day this old house will be yours, with all the memories in it, good and bad. That seems to be the pattern of life the Great Mystery has dealt out for us.

>   Your loving father
>   Harold

ps Any day next week will do. I'm free all day, and every day.

*

Euston,
with Brother Robert

Brideswell went back to his room, packed his bag and rejoined the older man. Brother Robert had left off his cassock for grey trousers and an open shirt.

They crossed the rail bridge into Farringdon Street.

"So, what about Smolensk, Michael – thought any more about it?"

His companion shrugged. "I don't seem to be having a choice – the city is forcing itself on me."

After some distance Brideswell sensed that his friend was finding the pace hard, breathing heavily and stopping when he wanted to say something. In St Andrew's Gardens they paused and sat on a bench shaded by a plane tree. The small park had once been a graveyard – slabs and tablets lining the stone walls running down the side of the dental hospital. Behind them, empty and a reminder of more human days, the resident gardener's cottage gave out a rejected, abandoned complaint – lower windows boarded, cold frame in the narrow strip of garden smashed. Yet from within those frames, unmindful of the ruin they grew in, stood tall onions, seeding and renewing in a cycle man had not destroyed. A spreading clump of half-wild alliums. Robert lifted out his inhaler.

"Ah ... what a gift this little blue fellow is. I thank God every day for allowing mankind to discover this wonderful easing pump. Without it I should be hopeless for any walk. Excuse me, Michael, while I do a spray."

Brideswell lifted his hand and moved his finger from side to side. "You stay here, Robert, and get your breath back – I'd like to go over to Maria's guest house and say I was there, at the funeral – to give her my condolences. She's a good woman – she was nice to my wife ... the loss of her husband must be really hard. We lived near them ..." He pointed to the far side of the Gray's Inn Road. A flat over an off-licence. "That hasn't changed." He stood up. "A daughter in Smolensk ... but neither came, did they?"

Robert pushed the inhaler down into the depths of his trouser pocket.

"No. The daughter Ivana was from Boris's first marriage. The vicar asked me to write to her once – he knew our parent house was in Smolensk. I wrote there and one of the Lexikon brothers wrote back. He said they knew of Ivana, that she was a cathedral cleaner, always scrubbing the steps. He was impressed by her devotion."

"Could you get a message through to him that her father has died?"

"It was a long time ago. When you go, find her and tell her the news. It is better coming from a family friend."

"Don't come on with me – relax here where the air is good and the sun's warm. I shall need to hurry on after seeing Maria – for my train."

They shook hands, then embraced. Brother Robert

watched his friend and helper walk away and offered up a silent blessing for him – his life and the burdens he seemed to be carrying. He found a packet of oat-cakes in the other pocket, eased one out, broke it into small pieces and scattered them at his feet for a waiting sparrow. He smiled at the bird. "You see, my friend, we are both birds of a feather. Both of us have found a place that suits us – you in this old graveyard, and me in a house without cloisters surrounded by more grass and fields than you could ever imagine. We are both free to move unhindered by a world rushing past us – you in a brown, mottled gown and me in one of a lighter colour I have not put on this morning because it makes me too hot if I have to walk far. We are both alone and we are never alone."

A woman passed him with a pram and a sleeping baby. She heard his final words and thanked her God that she too, with her new baby, would never be alone again.

Brideswell crossed the busy main road and paused on the corner of Guildford Street. The off-licence was just the same as ever, neither modernised nor decaying – he pushed the entrance door open. A thin bell rang. A man looked up from the counter. The dog at his feet stirred and watched.

"Hallo ... it's been a long time since I used to shop here." He looked around the shop. "Flo and Harry gone?"

The man turned the page of some papers he was going through. "Never 'eard of them, mate ... before my time." He returned his gaze to the receipts and order forms.

"Nothing's changed. My wife and I used to have the flat upstairs."

"Yeah? It's there, too. Some kids have it. Students over at the hospital."

Brideswell left without buying anything. A low mood had advanced towards and around him – the disinterested man, the flat where Kit had walked away from him never to come back – finding a man who suited her better and who gave her two children. Near the front door to Maria's guest-house he saw three large men come out and leave. The pall-bearers at the funeral – no sign of the fourth that had given him such a bad feeling. Indecision tugged at his resolve. Would Maria want to see him now? Would the mood he had sunk into be no good for a comforter. No – not the time, not today. When he was back here again. A sympathy card from his flat. He jotted down into his diary the house number and retraced his steps back to the gardens, to his friend and a more orderly, less invaded world.

Brother Robert saw him coming back. He could see that something had changed – the walk not so brisk, eyes lower.

"Well, how is our Maria?"

"I decided not to go in. Not in the right mood. I thought she might want to be on her own. Three of the pall-bearers were leaving."

"Not the fourth one – the man who looked so much like you?"

"No. Just the three." Brideswell stepped back and raised his hand. "Thanks. I'm better for having seen you again. You're a bridge over dark waters." At the gateway in Brideswell turned and waved. He could feel the warmth of Brother Robert's smile. The distance apart did not diminish it. He stepped out more firmly for the train.

Two other men, just as like him as the fourth unknown pall-bearer, were also hurrying for the same 3.15 pm Manchester train. One had been robbed by a King's Cross canal and had a deep wound on his neck covered by a plaster and a roll-neck jumper, the other was a man who had fallen in love with a Russian woman Anya ... Alice. The fourth man, the coffin holder was not yet near, but was beginning to hurry.

*

Grave carer for Brideswell's sister

An elderly man. An old car but reliable – one of the early Cavaliers with a vast mileage on the clock going round for the second time. A man who prided himself on his eyesight. Afterwards he wore glasses for driving but there was no need – vision like a hawk. The hospital had said so.

Lewis – a name not easy on the lips – a first name for some, a surname for most. A man with sharp reflexes. He played a reasonable game of squash with his grandson but not racquets anymore. His squash game now was from the back of the court. A man who had survived the war in Italy, France and Germany – front line – quick and decisive, brave but not stupid. It was always better to challenge Death than wait for her. He had killed men before, never a woman. Memories, dreams – sleepless nights after too much wine.

Lewis had driven all the way with the window half down, even on the motorway – something wrong jammed it, a detachment of the rubber seals. He didn't mind – cooled things down. Everywhere so hot. A heatwave. Didn't sweat like he used to – sweated like a pig at Anzio. No respite in the suburbs, just as hot as the city – should have taken the M 25, but never liked it.

Seventy five – how he used to sweat playing racquets at Queens. Yes, you dried up as you got older. Desiccation and no perspiration – well, not much, some across the forehead. Not a dried-up Bombay Duck ... not yet. Makes you feel the heat when you can't sweat. Knew a chap who died of that. Heatstroke. He worked in a gas-works. No other work around in those days.

So bloody hot. Thank God for the North Sea and the wind across it. Shirt too thick. Too slow to change them after the winter.

He pushed in the key and lifted up the hatch back. Not his words, new-speak ... just a boot. He had never understood. Never understood why she had stepped out onto the motorway in front of him. Why him? Why the wave and smile? Never understood that. So sudden, so unexpected. He saw everything, seen her walking up the hard shoulder, thought she was going to phone. Could have stopped. Might have done years ago – not now. Then she stepped out right in front. No chance. Threw the wheel over – a terrific skid. Car on its roof. Dead woman. Ghastly inquest. Like the night after a push forward into mortars and machine guns. Dead men everywhere. One dead girl. The father had spat in his face ...

From the back of the car, Lewis took a trowel, some bush lobelias, a lilac, some snap dragons and two dwarf fuchsias. He spoke to them.

"I shall have to water in you lot, and every day if it stays as hot as this. Lucky beggars." He walked from the parking space and with a dampened cloth wiped the face of the obelisk, the small marble headstone. Been through seas of those. This was different, a girl. Only the age was the same as the kids in the cemeteries over there. He let the cloth linger: 'Josephine Brideswell'.

Needed this Saharan dust taken off. Bloody stuff from Alamein. Knew the girl well now. Came three times a week. Had to, in this heat. Brought a packed lunch, sandwiches and a can of 'Lilt.' Had them under the willow trees. Somehow it had all become part of his life – the cemetery, Josie, his plants, the taps every fifty yards. Grenade distance, with a bit of rolling.

Water there, not men. Holy water, drinking water, watering water. Lewis filled his watering can and took the cold water to the grave. As he planted, puddling in his lobelias, he addressed the young woman who in two quick steps had changed his life.

"Josie, I have some news for you today. I thought you'd want to know what's happening to Michael as he doesn't come here much to tell you himself. In fact, I am your only news man. And I'm sorry your father doesn't come. He loved you, but it's too far from Dorset and he can't drive those distances anymore. Besides, think how sad it would be for him to come to you on his own, sit here in sadness and silence. We both understand."

Lewis took his eyes from the small grave marker, from name, a young woman he always talked to each time he came to see where she slept in eternity. He pressed the soft wet earth around the plants and wiped his hands on a cloth.

He liked to come at this time in hot weather, when a band of shade was thrown across the grave from a silver birch. In the strip of shadow he unclipped his folding stool, set it firmly on the cut grass and would take out his pipe. It was a moment in the day he enjoyed. Anyone close would have thought him mad or lonely – he was neither. Nor was he steeped in guilt – only a need to be near the woman who had chosen him to step out in front of, smiling.

"Didn't I tell you – do you remember – I met your brother Michael here once while I was cutting your grass edges. He thought I was a council gardener and handed me a fiver. I said it wasn't necessary, that I enjoyed being in the cemetery, keeping the grave neat. He told me it was hard for him to get down from the north … he'd come more often if he could. I said I kept the grave looking good all the year round. I could see he was pleased and he pressed the fiver back into my palm again. This time I took it. So, Josie, these lobelias are his… Michael's."

In the space remaining Lewis planted the wallflowers, bulbs of a dwarf gladiolus, ones that when they grew up wouldn't be flattened by the wind and rain. He was a tidy man. He liked order. "After that meeting I phoned your brother's publishers saying I was one of his readers, a fan if you like – I've read all his books. I said when is the next one coming out. The woman said there'd be nothing for two years, but she put me over to this other man, someone called George Lev. He had that superior sort of manner – still, it was good of him to speak to me. So, Josie … this is it – there is a new novel coming out. I thought you'd like to know that." Lewis smiled to himself, said nothing more for a while, and drew on his pipe. "I asked where it was set. At first he didn't answer. Perhaps he was fed up with me, a busy man and an idle caller. I admit I pressed the question. Then he was cold. Phone call at an end.

"You can buy it next year. It's set in Smolensk." He firmed the damp soil around the final plantings.

"Josie … why did you smile at me when you stepped out?

Why did you choose me out of all the traffic going past? Was it just chance? Did you see my face and think he won't mind doing it? Was your smile for me, into my eyes, a thank you for ending your life ... or something else. An irony ... but an irony about what? About life ... and chance?"

★

With Alice
to the Manchester train

Brideswell said goodbye to Vladimir and was glad to get away from the ward – its smells of disinfectant, rows of beds with old men and the sounds that erupted from them. The stale, unhealthy air of sickness and finality. Alice was waiting.

Out of the hospital they entered a living day, one of familiar things, sunlight and ordinary noises, no voices calling. A day still hot from a continuing late heatwave. He felt an uneasy lightness in his head – not that of a fit with its own accompanying smells. He offered up a silent prayer for that. Nor was it the brightness before fainting, more a lightness of the body, a floating of his footsteps, a tie drawing him back into a world known and familiar. In the hospital he had no past; here he did. Memories of his mother, a goodnight kiss, a cold drink on a hot night when he cried out after a bad dream, and in these streets were imprints of later days, parks, squares, trees, Indian food and favourite pubs. Alice was walking close to him. Her presence evaporated two years of greyness since Josie had thrown away her life – the rift with his father, the fading memories of a marriage that became doomed and another man father to children he hadn't been able to give to Kit.

Among the groups of students they were unremarkable and unnoticed. He took her arm as they crossed Gower Street. Brideswell was the first to break the binding silence between them.

"We have more than two hours before the train goes – I thought we might have something to eat in the café I went to last night. They know me there from the old days. Luigi ... a great memory for his old customers. What do you think, Alice?" She looked up into his face and smiled an assent with her eyes. "Good. That's fine ... it's not far. I used to go there a lot. Last night it was as if I'd never been away – no years and a life between. I was married then. It wasn't working out ... used to get a calm space and sort myself out a bit with his café – all so normal. No emotions ... only welcome and friendliness. Maybe I was always more suited to that. A sort of man a woman could find very irritating. It's funny isn't it – two people come together as virtual strangers – all different kinds of chemistry drawing them together, and then chemical reactions push them farther and farther apart."

She made no response. He loosened his arm. Instead she asked, "Vladimir – does he play a good game of chess?"

He smiled wryly at that – moving from Kit and their broken past to now, and chess. "Very good. We didn't move on very far – he likes to survey the board, the arrangement of the pieces. I believe he sees a kind of beauty in it – the patterns and the infinite possibilities of each move. He wants me to go to Smolensk." Still she made no response. A woman for whom words seemed of little importance. "He was in a strange mood. We put the game to one side and then he said he wanted me to do something for him, something he needed to know ... before he died. "Brideswell hurried on. "Of course, he isn't going to die soon – not in that kind of danger."

"What did he ask you to do in Smolensk, Michael?"

He liked the sound of his name on her lips, the tenderness in her voice –

"To find your father."

"And will you go?"

"I have to."

"Why?"

"For you and for Vladimir. I shall work on my book."

"Yes ... but do you want to?"

"I do."

They entered the restaurant. Luigi shook his hand and looked admiringly towards Alice. "Welcome to Luigi's"

For an instant Brideswell thought he would comment about his wife – think Alice was her – but the old restauranteur was worldly and wise. With a friendly sweep of his arm he guided them to a table, pulled out a chair for Alice and flicked the tablecloth with his napkin.

"To start with something, Signor Brideswell ... and Madame? I have a very good sweet melon, fresh – is very good for a hot day. I recommend. I prepare myself." He brought his finger and thumb together, "No sugar – a little lemon only and two drops of amoretto."

He served them with concern and kindness, as if sensing a need for it – a half carafe of cold white Venetian wine, the pasta strong and hot. Alice returned to Smolensk.

"Did Vladimir tell you my father's name?"

"Yes ... Kutsov. Andrei Andreyevich."

"I was Anya Marianskaya Kutsova. My father is dead. You

will not find him. How could Vladimir ask you to do such a thing!"

"There must be a chance. There is always a chance."

"A ghost in the whole of Russia?"

"But didn't you live once in Smolensk ... wouldn't he come back there if he managed to survive Siberia?"

She shook her head, a reproof in her eyes at his naivety. "One does not manage survival out there, Michael. You do not know the KGB, the camps, the brutality of the guards. When they arrested my father, they shot my mother. You see – choice does not come into it."

Brideswell was shocked. Silenced. He reached forward and covered her hand with his. Suddenly she had aged. A bleakness, a wedge of coldness had inserted itself between them, removing him to a distance. A very private and unresolved grief ... and rage.

"But Alice, Vladimir has asked me to try, to find out what happened ... where you father is. I have said 'yes'."

"Yes." She repeated the word softly to herself as if she were listening to another voice deep within her memory. "He is trusting you, Michael, as I do. But what does Vladimir really know of Siberia – only what people say who never went. The dead ones take their violations with them. What can he know about you that he can ask a thing like this!"

"But I am also going for my book. Maybe there is nothing to know. I have made a promise. I shall go."

The sadness of words lay a heavy weight upon them. Brideswell poured out the chilled wine. It cooled and misted their glasses. Alice did not look at him.

"Yesterday morning I saw you on the train in the seat across from me. You were worried about the old monk in his brown cape and case too big for him. You saw his bad breathing when he sat down and pulled out his inhaler. When you got up to go to the toilet I saw your book had fallen onto the floor, a paperback. I was amazed at the title. Turgenev, a writer my father loved and always carried in his pocket. I knew then that we had been drawn together."

"Yes."

"Your new book, the Russian one – what's it called?"

"The house at Spissikoye."

She was looking at him closely now. "This book … is it about a man or a woman?"

"A man who doesn't fit in. A superfluous man."

"His name?"

"Maxim Ivanovich Davidov."

Her smile was ironic. Yet the eyes were softer. For him. "How very Russian." Her leg moved forward and brushed against him. A sudden heat entered from her touch. The moment of contact passed and they remained in silence, but together, with no need for words after the eloquence of bodily pressure. Perhaps her mind had retreated again, travelled back in time to scenes she was reluctant to revive, revisit. "Are all your novels set in my country, Michael?"

"No, only this one."

"Why Smolensk? Why did you choose my city, the home of my family?"

He looked over her head and through the upper part of a window into the summer sky and for a moment followed the passage of a cloud being moved slowly in the easterly breeze. "I don't know. It chose me – whether it was chance or something else set all that off – these things are mysteries. Perhaps, Alice, all is chance and nothing is set in stone – all our lives in some kind of random movement we have no power over. No say in anything."

She shook her head. "That sounds like ancient Greek or eastern fatalism and I don't believe it. There is nothing of chance in the way we met, the way I feel about you." She placed upon him the tenderest of smiles, "The way I need you. I have waited so long."

Brideswell paid the bill and promised Luigi they would be back, that his melon and pasta were the best in London. He walked slowly with Alice to their train, his arm through hers as if they were a couple already bound and loving after years of marriage. On the concourse she pulled Brideswell into her and kissed him long and searchingly on the lips. The train was posted on the departure board with its platform. 1515 to Manchester Piccadilly. They walked through.

He said, "I did reserve a seat but it won't be any good, only for one. We'll need to go on farther down."

They paused at the carriage door where the booked seat was but not knowing from the platform which one precisely, they did not see the man in it. He had arrived ten minutes earlier. A thin maroon roll-neck jumper covered a plaster on his neck where his throat had been cut the day before, the sleeve covered bruising on his left arm where a drip had replaced so much lost blood. The seated man did not see them; he was reading a book of short stories by Ivan Turgenev, a thin paperback with a blue cover. But the man's eyes were not taking in the printed words, his mind was elsewhere, a different station which also had four exits to a great city. Four exits to Smolensk.

★

Spring 1992
Nizhny Novgarod

A favourite seat. When he was old he would come here, to this table with its clean white cloth and new lamp – come here in the spring, sit and watch the world being reborn. New light, new warmth, snowmelt.

He ran his fingers along the edge of the table and felt a pleasure of familiarity. A room more gracious now, the chairs upholstered, patterns on the fabrics, the neat white cloths on every table and each with its new lamp, softer lighting. Small things but changes for the better – a gentler world where there was time to look at the sky. The room reflected the changes sweeping Russia. The decorations and prints on the walls had no angularity, no geometry with a social message, no exhortation to work with tools, no idealist shouldering a Soviet flag – all gone. Just a simple restaurant doing things it had always done best – giving customers good food, warmth and a restful place to eat in. In this new world there was a place for good linen for a room where the eye could travel outward into a world of unfolding beauty coming back after fifty years of being forgotten. The doctor shrugged – how could such dogmas have survived when all that is beautiful was dismissed?

Liadev was in a tranquil mood. Even the café had emerged from endless winter. Now it was owned by an Armenian – Grigori Basilievich Avazian – a big man. And like Liadev he sweated easily. He could need to change his shirt three times in a day. He had bought the café when market forces knifed their way into a failing economy. With his wife, they changed everything. Their platform restaurant welcomed travellers with the aroma of strong Georgian coffee, the smell of garlic kebabs grilling on a roasting spit – southern dishes for a cold city beside the Volga. It had become a haven and refuge for passengers arriving tired from Moscow, for those changing trains with hours to wait and half a century of grey paint stained by a million cigarettes had in one week of painting been banished forever.

The owner came to Dr Liadev. He smiled with a warmth of welcome and recognition. He had always liked the large unassuming doctor.

"What will you have today, Dr Liadev?"

"It's good to be back, Grigori. What do you recommend? – some baked fish? What are those herbs I can smell?"

"Doctor … my wife sees to all that. The fish is good, we sell a lot of it. Garlic, maybe, you can smell. But she's a Georgian and I forgive her … not like me an exiled Armenian. Yerevan."

"I'll have some." Liadev looked about him with appreciation. "Your place is looking good. I like the new lamps and the window curtains."

"A wife and three daughters. Between them they'll bankrupt me … and then the weddings – ay ay. That will finish me, Doctor."

"They won't all get married at once, Grigori – unless you have three brothers lined up."

The café owner laughed. "Are you mad, Doctor! What a thought! Now what'll you have to drink? We have some good Bulgarian wine. I like it ... or some beer?" The patron spread his arms. "But I won't bring you vodka ... then you wouldn't taste Maria's fish properly." He moved the napkin on his arm, a gesture as if he was already thinking of polishing a wineglass.

The doctor smiled. "Some white wine I think with the fish. And tell me, Grigori ... can I still catch a bus outside the station to Ulitsa Pushkina?"

The big Armenian didn't answer at first but raised his finger. "Next time you come to me, Doctor, you taste my elder daughter's chicken tabaka. Now that is a real Georgian dish. Buses ...? You don't catch any bus. A man can wait for ever and freeze to death waiting for a bus. My friend Nikolai will come round for you with his car. He's an honest man. I won't let him overcharge you. Let him rob the tourists for the Volga steamers, not my Dr Liadev!" He burst into a deep bass laugh. The whole body shook. "He has to live, Doctor ... and petrol, good petrol – it's not easy to get."

The fish was good. The sharp wine relaxed the doctor and brought into his mood an added mellowness. Liadev's mind drifted outward towards the city – a large industrial conurbation with its feet securely anchored in its past. It had its slums which fed labour into its mills and factories, and where a boy Alexei Peshkov- to become Maxim Gorky – grew up.

The revolution – huge, idealistic with all the ruthless cruelties of change. The city slums were exploded and cleared, blocks of flats no more than five storeys high were erected for people to live decently with warmth and water. Then Stalin, a Georgian with a hunger for power, and ideas fixed. Millions died. They renamed the city Gorky. Liadev shook his head, dabbed his lips with the serviette and drank from the misted glass. A good wine. The baked fish perfect, just as Grigori had said. The city's old name, Novgorod, was coming back, just like St Petersburg. Not a beautiful place but fine, firm and solid, its roots secular not spiritual. A city with one of Russia's greatest rivers – a city Liadev was about to enter again after an absence of more than six months, a place for exiles, textiles, trauma and tractors. Its shipyards built the great Volga barges with powerful engines to breast the great river's currents. She refined oil for those engines, made the tools that repaired them, made the paper they transported and the tractors which ploughed deep the black soil to grow the grain for Russia's bread.

He finished the wine. Liadev loved the city, its energy, its life of so many facets, its people and its rivers, the huge volume of moving water which laid a presence and vastness upon the small human activities along its banks. He folded his napkin, in no hurry to leave his table of thoughts.

Liadev sighed; such a strange and mysterious thing was life – so subject to the whims and thrusts of chance, so surrounded by questions unanswerable. He thought of his own work. Would he still be doing it in five years ... and the future, how could anyone look into a glass which had been so darkened, only now a handful of summers and springs to bring in a sweeter wine. Appointed doctor – but for how long? A brief to recover Russian artists from the punishments and the dictatorship of their minds. So long as he was wanted, he would carry on, and from Gorky – central to the rail network – east to Kirov, west to Moscow, south into the Volga basin, to Kharkov and the sea. How fortunate that he was a man who loved trains since he spent half his life in them or on platforms waiting. And Gorky was the home of his family.

Six months before his mother had taken in as a lodger and companion his widowed cousin, Natalya. Very shortly he would be meeting her himself – friends as children though he had been much older. Now they would meet half as strangers with a lifetime as wide as the Volga inserted between them.

Suddenly Grigori was there, in front of him, with Marya.

"I have brought over Marya, Doctor. Tell her what you think of her fish."

The woman was shy against the bulk of her husband. She wiped her hands nervously as if expecting a rebuke.

"Delicious, Marya. My mother couldn't have cooked it better."

Her husband turned to her and softly touched her cheek. "There you are, Marioushka, what a compliment! His own mother couldn't have done it better."

She smiled and was pleased. "It was also my mother's recipe, Doctor. We ate a lot of fish as children, my father caught them."

*

Malenkova District

The cab driver Nikolai was a silent man. He smoked strong Turkish cigarettes. Liadev wound down the window. The man turned his head round.

"There are three streets called Pushkina."

"Malenkova district."

They drew up outside a block of flats, one of a group of six all identical, all built in 1960 when the land was cleared. He gave Nikolai a larger fare than Grigori had suggested. It wasn't easy to make a taxi bring in good money. The man nodded and pointed.

"Does she live up there ... your mother?"

"The smaller block behind. I'll walk through."

"I never come here. These people don't use taxis."

"Follow the 37 bus back. You won't get lost."

"I never get lost, Doctor."

Liadev waited while the car drove away – a well-cared for car, unhurried in its passage through the anarchy of city traffic, leaving behind a faint smell of exhaust, Turkish tobacco and wax polish. Where he obtained his petrol, the doctor did not dwell on – these days everything seemed to have a price. Calmed by the café and relaxed by the soft-seated car, he walked through the estate of flats, past playgrounds and empty football pitches to an older block, left standing. Either money had run out for its modernisation, or it had been just overlooked.

A box-shaped iron grill on a steel platform passed for an uncertain lift, wide enough for three persons, one pram and a mother or a large man with a small dog. With Liadev in it there was no room for anyone else. Yet it arose silently and swiftly, as old as the block itself, mechanics sound and built by the first Soviet lift engineers to last. It had done. He knocked on his mother's door rather than use his key – to give her a moment before his arrival and to signal to Natalya, if she were there and not at work. Her factory like most worked shifts. The door opened. His mother – small enough to be a child – stood before him. She looked up into his face, tears surging up into her eyes.

"Maximoushka!" He kissed her on each cheek and held her for a few moments in his embrace. She examined him with concern. "Why didn't you telephone and leave a message with Irina Bloch? I could have had something ready for you to eat!"

"Mama! I'm not a child … do I look as if I need something to eat?"

She pursed her lips unconvinced and drew him by the hand into the hall. "Why do you always have such a little bag. It's much too small! Have you been robbed? Where is your father's suitcase?"

"I left it with the Holy Father in Smolensk."

"With who? How can you leave Papa's own case with a stranger?"

Her son protested. "But he isn't a stranger – the Holy Father is a friend and head of the seminary. It is the school for the cathedral and all the city's churches."

She let go his hand and admonished him with her finger. "Maximoushka ... there are priests and priests. A bad one will lock it away and a good one will give it to the poor. Whichever way you'll have lost it." She sat at a table and moved her sewing to one side. A gesture he loved. Vavara always moved her sewing over if anyone entered the room just like another woman might turn off the television. He lowered himself into the large wicker armchair by the window. It embraced him like an old friend, like a shoe that fitted – a chair comfortable, wide and kept especially for him. "How do you know such people, darling ... are you coming back into the church?" She looked deeply into his eyes. Her only son, now so strong and handsome and looking more and more like his grandfather. And so Russian. "So many changes everywhere. Here in Novgorod – we call it that again now and like your friend, all our own churches are being repaired and opened up. You wouldn't believe how full they are, It's as if the old city has taken back her name and her faith. And it's just the same with Irina Bloch's synagogue – full every Saturday."

"Holy Russia, Mama. When the lid is pressed down the lock wears out. I wrote and told you about Father Adrian ... don't you get my letters?"

His mother moved her head to one side and tensed her lips. "Sometimes. When you write."

"I see the Holy Father whenever I visit Smolensk, and he's very kind to Papa's case. It's safe and dry and there for when I shall need it."

"Well, I just hope so. Why do you go there?"

"He's looking after a composer for me."

She sighed and stood up. "I shall make you some tea with sugar. You'll wear yourself out with all this tearing about all over Russia. I should have found you a wife long ago … she wouldn't let you spend all your life riding about in trains – rushing around like an ant in ointment!"

"Mama you're mixing your metaphors – a fly in a bottle, or stuck like an ant in ointment. Anyway, I would have made a poor husband."

"Nonsense." Vavara smoothed the hair from her brow. "You will make a lovely husband. A sensible man at a sensible age … and it's time Papa's paintings were given a proper home, not kept hidden away in a dark cupboard. What are you doing, Maxim? – giving Papa's best leather case to a priest, and keeping his beautiful paintings in a broom cupboard when you should be a proper married man having them proudly displayed in your best room!"

"You're right, Mama." He was coming over drowsy – the wine, Marya's baked fish and the spring sunshine that was entering the room. "How's Natalya?"

"Wait." His mother's voice echoed from the kitchen, "I'll tell you in a minute … she's at work."

Vavara came back in with a tray, two glasses of tea in her mother's old-fashioned enamelled holders and a plate of the sweet cakes Maxim loved as a boy. She passed him the tray, moved out a low table and addressed him by a name from his childhood. "Maxi, why do you leave it so long between coming back home to see me? I'm not a young woman now – I want to see more of my son."

"It's my work, Mama."

"Couldn't you have stayed in the hospital?"

"This is more important; Moscow chose me to do it. Papa would understand, he was an artist – and suffered for it."

"He gave it up, if that's what you mean. Never mind. I have you now, darling." She kissed his cheek and passed him his lemon tea. "And what about my letters ... I went to a lot of trouble with my last one and I told you all about Natalya. It took me a long time to write all that down."

Liadev took two sugar lumps from the basin and lifted his glass of tea thoughtfully. "Yes, I did get that one – a very good letter, Mama. I read it in Smolensk by our great river Dnepr... I enjoyed reading it so much. And such a lovely morning. Three ducks were watching me – and a lady with a dog. My secretary does her best, she sends everything on, but I'm like a bird in flight. I'm always moving on. She knows to keep them for me until I'm on my way back. I'm sure none have gone astray, and I do love getting them."

His mother was reassured. "Yes, that girl of yours ..."

"Sasha."

"I know her name's Sasha, don't be so quick. You're becoming like all those Moscow men! I was about to say that your Sasha is a nice girl – Irina Bloch says so. And she has a good telephone manner, and respectful. Irina likes her." She sipped her tea. It was too hot to drink. "Irina's son, Ivan – do you remember him, he had a trial for Dynamo? He's in the telephone business now."

"Telephones, Mama?"

"Yes, those little ones you carry around in your pocket. He could get one for you at a special price."

"I'm happy as I am. I don't think they work well in Russia – everywhere is so far apart. Maybe for the Moscow Men, not for me."

"I don't like telephones, but you should phone Irina more. She brings every message up to me straight away. She likes doing that, it makes her day important."

Liadev was enjoying the hot, sweet tea and was glad to be home with Vavara, listening to her and seeing how happy she was to have him back, feeling her love and concerns. Now he need not worry so much about her, those guilty feelings of being always so far away. Natalya was here. "You'd like Smolensk, Mama. It's a really old city, lovely in places and so timeless. Different from here. It's not much bigger than your Malenkova district."

"It may suit you. This is where I live."

"I made a friend there."

"You said, darling ... the priest."

"Another friend; a woman who cleans the cathedral."

"Are you mad ... a cleaning woman!"

"Mama! Aren't you a democrat? She cleans the cathedral because she loves it."

"My son, a famous doctor, has a friend who is a cleaning woman. What is the world coming to!"

Liadev shook his head, smiled and said softly, "She knows the Archbishop."

"Well, don't upset your cousin by telling her that. You remember how much she admired you as children ... and she's longing to see you. Natalya is so excited."

"Where is she?"

"In the factory where she works."

"What does she do?"

"What do you think she does ... makes motor cars, of course." Quickly she raised her fingers to her throat, "But, Maxim, what have you had to eat today ... did you have any breakfast – are you hungry? Natalya has made some goulash for you. She insisted on cooking it herself." Vavara Davidovna lifted her palms upwards. "What could I do … she was determined to make it. I said 'I don't know if Maxim likes goulash.'"

"Of course I do. Is she a good cook?"

"We get along all right in the kitchen – but she's got a lot to learn. I said no to dumplings. Maxim hates dumplings."

He laughed. "Do I, Mama – hate dumplings?"

"You know you do. The slimy outside makes you sick. You only eat them when I bake them separately."

Liadev nodded. "I shall be hungry for it by suppertime. I ate something at the station."

Vavara Davidovna was shocked. "At the station! The food there is disgusting. Do you want to come home and be ill? How could you eat at the station when you know your mother and your cousin would be preparing food for you. I mean proper food! Home cooked by women who know what they're doing!"

He reached forward and placed his hand on her arm. "I'm sorry, Mama. I came off the train and needed something. And I wanted to enjoy that special time of arrival. To be back, to see the spring everywhere outside the windows and the wonderful Volga, the sunlight on it, its great and mysterious movements … besides, the food is excellent there now. The buffet has been bought by a Georgian Armenian and it's a restaurant now. I shall take you and Natalya there. His wife and daughters do the cooking – and they know me."

"Georgian … I might have guessed it. They get everywhere … look at Stalin – what a dreadful man, no education and a disaster for our country. Holy Russia with a Georgian Tartar at her throat!"

"Grigori is a good man. His wife is called Marya and she does a good baked fish in onion with lots of paprika and garlic."

"Maybe. You should eat at home when you come back to Gorky."

"Not Gorky, Mama … Nizhny Novgorod."

His mother took his glass and went back into the kitchen.

After supper when the two women came away from the kitchen, Dr Liadev unzipped his travel bag. "I have a few little presents. For both of you."

His cousin flushed. "For me as well, Maxim?"

"Of course for you as well, Natalya – we are a family of three now."

She lowered her eyes, embarrassed, and said quietly. "That is better than anything."

"So," he said, looking at her from under his eyebrows, "shall I take these presents back to the shops in Smolensk?"

They laughed. The women sat at the table. The colour remained in his cousin's cheeks. He passed his mother an amber brooch set in an old-fashioned Russian filigree, oval with gold settings and which opened for a photo of a loved one. Vavara Davidovna kissed him; she tried it on in front of the mirror and touching either side of it asked her niece.

"What do you think of it, dear?"

"It's beautiful, Aunty. The amber has such a lovely colour. Is it Russian amber, Maxim?"

"No. Lithuanian. The man who sold it to me said it was better quality. I didn't believe him, but I rather liked it." He delved into his bag and brought out a small box for Natalya. She looked at him with shy pleasure. "For me?"

"Yes. Open it."

She drew from the cotton wool covering it, an amber pendant. "Oh ... I love this!" She passed the chain over her head, lifting her hair clear at the back. She touched it as it hung into the V of her dress, in the folds between the breasts. She went to the mirror just as her aunt had done. "Aunty?" She pressed the cool resin and allowed her fingers to spread the softness of the framing skin.

"Yes, Natoushka – it's right for you. For your hair and your eyes."

Natalya bent over the doctor. He smelled her washed hair and faint perfume which surrounded her. A rounded, warm woman. She kissed him softly on each cheek with tenderness. "Thank you, Cousin Maxim. I have never been given such a present before." A love in her eyes. Vavara Davidovna saw it and there came up into her heart an unwanted shaft of jealousy. She retorted with a sharpness, becoming milder and more accepting. It was what she had wanted but her jealousy rising up so suddenly disturbed her. "Both of us, Natalya, are going to lose Maximoushka's affection. He has a lady friend in Smolensk ... a cleaning woman!"

The doctor touched the softness of his cousin's arm as she straightened up, as the pendant he had given her swung back away from him into the roundness of untouched, unloved breasts. His look reached into her but his smile was unreadable.

"Men of my size have a big heart – there is room enough in it for three women."

Vavara Davidovna admonished him with her finger – she

looked towards her niece with all jealousy gone. "Natalya, I don't like the sound of all this. Our Maximoushka is becoming a Moscow Man. We shall have to very soon find him a wife!"

*

Euston, after leaving Brother Robert

As he walked slowly along Platform 7, Brideswell's mind was already travelling lightly and at random – thoughts triggered by the sight of the waiting train. A memory, a picture – the quietness of a different platform opposite a Russian city subsiding into the end of a day. The Moscow train had terminated at Smolensk, people were gathered on the platform waiting for a connection, the train to take them on to Poland and Berlin. The same silence and expectation that was invading him now. And the silence he had felt in the great Russian cathedral within a vast and meaningful space, where the waiting was spiritual, a service beginning, the Cathedral of the Assumption.

His mind returned to the moment and to Robert, how he had met by chance a Lexikon brother from a religious house, the monastery of St Chryostom, in that same city, the parent house of a distant monastic building in Mobberly not 10 miles from him.

He nodded to no one but himself. Smolensk was a city he would have to return to now – it had reached him with a grasp and grip unimaginable only three or four days ago.

It had come to his left hand, held his right and threw the image of itself into his eyes. The platform he was walking down had risen up like a reflection, a mirror for Smolensk, and a cooler space, respite from the heat of the huge city he was leaving. Brideswell took out his ticket and checked the number of his reserved seat. The heavy doors of the carriage were wide open but few people were boarding – he was early and the part of the train he was passing was first class. He hitched up the strap of his shoulder bag and prepared to board further down, behind an elderly woman having difficulty with a white leather case. In her other hand she gripped a deep Hessian bag made cumbersome by protruding newspapers.

"Here ... let me take your case. That bag looks precarious. Not the place for a spill."

She gave him a smile, easing the anxiety in her face. "The newspapers are so silly now. Why-ever should I bother to read them. It's only habit. I don't seem to be able to enter a train without them." In the wideness of the carriage-end, she carefully set down the bag so it wouldn't topple over, and waited for him.

"Well, I must say I've given them up, too. I'd rather a book."

She lifted the bag. "Did you notice ... this is 'E', isn't it?"

"Yes. There's a sticker on the window. What's your seat number – I'll put this one up on the rack for you if you don't need it for the journey." They walked towards the double glass doors, which flew open with a hiss.

"Thank you. You're very kind. I can't read a book in a train, all that shaking about of the small print upsets my eyes." She stopped and rummaged about, lifting out a small handbag. "Would you hold my shopping bag. I need to find the ticket with the seat number." He waited while she searched. "Here ... this is the one. I'm number 24 A."

"Good. Then you'll be quite near me, I'm 37 on the other side."

The carriage was filling up. Ten minutes before departure. The aisle ahead of them was blocked by passengers stowing away bags, removing coats and settling into seats. They edged their way past. The woman sighed.

"The old trains were much better – at least you had a corridor and room enough to get through." She peered at the numbers above the seats. "Thank Heavens ... here I am. I shall be glad to sit down!" A seat for two, a reservation card – only for the window seat. She sat down awkwardly, looked back at him and smiled. "You've been a wonderful help. Thank you." He lifted the case up onto the rack and wedged it in firmly.

"I'm going as far as Stockport – I'll lift it down if you're going further on."

"Thank you. I stay put till Macclesfield." The swell of people behind them was becoming restless and pressing towards him.

"I'd better be moving along – people want to get by. I'll find my place. I'm not far away." He raised his left hand and gave a sort of goodbye with a shake of his fingers. At the midway luggage recess he leaned in out of the way to allow the passengers behind him to come through. He found 37. In his reserved seat was a thin man in a maroon polo-necked jumper. Brideswell looked again at his ticket, rechecking the number.

"I can't quite understand this ..." He did not engage the man's eyes but kept his gaze down ... "are you sure you're in the right seat?" The man he spoke to also had his attention elsewhere, on a book with a blue cover. He glanced up in a leisurely way, a man certain of his place. Brideswell was taken aback, overwhelmed by the man's face and disturbed by the large plaster showing above the pullover rim. The man's neck. And the sight of the book; it chilled him. He instinctively felt in his pocket to feel his own – so similar. Still there. The meeting had unsettled the seated man too.

"I'm sorry. I can't prove it. I was robbed in London and they took my wallet with the ticket. I have this replacement, but no seat reservation. Sorry. I remembered the seat number." As the man moved his neck round more he winced, shut his eyes, raised his fingers to ease the pressure of the jumper on his wound.

"Don't worry," said Brideswell, "you stay put. Sorry about your neck."

"Thanks. It's better than it was. Glad you're not turfing me out. Still get dizzy. It happens."

"Yes. Bad luck. I'll go back to a woman I helped on – the seat next to her is free. That book you're reading ... may I see the cover?"

" Certainly. I haven't taken your book as well as your seat, have I?" He gave a wry smile, closed the book and showed the blue cover. "Turgenev."

"How extraordinary!"

"Why?"

"I am reading the same one."

The man raised his left hand, cupped the palm and fingers in a gesture of surprise, acceptance, welcome and valediction. Brideswell returned to the woman with the white case and sheaf of newspapers. She had not moved, papers unread beside her.

"Excuse me ... would you mind if I sat down beside you – there's a chap in my seat." She lifted her bag and papers.

"Please do. What bad luck. You left him in it?"

"Didn't want to make a fuss. He's been in an accident and was mugged. They took everything, and his ticket." He sat down. "The funny thing is, he's some kind of doppelgänger – my pullover, my book ..."

"Three things. Your seat as well?"

Brideswell smiled and nodded. "You're right. One big difference – I don't have a huge hospital plaster on my neck!" He sat down. "Thanks."

"You can get out your book. You don't have to talk to me unless you want to. I always start by looking out of the window. It's special for me – a luxury."

"Yes? How's that?"

"I could never sit in this place as a child. My older sister always demanded the window seat."

★

Alice

The 15.15 from Euston to Manchester Piccadilly slowed and smoothly came to a halt at its first stop, Milton Keynes Central. Alice opened her eyes. She had fallen asleep, her head on Michael's shoulder. She remained still and motionless, unwilling to break the pleasure of waking and being held. She could see he had read hardly anything of his book. "Where are we?"

"Milton Keynes."

The swish and clatter of the automatic doors invaded her feeling of love and security. Several people came down the train, large people who held their cases in front of them to negotiate the narrowness of the aisle, pressing the luggage forward with their knees. Peripheral and inward people, searching not just for a free seat, but almost for comfort and respite and a way in from the margin. They passed her as a bird will cross in front of a wide moon in a night frost, a silhouette of movement, a memory of passage.

"You haven't read much, Michael?"

"A little. I've been looking out of the window mostly."

"What have you been thinking about?"

He did not answer at first. "How my life has changed. When you look for love it's not there – then when you least expect it, it arrives. Yesterday when I came to London I wanted to escape from everything – a sort of grey bleakness all around me. Now it's all changed. What I see out of the window pleases me, all the colours are brighter. I even like the people in this carriage ... and especially you, Alice."

She smiled up at him and eased herself back into her seat, smoothing the loose hair away from her face. "We know each other so well, and so little."

"It doesn't seem to matter. I do want to know a lot more about you, but there's no hurry. I feel time isn't a factor – perhaps that's why I'm happy with the countryside streaming past our window. I don't feel it is some kind of unreality, I don't overlay it with negative thoughts, only see it as a view from a train hurrying through England on a summer afternoon. I am a writer – I've spent most of my life struggling with the passage of time. At last that has stopped." He took her hand in his. "I've lost interest in such things with you next to me."

The refreshment trolley came to them and Milton Keynes was left behind. He bought two coffees and a packet of biscuits. As he passed her the covered carton he said, "You have unusual fingers."

"Have I? I wasn't aware of that."

"I notice hands ... hands and gestures. It's a peculiarity of writers. Sometimes they watch too much and feel too little."

She moved her fingers loosening their tips. "Fingers of a fiddle player. I practise every day. You have to."

"That explains it ... why I like your hands."

She looked into his eyes. "I notice things about you, too."

"Not bad things, I hope."

"You like to be on your own."

"Really? Are you sure?"

"I'm certain. Some women would find that difficult – not me. Too much closeness can break up a marriage ... not enough space and respect. After all, we're all very private deep down. Even people married for years and years – they still need somewhere private to be, sometimes. Don't you think so ...?"

"I don't know. I was no good at it. Marriage."

The train rocked over points and raced through a station. He took Alice's coffee from her and steadied them both on the seat shelf. When they slowed, she picked hers up, took off the cover and stirred in a tube of sugar, a luxury she did not allow herself at home.

"My husband loved me at first – but there was always a gap between us. You see – too wide a space. It seems a marriage needs some kind of balance. I used to think it was because I was Russian and he was so English. Frank loves all those things Englishmen think so much of – rugby, cricket, his work, his car, his pub ... and he loves television. Not me. I can do without it."

"I see that. Too many places of non-meeting. You grew up in a different world."

"I grew up in Russia. We knew nothing of sport ... except chess. My father was a disgraced composer. In any country where marriages are planned, mine to Frank wouldn't have survived the first report of his family's detective. An unsuitable marriage – an Englishman with a deep love for his own country's traditions, a boarding school boy, with a Russian refugee who practised her violin before breakfast in the kitchen with the door shut." She smiled bleakly and raised her hands in a muted protest. "I'm not looking for a defence or excuse, only saying how it was. Because you understand. We are alike."

"Yes."

"I'm glad Frank has found another woman who suits him better, who loves him the way he wants to be loved – but why did he have to choose a woman who is so stupid, and break his son's heart by going to live in her drab and tasteless house?" Alice sighed, reached for his hand and pressed it against her face, kissing his fingertips. "I think you're going to get on very well with Kenny. He likes a quieter sort of man." She shrugged. "He has a bad time at school now ... they think he comes from a one-parent family – only a mother. No man to look up to."

Brideswell did not answer her at once. His gaze through the window was distant, perhaps travelling westward towards his own father. He also had one parent, a father whose love he had never known.

"Tell me about Kenny – what's he like?" He let go of her hand and put the hot coffee to his lips.

"He's not a boy easy to describe – so many different sides to him. I'd say he has become far too serious. He doesn't laugh enough. You'll cheer him up. Come with me this evening when I collect him from Carol's."

He shook his head. "That would upset him. It's only you he'll want to see, not a stranger as well. He'll need comforting after that haircut. No ... I'm the last person he'd want to see with his mother ... another man."

She touched his cheek. "You understand already."

"Maybe I could come to the match with you tomorrow? You could both come back to my flat. I'll get some fish and chips in."

She laughed lightly. "He's set his heart on MacDonalds."

"I'll just come for the match. That's enough. He won't mind that."

They became quiet. The train stopped at Rugby. No one got on or off. A train unwanted there, waiting like a long fish in a current before moving on upstream. Alice touched his arm.

"Read your book and have some peace. I don't think you want to have me bothering you all the time with our endless problems. Now I've found you, I don't want to scare you away. Already you're precious."

A thinnish man with hair greying at the temples, thoughtful with inward looking eyes, came down the aisle, as if he had got on unseen and was searching for a seat. When opposite them, the train started with a jolt and he grasped the top of Brideswell's seat, lurching across him.

"Sorry. Sorry – the train. Caught off balance."

Brideswell looked up and closed his book, displaying its blue cover and picture of a woman by Korovin in a nightdress, by a window. The stumbling man saw it.

"How strange ... you as well. Reading that book! It is totally improbable that three people on this train should all be reading that one book."

Brideswell looked up. The man gave him a start – someone who looked so much like him. He shrugged. "It must be all these Mancunians ... we all love the classics."

The man nodded, humour in his eyes. "Your right. That's the answer." As he moved off Alice watched him.

"Do you know that man, Michael? He could be your twin, except that he's wearing a maroon jumper, and his hair's a bit greyer. And something's happened to his neck. He has a big plaster."

Brideswell re-opened his book but his mind was on the

man. Everyone, he thought, has a double. Not the first time he'd seen someone he might be related to.

"I don't know him but we're reading the same book and he has on a jumper exactly like the one in my bag. Thankfully my neck is OK."

But the man who had stumbled across them was mistaken about the number of people on the train with Turgenev's book of love stories. A fourth man, a novelist also had it in his pocket. He had been to a funeral, carried a coffin and had promised the widow of the dead man that he would go to Smolensk. To try and find her other daughter. A step-daughter named Ivana.

★

Brideswell at Altrincham FC

Brideswell bent down towards the boy sitting beside him. "I've brought you a few stamps, Kenny. Alice said you collected them." The Altrincham football ground was summer-green and bathed in strong sunlight. The heat of the week had passed, blown away by a cooling wind. The stand was two-thirds full – quite good for a pre-season friendly with Crewe Alexandra, a team climbing back up the league table after falling fortunes. He passed the boy a brown envelope. "They're oldish ones … you can use them as swaps if you have them already – or don't like them all that much."

Kenny looked up at him, surprise in his eyes. He was never given stamps old or otherwise. The question in his gaze was unreadable to the man, nor was it any clearer when he rested it on his mother – a slight lift of the chin, a barely perceptible movement of the shoulders, gestures he learned from her, not at school. Perhaps he was asking if he ought to accept a present from a man that he'd only met for the first time half an hour before. Perhaps he had been warned about such things – gifts from strangers. In the event she took the envelope from him.

"I expect Michael collected stamps when he was a boy. We'll open it and have a look when we get home. Here they might blow away in this wind."

Kenny did not smile, agree – or say anything. He watched as his stamps were shut away in Alice's handbag, for later. He was saddened and elated. All jumbled up. "Where are they from, Michael?"

"Commonwealth, and some English pictorials."

"Are there any dogs?"

"I think there's one."

"Are any from Russia?"

"I'm afraid not."

"I should like some stamps from Russia. I am a quarter Russian."

"That sounds good to me. They're so brilliant at lots of things."

"What things?"

"Space ... that's just one. Brilliant at music and composing, at art. Some of their writers are the best in the world. Their old books are classics."

"What's a classic?"

"A book that people admire years and years after it was written."

"Like Alice and Wonderland?"

"Exactly."

"Have you ever been to Russia?"

"Yes ... as a writer."

"Alice was born in Smolensk."

"That's where I went."

His being there, in Smolensk, seemed to satisfy the boy. That it was all right for him to be friends with his mother

– he knew the city where Alice was born, and knew a lot about stamps. "Do you speak Russian?"

"A bit – to get by ... but not like Alice."

Kenny took Michael's hand. Crewe were attacking. In the penalty area. When they scored tears flooded into the boy's eyes.

"Dead lucky goal that," said Brideswell. "I'm sure their striker was miles offside."

Alice left them to buy ice-creams. Kenny had retreated into himself. The goal upset him and he stared down at the programme. Fortunately the whistle blew then for half time and Crewe's corner was not taken.

"Second half," said Brideswell, "Altrincham will come back. Anyone can see they're a good team – but Crewe is tough opposition – top end of their league."

"They were lucky. The linesman should have disallowed their goal." His mind left the programme and the match, reverting to another insult. "I hate Carol."

Brideswell nodded. "I don't blame you. So would I."

"Look what she did to my hair."

"Yes. It does look a bit bare, but hair at your age grows fast – a couple of weeks. There are lots of boys with that kind of haircut. It's a sort of style."

"D'you think so?"

"Why ... yes. Look at footballers today – lots of them have haircuts like yours."

"Are you sure?"

"It's common sense. If you're scoring goals with your head, the top needs to be a bit smooth. Good contact." He flicked his head as if scoring in a top right-hand corner. "You can't be a top striker with hair all over your eyes."

"The man who did it was horrible."

"Some barbers are like that."

"He made me sit on the babies' chair and kept saying yes to Carol."

"What was Carol saying?"

"Stupid things. That my hair was too long for a boy of seven."

"I don't think I would like her," said Brideswell.

The boy looked up at him, smiled and relaxed. "My father's name is Frank."

"I like that name."

"He plays rugby."

"Not my game, Kenny."

The boy paused as he heard his name. "I don't know anyone called Michael."

"I don't mind it ... the name."

"Sometimes Carol calls me 'Kenneth'. That's not my name. I hate it. I don't know why Frank lives with her. She's a show-off. Like Graham."

"Graham?"

"He's my friend. He always wants his postcards back."

"Why?"

"The stamps. And he collects postcards. I wouldn't go and live with him – and Frank shouldn't go and live with Carol. No one should live with her."

Brideswell nodded. He could see that. After a moment he said, "I wouldn't have been much of a father."

"I should think you would have been all right." Kenny looked Brideswell up and down to check his assessment.

"Thank you."

"Will you come from Russia to see us again."

"Maybe you'd come and see me. I'm living here at the moment, the other side of Knutsford."

Kenny was puzzled. A name he had heard. They had no football team. "Is that near Manchester?"

"Not far. A train from Piccadilly, then you change at Stockport, then our line there on to Knutsford – and for me another bus ride … a few miles."

Kenny suddenly remembered. "I went to Tatton Park once. When I was small."

"That's it. You're right there."

"What would we do if we came to you?"

"I've got some games. Have you ever played chess?"

"No."

"You might like it. The pieces you move are exciting … castles and bishops, kings and queens – and then there are the horses, the knights, they jump a bit like a frog or crab. Forwards and sideways – all at the same time."

"Have you got any football programmes?"

"I'm afraid not. But we could make some."

"Could you teach me some Russian words?"

"Wouldn't Alice be better at that?"

"No." He shook his head and watched his mother approaching, holding three ice cream cones. "She never speaks Russian. We never talk about Russia at all." The two teams ran back onto the field. Alice apologized.

"Sorry to be so long. Such a long queue!"

"Michael is going to teach me chess and Russian."

Alice looked into Brideswell's eyes. "I'm glad of that."

*

Unreserved seat

"I have a sister living in Russia. She would have read that book you're reading."

"Really ... Where might that be? Which part?" Brideswell forgot himself, and everything else – astonished to find that the woman sitting next to him had a Russian sister.

"Gorky. Now they call it by the old name again, Nizhny Novgarod."

"You do surprise me. That seems amazing!"

"Yes. Your book made me think of her. We're a Jewish family. My sister went back and married out – a big Russian mechanic who repaired buses in Moscow."

"That's astonishing ... but you said she lives in Gorky not Moscow?"

"That's right. Her husband died and she went back home."

"I'm sorry."

"The flat was still there. Her son didn't go up with them. There was a neighbour who was her best friend. It was right to go back."

"I don't know that part."

"On the Volga. Her friend who has the flat underneath has a son who is a doctor. He travels all over Russia in his work."

"Ah. Yes …"

Brideswell lapsed into silence. The train gathered speed as it left Rugby station far behind, a memory being effaced and ever diminishing. "Life is so strange. My name is Brideswell … I'm a writer. I've written a novel. Parts of it are set in Russia … Smolensk."

She did not comment. Her thoughts remained with her sister. "I have never been there either. Irina was the idealist in our family. She wanted to go back and show solidarity."

"Yes … I do have to go back, though not for that reason. The Russian chapters in my book have upset my publisher. He is a Russian. He called me down yesterday to tell me they were no good – but life intervened. Life or death. I had to go to a funeral. But I was going back in any case. There's a girl I need to see."

"You're a romantic. Like my Irina."

"No – not quite like that. She's the daughter of the Russian man whose funeral I went to." He sighed and watched the passing fields and ever-changing scene. "It was sad – almost no one came – just four friends carrying the coffin, the widow and a nephew. She has three children, none of them were there … one daughter in Smolensk, one in South London who has fallen out with the family, and the son in Italy."

"It seems to happen so often now. There's an excuse perhaps for the ones abroad not coming. Not for the daughter in London."

"The step-daughter in Russia hasn't yet been told. She's out of contact. I said to her mother that I would find her and break the bad news."

"How can you – if there's no contact?"

"Ivana works in the cathedral. I have the name – it shouldn't be hard."

The train rocked across points at speed. It shook, swayed and threw up a soft grating sound. They did not resume talking for some time.

"When are you planning to go over, Mr Brideswell?"

"Soon. In a couple of weeks."

Approaching Crewe, the train slowed at signals. Two young women in neat uniforms stopped by them with the refreshments-trolley.

"Tea or coffee, madam ... and for you, sir?"

Brideswell turned to his companion. "Do you fancy something from the trolley?"

"You choose something for us."

He bought two coffees and a packet of custard creams. The younger woman pushing the trolley said to her friend as they moved farther along the aisle –

"Did you notice that man? He has a twin on this train. I wonder why they're not sitting together? Funny – he also bought two coffees and a packet of custard creams." Her friend didn't remember. "You must ... he was with his wife. I gave him all those pound coins in the change."

Brideswell placed the coffees on the window shelf. The trained eased down some more and came to a halt at a signal just outside the station. He passed her the carton. "It'll be boiling hot. They usually are. Be careful with the lid if you put in sugar."

"Thank you. You're a kind man. You gave me your name but I haven't told you mine. I'm Miss Oman. Sarah to most people. Sasha to my sister and to my father. Tell me, what is the name of this young woman you have to find in Smolensk — I didn't quite catch it."

"Ivana."

"Ah yes ... and the family name?"

"Ivana Petrovna Madiewska."

"That sounds more Polish than Russian."

"He was born in Kaliningrad — Königsberg that was — and he must have been one of the handful of remaining Russian Protestants." He slipped his book into his jacket pocket. "This has been the strangest away-day in my life. I seem to be surrounded by Russians at every turn. And every which-way is leading to Smolensk. The Fates are playing with me, Miss Oman."

"Irina says Mrs Liadev's son — the doctor I told you about — he goes to Smolensk sometimes, to a seminary. I believe he has a patient there. You could ask the Father in charge if he knows your young woman. I mean — as she works in the cathedral."

"Yes. I could."

Brideswell took out his diary. He wrote down a list — Dr Liadev, the seminary at Smolensk, Irina, Gorky and Miss Sarah Oman. The woman at his side noted his writing.

"What a careful and precise man you are, Mr Brideswell."

"It's a fault of novelists, Miss Oman. Should I leave you my number in case I bump into the good doctor?"

She opened her handbag and found a small card. "You can find me at Huddersfield University. I lecture in piano and composition."

He took it and thanked her. "A composer and a pianist. These are Russian gifts."

"I could give you a lift from Macclesfield if you were to stay on. I don't have a car but I have a driver who always takes me everywhere. His name is Ilya ... you might like to try out your Russian on him."

*

Letters

The flat was hot. He had forgotten to close the front room curtains and two days of midsummer sun burning in had left it airless and unfriendly. He threw open all the windows then went downstairs to collect his mail from the pigeon-hole in the hall recess.

Two letters – one from his father the other in a neat hand he did not recognise, forwarded from Mannings. He eased off the clammy roll-neck sweater, winced as he lifted it up and over the neck plaster then settled back into his window chair to read. He opened first the letter sent on from his publishers.

> Hatch End, Middlesex
> HA9 3AW
> June 28th 1995

'Dear Mr Brideswell,
                    Please forgive me for writing but I'm one of your devoted readers ...'

Brideswell sighed. Devoted readers only wrote to point out errors.

'... I spoke to your publisher Mr Lev about your next book, which I look forward to very much. Good luck for your trip to Russia, you'll find it a very different place under Boris Yeltsin.

You may remember seeing me some time ago at your sister's grave. I keep it tended along with one or two others. I wanted to write to say I've been called over to Swansea to my sister's and wondered if you'd splash some water on the plants when you come down this time. I'd be grateful. The council are generous with taps, there's one close by.

Best wishes to your father. I know he can't get up here from Dorset. Perhaps when you do come to water you might take photo of it for him. The penstemons are coming out and the lilac lobelias look well beside them.

> Yours sincerely
> EV Lucas (a friend of Josie)

Strange letter. Brideswell dimly recalled a gardener at Carpenters Park Cemetery. He had wanted to give him money for tending the grave but at first the man had refused. The letter touched him – a third act of kindness he had received from strangers in the space of a few hours. But puzzling – how did EV Lucas know his father lived in Dorset and was too old to visit his daughter's grave. And a photo? What a strange idea. There was something about the letter that disturbed him. Something metaphysical?

He picked up the envelope containing his father's letter. For a long time he did not open it. An uneasy shiver passed through him – a few hours ago he had been dreaming of

Josie and her suicide. Now there was a letter from a stranger who tended her grave, asking him to water the plants around it. And on top of that, a letter from his father who never believed his own beloved daughter had taken her own life. At the inquest he had been told his father spat into the driver's face.

*

Lyskovo
May 1995

A hot day in late spring. A holiday without the bombast of former years. As they came alongside the quay at Lyskovo, the balalaika band played a quiet wistful Hebrew melody as if addressed to all arrivals, each one with a mixture of time present, time past, time lost. Dr Liadev was affected by the music, how Russian to be questioning arrival, how poetic the melody. Unaccustomed tears came into his eyes. His smile was like arrivals – a wry comment on their enigma. He touched his cousin's arm.

"What a lovely tune that is, Natalya. Why do they play with such sadness for our arrival – surely the tune should be more joyful?"

The woman at his side had no answer. Perhaps there was none. She did know the band though – three of them worked in her factory on the assembly line, but at heart they were country people. "Some players remember different days when they didn't spend all their lives in a car factory. They remember a different life ... coming here must remind them, Maxim."

"What a sensible and sensitive woman you are, Natoushka." He touched her hand, "I hadn't thought of that."

They stood up leaving Vavara Davidovna asleep in her deckchair – the midday sun had moved from her leaving an avenue of shade. Liadev took some notes from his wallet. "Here, Natalya ... give these to the band for their lunch and some drinks. They play well."

She took the roubles and handed them to the leader, a man from the works office. "Yakob, the doctor says your music is sad."

He smiled, took them, nodded towards his band and thanked her. "Natalya – so you are travelling with a doctor now? Has Mr Yeltsin also got plans for you?" He lowered the finger of humour and irony and looked towards the big man leaning on the steamer's rail. He lifted both hands towards the doctor in a gesture of thanks and of surprise. The soft laugh he gave came from a century of Russian surprises, most of them bad.

"The doctor is my cousin, Yakob."

"And a good man to think of my players."

"He said it was a beautiful tune."

"Thank him for that. But tell your distinguished cousin that the music is sad, but my band is happy." He spoke gently and walked back to the musicians. Natalya rejoined Liadev. He asked her a question.

"Do you know this town, Natoushka?"

"No ... how could I know it it?"

"We're here for three hours. It is a great mixture – a soup of cultures. They have an Armenian church, a market full of Ukrainians and ..." He stopped as a short woman with a large bulging bag pushed past. "... and a Georgian café where I'll take you both for some real tabaka."

She took his hands in hers and lifted his fingers to her cheek. "I wish you didn't have to go away. Will it be for long? These absences, Maxim, are too much for us. We miss you and they break our hearts."

For the first time he put his arm around her, held her and comforted her. Natalya leaned against him and let him feel her love, her warmth, and her strength. They remained quiet while the noisy exodus down the gangway continued. His mother, in her embracing deckchair, remained asleep, enfolded within the canvas arch, brushed by the afternoon heat. He eased his arm away and reached into his jacket pocket for a handkerchief – a sweat had broken out across his forehead.

"You should take your jacket off, Maxim ... there's a breeze off the river. It'll cool you. Here, let me hold it."

He hesitated, then with the smile of a child passed it to her. "It's true – I've been away too much. Yet I have neglected Smolensk and been too much in Moscow and St Petersburg. I believe I have achieved something." He paused and looked down into the slow flowing waters. "We have now some respite houses for our Russian artists to recover in. I've had to fight hard for them. I've been informed my office is closing down. I've had to tell Sasha to find a new job. She is upset and I've been doing my best to persuade the director to place her in another department, but no promises. That's how we are now. Everything uncertain, no money, cut backs. I shall carry on as long as I can without an office, Natoushka. The work will have to go on. The need has not gone away. Some people will need help for decades ... some for the rest of their lives."

She placed her hand over his. "We all know you'll fight everyone for your patients, dear Maxim."

He sighed, shook his head and looked across the wide river to the far bank and beyond, into the distant hills which had bent the course of the Oka River northwards. "You know, Natalya, how things are in Moscow – a different sort of revolution – Boris Yeltsin, the Parliament ... so much chaos, so many criminals undermining everything. I shall be glad to leave Moscow behind and take with me half pay and a free railway pass."

"But, Maxim, you must have somewhere to work from, a telephone and someone to take down your messages when you're away. Will you work from home, from Gorky?"

He turned and saw his mother was still sleeping. "I haven't told Mama any of this yet. I have had an offer. Perhaps it's time for all of us to move on. Papa's paintings need to be hung up properly. They've waited a long time."

"You mean, you'll stop working with your patients and poets?"

"No. How could I? I shall never stop working. I have responsibilities all over Russia – our great and beautiful land – to the people I've found and tried to bring back ... some are very damaged souls. I have my two respite homes. I shall not abandon them."

"But what of this offer, Maxim. You said 'us all' – what does that mean? – you are being mysterious, and secretive."

"I shall tell you both together, over our meal." He paused, put his arm around her shoulder and drew her into him. "I want to move all three of us to Smolensk."

The centre of the square was never used by tradition by the market traders. Nor did any grass grow on it – bare, hard, baked soil. It was in other times, other days, the practice pitch for a football team – Sparta Lyskovo. But no players on it today – May Day holiday, the special market overflowing outwards – extra stalls, fortune-tellers, jugglers, acrobats and musicians. A fair more than a market and the crowds swelled by 200 passengers from the Novgorod steamer 'Sergei Aksakov'. And so much buying, so much bargaining and selling – carpets from Kazakhs, woven and printed Uzbek blankets, white linen and lace at the Romany stalls, watches from Odessa, goat cheeses from the slopes of the Carpathian mountains. There were Russian hats, mats, long-haired rabbits and marmalade cats. A place to buy anything and everything, cakes, jam and Armenian honey – the whole market was as much a hive as any apiary. The bees – human.

The restaurant 'Azov' was one of many cafés which bordered the market square – full on market days and on every warm evening in spring when the wind came up from the south. A place of welcome. The wind which fanned and cooled Liadev was a blessing on a hot May day coming in from the north-east and tracking down the Volga. The sun was shaded by high cloud and in the café forecourt by large wide parasols. The doctor and the two women waited to be shown to a table for three.

Liadev ordered – chicken tabaka with potatoes baked in garlic and herbs each with a centre of cream cheese. The waiter was quick and attentive – he brought a sparkling white wine in a canister of ice, opened it by unwinding the wire and easing off the cork. It exploded with a crack of a starting pistol. The out-flowing wine was deftly caught in a long tilted glass. While they waited for the meal to come to them, the doctor proposed a toast.

"To both of you whom I love very much … and to our future."

They clinked glasses. The women looked at each other. A flush had spread into Natalya's cheeks. Vavara Davidovna intercepted the quick glance between her son and her niece.

"What exactly are we toasting, Maximoushka? What future are you planning for us?"

"Ah ... well, this is a good time to tell you, Mama. I do have a plan for us, for our future lives together."

"So tell me. I should know."

He did not hurry but drank deeply into the chilled wine. "I have to leave my office – the Moscow Centre is closing down. I have been put on half salary."

Vavara Davidovna put her hands to her throat. "Half salary! I can't believe it. You are a doctor, your work has been ordered by the Kremlin! What are they doing? I can't believe Mr Yeltsin would do this, he wouldn't allow it!"

"Everything is changing in Moscow, Mama. I have to leave. My Sasha has been told to find another job."

"But she's your secretary ... for years. Poor girl! Irina Bloch will be very upset – she speaks to her on the phone like a daughter. This is monstrous, Maxim darling. Outrageous!"

"What can I do, Mama? No office, my work downgraded – I don't even know how long they'll keep me on. There's no money. I have to take a salary cut like everyone else ... and find a cheaper place to work from. And as you say, poor Sasha – I am asking around and doing my best to find her something. At least I have a role still – they want me to carry on."

"It is a complete disgrace that they can treat you like this, a senior doctor working directly for a government minister. What is Russia coming to?"

"At least I still keep my free travel on our railways."

"All the years you have worked for the Office of Soviet

Culture. Your father will be weeping in his grave ... to be treated like this!"

"Russian culture, Mama, the Soviet days and ways are over."

His mother shook her head, upset. "Did you know about all this, Natalya?"

"Only just now, Aunty. Maxim told me while you were asleep on the boat."

"So what is our future to be? I hope your dear Papa would approve. You're not abandoning all his friends I hope. He wouldn't like that."

"Mamam ... of course not! I shall still look after them. Listen ... I've had an offer. The chance to rent a large flat in Smolensk."

Vavara Davidovna was astonished. "Smolensk ...? What are you saying, Maxi ... are you taking us there? We can't go to Smolensk, it's the other side of the earth. Those people are not a bit like us, all the war and everything. It used to be part of Poland – we are Volga people. Their ways are not our ways!"

"Mama ... listen, and don't get so upset. Hear me out. I want us to move to Smolensk because I've been offered a church flat to work from. It is unwanted by the priest – too large and he wants to return to the seminary – he's used to being with people around him he knows, not marooned in a large empty flat."

His mother gazed at him in continuing disbelief. "Maxi, you don't even go to church! Why are they giving it to you?"

He did not answer her question but hurried on. "The flat is on two floors and is attached to the church. The upstairs has a tenant ... he has his own entrance."

"I have 20 people living above me. Should we worry about that?"

"The tenant is not a priest, but he is from the seminary. He is in the upstairs studio with the piano, a small bedroom and little kitchen. You'll like him, Mama. His name is Andrei Andreyevich... a musician. He has no memory of the past – it was beaten out of him in a prison camp."

Vavara Davidovna turned to her niece. "We might like him ... if we go!"

She raised her finger to her son, severely. "You've been working all this out, Maxim, with not a single word to us, your own mother and our Natoushka. You've been very secretive. It's not like you. Your Papa and I expect better than that."

Dr Liadev's eyes had humour returning to them. He reached forward and touched her arm, left his fingers there and with the other hand drank from his wine-glass. "It's quite wonderful, Mama. The church is St Peter and St Paul and is very beautiful, the oldest church in Smolensk. Andrei, our composer, is upstairs – he'll be teaching the choir and composing again. He's been put in charge of all church music. There's another thing – he has suffered so much and with us beneath him, he won't be alone at night."

That reached the soft heart of Vavara Davidovna, but not enough to convince. The news of moving shocked her. A bombshell from nowhere. "Maxi, how can we possibly go – Natalya has her job at GAZ and I have my dear friend Irina. Think of her left alone with a son who sells baby telephones." She shook her head and was adamant. "No, it would break her heart."

"But I have thought of her, Mama. I shall speak to her English sister Sarah and explain everything. You can invite them both to live with us from time to time. You know her sister won't come to Gorky ... but Smolensk – it's no farther for her than flying to Scotland. This is no ordinary flat, it is large enough for all of us. I should think it was built for an archbishop."

"Irina Bloch doesn't even go to Moscow. She would never come with us – half way to Warsaw!"

But he knew she was weakening. "We have to think about our future, Mama. We will at last be able to hang Papa's pictures, like they should be, like you were saying last year. We will have three bedrooms, a large sitting room, a library-study for my work ... even a telephone. I have seen it twice and I know you'll both love it. Ground floor – no lifts to break down. The sitting room looks out onto lawns and it's all part of an all-white building, with a cloister. It is a lovely place, so beautiful. A chance in a lifetime for us."

Vavara Davidovna's voice changed. Its tone was no longer in protest. She was, among her other many qualities, a practical woman. "Then tell me, explain how we could afford such a palatial flat, darling. Things are not the same as they were, you know that. Market rents, rising all the time. We can only manage now with Natalya's extra money."

"Ah, but I do have a job for you, Natalya." He smiled into her eyes.

"A job?" His cousin was surprised, and excited. "What kind of job ... another car factory, Maxim?"

"Not at all."

Three waiters came to their table. One brushed away invisible crumbs then placed in front of them, one at a time, a dinner plate, polishing each one hard as if to make it shine. The man behind him came forward with a metallic, oven-black hotplate. The third member of this wedge of waiters set down the chicken tabaka. A young girl came into the trio bearing baked potatoes smelling richly of garlic and roasted herbs. Also from her tray, she took a jug of iced water and three glasses. They then formed a line just as if they had served a Tsar or General Kutusov himself. They bowed, smiled and left in a military file.

"Thank you," exclaimed the doctor. "Thank you very much."

Vavara Davidovna asked her niece to serve. They passed up their plates, stinging their fingers with the heat of them.

Natalya served out as a mother of a family might do. When she saw they had what they wanted, she asked, "So tell me, Maxim," a half-smile, part humorous, part affectionate animated her face, "I am not to work in another car factory in your beautiful city?"

"Now, Natoushka, would I do that to you?" Liadev laughed softly. "No – a complete change. I have a friend who works in the Smolensk cathedral."

"Oh, yes ... we know all about her." Vavara Davidovna sent a dry, knowing look towards her niece, "... a cleaner!"

Liadev protested. "Mama! How can you be so high and mighty! Ivana is a good woman, and she knows the Metropolitan Bishop, which is more than you do."

The two women looked at each other, almost laughing.

"He likes cleaning women – my son."

He ignored their teasing and continued. "Your job won't be heavy work like you did at GAZ. You'd be a verger under the sacristan, assisting with the candles, helping all the different kinds of people who come in to the services or just to pray, keeping an eye on things, yes ... there would be some polishing. It's a different world. I'm certain you'd be just the person to do it."

He paused and they ate the hot food, enjoying the flavours

of the south. The job description seemed to have silenced them both. "I have already spoken to the Holy Father. I've recommended you, Natoushka."

She laughed and touched her aunt's hand. "Supposing I say no, Aunty – whatever will become of us?"

Liadev was like a man with two wild horses, unsure if he had won the battle to win them over. He poured more wine into each glass, almost as if preparing for a toast – happy, yet flushed, invaded by an embarrassment, a proposal that sent his heart beating quickly. "How could I marry you, Natalya, if you remained at GAZ, living with Mama, and me in a priest's flat large enough for all of us, so far away in Smolensk? A husband wouldn't want to be with those he loved looking at the Volga, and not at him."

A deep redness coloured his cousin's cheeks. She gazed at him with love and astonishment. "You are going to marry me, Maximoushka?"

Vavara Davidovna stood up. She leaned over her niece, embraced and kissed her. And wept.

*

Eric Vernon Lewis
July 8th

The east wind had been blowing lightly all week bringing in a faint morning haze under a sky of muted blue. When the sun rose above the trees, it lifted the mist and released the colours and shades of high summer. Before 10 am a heat was parching a country more used to grey, cool days and rain. A summer of tradition, Henley, Wimbledon and the second test at Lords, unchanging, but on this year it arrived arm-in-arm with a heat wave.

The man watering the graveside flowers returned to his car for his wide-brimmed hat. In the cemetery not far from where he was working stood a bench in shade beneath a tree still in flower, a white wayfaring tree planted half a century earlier, marking the grave of a loved-one now forgotten. But the bench kept a different memory alive. It had a name engraved at the top – a young man, snatched and whisked away from a life only beginning to be lived. How he died was not stated, only a name without dates – 'Johnny Wallis, who loved trees.'

The inscription had become soft-edged by rain-wash and the circularity of seasons. Leaning his back against the name was another young man who had also been visited by death, but left behind until another time. A morning chill decided him to wear a roll-neck jumper but the rising heat had forced him to take it off, exposing a red scar on his neck.

The grave-carer approached him with a thermos. "D'you mind if I sit here with you? Lovely weather ... but there's not a lot of shade."

The man he had joined was not as young as he had first imagined, some greying at his temple and eyes that had seen sadness.

"Not at all – you have a thankless job trying to keep everything alive in this heat-wave. I suppose a sprinkler wouldn't be allowed."

The gardener nodded. "It isn't easy. There's plenty of taps. I wouldn't normally put water on in a morning, it's burnt up in half an hour. But I can't come back this evening."

"The cemetery is lucky to have someone who'll try and come back later to water."

"I'm the lucky one. You may think it's pretty odd, but I like looking after the graves." He unscrewed the thermos cap. "Some lemon tea?"

"That's very kind. I haven't had lemon tea for years. Thanks."

"You're Mr Brideswell?"

The younger man was surprised at hearing his name. Then he smiled. "Yes ... and you must be Mr Lewis. It's my sister's grave you come to see to ... thank you for writing. I really appreciate what you're doing." Brideswell sipped the sweet tea. "Have you always been a cemetery assistant?"

"Only since your sister came here."

"Really? That really is surprising."

Lewis took of his cap and rested it on the ground beside

him. He poured himself a beaker of tea. "You didn't come to the inquest, Mr Brideswell. But your father was there. He was very angry with me ... grabbed me by the throat. I understood. I was not shocked or offended. It is a tragedy to lose a daughter, one so young with a charming smile ... but so sad."

Brideswell was shocked. "You? ... you were the driver! Is that why you come here? How amazing! Well...that has taken me aback – I had no idea." He took a deep breath and looked closer at the man who had written to him. "I've taken you for a council worker."

"Why not. I like to come and see her here ... make sure everything's all right. I have plenty of time. At my age." Lewis was silent while he drank the remainder of his tea. He hesitated. "I didn't tell them at the inquest and was pleased the coroner reached a kinder verdict. It was better to leave everything like that."

"I don't follow you, Mr Lewis."

"I didn't think your father should know, he was suffering enough. You will understand – you wear the same sadness. It was in her smile as she stepped out."

Brideswell shut his eyes, clenched his fists then released them to place his fingertips on his neck. On his scar. "She committed suicide, Mr Lewis?"

"Those definitions are far too precise, it's like putting a label 'china' on a dinner service. It says something, but not very much. When she stepped out in front of me, she was smiling and waving."

"Why ever would she do that?"

"I don't know, except she seemed very calm."

"Why of all the cars out there, did my sister choose yours, Mr Lewis?"

"I had the feeling that Josie saw me as a friend. How can I know what she was thinking, but I have idea that she thought I wouldn't mind." He closed the flask and took the spare beaker from the younger man. "That's how it was. Impossible to explain."

"There is a lot you don't know, Mr Lewis, that might help. My sister was a doctor. In the days before she looked at you and smiled, three of her patients had died. She had done nothing wrong. She was not to blame, but ..."

"Yes."

"You were an innocent instrument, Mr Lewis, and a man of courage — of exceptional tolerance, in my eyes. I'm glad you told me today, here, but I think I have always known."

Lewis touched his shoulder. "Come and have a look. The light's a bit bright for a photo but if you set the camera — and there's some shadow from the penstemons." They walked together to the graveside. A dampness from the earlier watering lingered in places still. Brideswell took the photograph.

"Would you mind, Mr Lewis, if I took your photo also ... on the bench? I appreciate everything you've been doing for my family ... the kindness to my sister's memory. For allowing that verdict of accidental death. It did help my father, but like me — he will have to know. When the time is right."

Brideswell caught a train from the junction, boarding quickly as it only stopped for two minutes. For some reason he chose the same seat as the week before, the same number, same way of facing. He shut his eyes and thought more about the driver his sister had chosen to end her life with. Eric Vernon Lewis, an unusual name, a remarkable man. Extraordinary courage. A belief in himself that seemed timeless, and wise. Good to have his photo. He might take it with him to Dorset, an olive branch – yet how to explain? A lighter thought entered his mind. Perhaps he could show his father something more than a photograph – a child, a boy of eight who was rather like Lewis, a rarity and wise beyond his years. And his mother – would they like a day out? With that thought in his head, he fell asleep.

A sleep with no dreams.

Kenny

July 9th

Kenny woke up slowly. He heard sounds made by Alice downstairs in the kitchen. He smelled the amazing presence of God in the upward drifting aroma of his breakfast being cooked. Sunday – he said a short prayer and thanked God for a sausage day. He cleaned his teeth, splashed his face with cold water and put on his watch. He went down, sat at his place, looked and smiled. A knife and fork day. Alice put her head around the door.

"There you are, darling. Good morning ... are you ready for breakfast?"

"Yes, please."

"Orange or apple juice?"

"Apple, please ... and am I going to learn chess today?"

"Michael has said so. You'll have to learn how the pieces move first."

"When are we going, Alice?"

"Jobs first, dear. Shoes and piano practice."

"No one else cleans shoes in the summer. They don't get dirty."

"Yours have done ... and my brown ones."

"Only two pairs."

"I have cleaned your trainers already."

Alice's car was a white Renault 4 with a column change. She had bought it from a doctor in Oldham the year before for £200. Already it was rusted around the windows, but she liked it – a lift-up back which wasn't heavy, plenty of room for her violin, scores, and a music stand that went with her everywhere, a sort of good luck thing.

After Wilmslow they took the quieter Knutsford Road through Mobberley. There, outside the Kodak factory, they stopped at a pedestrian crossing to allow two monks in brown habits to cross.

"Who are those funny people, Alice?"

"They're not funny, dear – only monks from the monastery by the station. There was one on my train."

"What's a monk?"

"A man who lives a quiet life of the spirit, and very simply. They don't have possessions like a car or home."

"Is Michael like that? He doesn't have a car or a home, only a flat."

"I suppose he is in a way. You're right." She glanced into his serious face and nodded with the hint of a smile.

"He knows a lot about football. Rugby's not his game."

"He liked the match, didn't he."

"Crewe were lucky. He said so."

"Michael has to go away soon, to do with his writing. To visit Russia."

The road took a slow right curve out of the village. Houses remained for some time but away to the right stretched unbroken farmland, fields of barley and repeated blocks of potatoes, whitened by their late summer flower-heads.

"Will he go for long, Alice?"

"I wouldn't think so. He has some chapters of his book to re-write ... his publisher wants them to be more Russian – so Michael has to live there for a while to pick up a better feeling about everyone's lives."

"Will he have to stay there until the winter?"

"No, dear, not as long as that. He is thinking about a month, maybe two if he has to. Not till the winter – he wouldn't want to stay away that long."

"Will he send us postcards?" The road became wider and more open. Kenny watched the speedometer flick round the dial, hoping it would reach 60 mph, but suspecting the interference of Dog to hold it back. "Why is Michael like a monk, Alice?"

"That's two questions. Yes, he'll send us cards – we'll ask him to. And he lives quietly because that's his way. People who write things have to be on their own a lot, and they don't have lots of money to buy things. He has to pay for his flat. I don't think he could run a car as well – they cost a lot of money. Lots of money."

"This one didn't. Only £200 pounds."

"That's only the beginning. They need so much more, servicing, petrol, road tax, insurance ... you need to earn a lot before you can run a car."

"Then how do we have a car?"

"Daddy helps us."

The final comment silenced the boy and he watched with disappointment as the needle was pushed back to forty. Even on God's day, Dog was here. He sighed and moved his seat belt so it didn't rub. "Graham has two grandfathers, two grandmas and loads of uncles and aunts. It's not fair. All I have is a mother."

"Michael is going to teach you chess, darling."

He became instructive. "Mrs Ranwell says that throughout history there have been one-parent families."

"She says that?"

"Yes. The fathers had to join the army and go to war – even in Roman times. A soldier could be in a Roman Legion for twenty years."

"That's a long time."

"And lots got killed. Once in Gaul a whole Roman Legion was killed by the Germans."

"I'm glad, dear, that Michael isn't a Roman."

"Graham's grandads see him every week and they're always giving him things. You must have had a mother and father, Alice. Why don't they send us postcards. Every card Graham sends me he wants back."

"Graham is a bit spoilt, and he is too bossy with you sometimes. We will ask Michael when he goes to Russia to find out what happened to your Russian grandfather."

"What was my grandfather's name?"

"It's a long Russian name. Perhaps we should call him Andrew."

"Alice! I can understand long names."

They slowed down more entering a 30 mph limit, and into Knutsford

"Then we shall let him have his proper name – Andrei Andreyevich Kutsov."

"Why don't you know where he is?"

"Because he was put into prison by the Soviet Police."

"What did grandfather do wrong?"

"He wrote music Stalin didn't like."

"They should have put Stalin in prison then."

Alice felt tears wash suddenly into her eyes. "Stalin was

the head of all Russia, and just like being a bad headmaster, no one could tell him off or put him in prison. He was a very cruel man."

"I would have done it."

"You're just like your grandfather, darling, and I hope you'll never change."

"I have to grow up, Alice. Everyone has to. When I'm grown up I shall be a vicar."

"Yes dear – and a very good one you'll be." She took a tissue from a packet wedged into her glove box. "You have plenty of time before all that."

They took the Chelford Road and after a roundabout parked outside a small block of flats. Brideswell saw them arrive from his front window, hurried down, embraced Alice. He took the boy's hand.

"Did you help mummy with the map, Kenny?"

"She's not a mummy, Michael, just an Alice."

"Of course ... and she would know the way."

"We stopped for some monks on the pedestrian crossing at Kodaks"

Brideswell held the door and they entered the hall. "What did they look like, Kenny – these monks?"

"There were two of them and they wore brown things like blankets."

"Real monks then."

The entrance hall was wide, cool and calm in a dark green paint. It smelled faintly of carpets and unchanged air. He said to the boy, "There was a monk on the train down to London – in our carriage. I think Alice noticed him. I should think he'd have been one of them." He held Kenny's hand as they climbed the stairs. "He also had a brown cloak which tied with a cord. And he had a green case that was too big for him – it puffed him out. He had to use his inhaler."

"What's an inhaler, Michael?"

Alice smiled and touched Brideswell's hand. "Kenny is the world's greatest questioner." A look of irritation passed across her son's face, but it left as quickly, like breeze after disturbing a branch.

"I just wanted to know."

He explained. "It helps you breathe when you have asthma."

Kenny didn't know what that was but his mind and eyes were on the opening door and what lay beyond. He did not release Michael's hand. Frank never held his hand now, and as for Carol – he stayed as far away from her as possible.

Inside he was not disappointed. Never had he been into a flat before. And now he knew why it was a flat – no upstairs. Yet when he looked down from the window it did confuse him. They were upstairs. Only bits of it were flat. The game with its strangely shaped pieces was on a small table. On a wider one stood a typewriter and a laptop. The appearance of the chessmen astonished him, some with the heads of horses, others with pointed hats, the kings and queens with their crowns and the small soldiers in the front line – a game with definite rules. He liked that. Slowly, with help, he played his first game.

"I think I'm going to like this game, Michael."

"Yes, I'm sure you will. You have the right mind for it, I'd say. It suits people who like to think and imagine things."

"Will it take me long to learn?"

"Yes, but you'll pick it up. You practice how each piece moves and imagine a battle where the king is trying to escape, and I'll ask Alice to come and help me with the tea. Do you eat crumpets or toast ... orange or lemon juice ... I think I have some Seven-Up."

The boy did not look up from the board. It was strange, a surprise – the chessmen held him in a fascination, like nothing he had ever seen before. He made no answer – the words reached him but sailed on, out of the battlefield.

In the kitchen Alice kissed Brideswell full on the mouth. She whispered, "If only you could come to me now." She released him. He went to the fridge and lifted out a chocolate cake.

"I have to go down to Dorset, Alice, to see my father. He's written and wants me to go. We don't get on – it's rare for him to write and ask me down. Something is bothering him. I was thinking ... it would be good if you and Kenny came too. An outing for you, a pleasure for me – a dilution between me and my father." He asked her to sit down on the kitchen stool. "It's an old house. I love it and don't see it enough. It's in a small village in Dorset, near Sherborne ... we could take the train and then a taxi from the station, though my father still drives and he'd probably insist on picking us up. I think he'd love to meet Kenny – he has never had a grandson. My sister was a doctor, she didn't marry ... and then died. He's never got over the shock."

Alice covered his hand with hers. "Of course we'll come. Which day? I have no orchestra rehearsal on Thursday of next week, and Kenny's school breaks up on the Wednesday. How does that sound? Would you father be free? I know Kenny will be thrilled – he loves long train rides. We've never been on a train to Dorset."

He leaned forward and kissed her with tenderness. "Thanks. Thursday it is. I shall ring father and tell him. He said any day was fine." As he moved to the doorway he saw the boy leaning over the chessboard deep in thought and making little sounds to himself as if he were talking to the men or giving them orders.

"Ah – you're giving those soldiers some good combat training I can see. Alice says we might all go down and visit my father next week."

Kenny looked up at Brideswell in surprise. "Oh? Where does he live?"

"In Dorset. We'd be out for the whole day on Thursday. I'd have to ring my father first but I'd sure that day would be fine – he's retired and spends a lot of time at home."

"How will we get there, Michael?"

"A train to Sherborne. In the south-west of England, but not as far down as Cornwall – about half way, I'd say."

"Will we be going just for the day?"

"Yes. An away-day. Would you like to come and bring in the cake. I don't think we'll let Alice carry it ... needs a strong chap."

Kenny gave him a radiant smile, from his heart.

*

Miss Sarah Oman, next Day

The Monday morning had felt its way into the day with drizzle. A greyness had blown in low and slow, from the north-east where it had begun as a cool sea fret on Filey sands, gathering up a darkness from the black sands of Seaton Carew. By the time it reached Manchester it had warmed, thinned and had begun to release soft films of water droplets. At Knutsford a summer sun leaned on it, burned it and sent it skywards, first as low cloud, later as a memory. At 10 am it was hot. He stopped for a moment where the pavement ended, crossed the road and picked up the path to the village. To the right of him the land fell away to a wooded vale with a stream, ahead a side road and a signpost indicating the station.

The house he wanted was on a block of raised ground between the stream and the road. A back garden ended in a gate and a wooden bridge. Time had laid its mark on the house. There had been changes. It was now a divided dwelling, split up into two homes, each one the mirror image of the other with high gables, ornate tiling and a patterned brick-mosaic around every window. Had it been a church it would have been labelled as over-improved Victorian meddling. Even so, it had its own charm. Beyond the low front hedge was a well cared-for garden rich in mid-summer growth, shrubs and flowers – hollyhocks, roses and clematis on a trellis against the house. The home of a quiet, thoughtful person.

Brideswell rang the bell, but couldn't hear if it worked, if it was ringing somewhere out of ear-shot. He raised the knocker and let it fall, checking its descent so that his presence should not alarm by sounding official or insistent. The door was opened by a young woman. She observed him with suspicion and distrust.

"Yes?" The voice flat; he recognised the dullness in her eyes. He had observed the same in his own many times. The dog which had barked became visible – it approached and examined him with curiosity and some disdain, a mongrel, head too long for a terrier, legs too short for a greyhound; a watchful, waiting kind of dog.

"I've come to see Miss Oman." He eased the file under his arm. He was holding it too tightly – a tension was entering him.

"Is the doctor expecting you?"

Brideswell looked at her more carefully. Her thin face and deepset eyes reflected outward a hostility and inwardly disappointment and sadness. Miss Oman had not introduced herself as 'doctor', perhaps she kept it for the music school and unwanted guests.

"She asked me to call this morning but didn't say what time." He glanced down at the dog. "My name is Brideswell."

"The doctor never sees visitors on Mondays. Wait here." Words from a small mouth and lips with no colour. The dog moved to bar the entrance. He waited, separated from the animal by a low, half-brass doorstep. The mongrel sat down with its head raised as if listening to his master's voice, a vacant look in the eyes. Brideswell addressed him.

"Hallo, old chap … what's your name?"

The animal responded by lowering its head and flattening his ears. For all its detachment, it would not have let him cross the threshold. He looked beyond the dog into the hall and felt a coolness coming out to meet him. No features within impressed him or told him anything about the occupant except that he carried still in his mind's eye the image of her well-tended garden. He noted a writing desk with a fold-down flap and top wide enough to take the telephone, some loose sheets of scrap paper and a pen. On the walls were floral prints. The length of the hall was served by a carpet faded and flattened by decades of feet, impressed by the passage of generations, giving off almost a worn sadness from days when families had rushed up and down it. Half way along stood a table bearing a Chinese vase, slender and delicate – from its white porcelain collar fanned out a spray of garden blooms. The girl came back.

"Dr Oman will see you. Come this way."

The dog picked itself up and seemed to sigh. It followed the girl with its nose close to the back of her shoes, unsure and disconcerted by the arrival of a man. The young woman moved effortlessly and silently down the length of the hall to a glass panelled door, each pane in a different shade. The sun shone into it and cast down strips and bands of every colour. It led outside.

They crossed a patio, walked on marble paving, until he was shown into a conservatory. The woman he had come to see, Sarah – Sasha – Oman, was seated in a wicker chair beside a glass-topped cane table. She was holding a sheaf of papers. She smiled up at him and put them down.

"It's a thesis and not a very good one. Too many inaccuracies – she hasn't checked her sources properly. It's rather a shame – all that work and now to be referred back for corrections. We'll pass her later– it sometimes happens. Come and sit down, Mr Brideswell."

He lowered himself into a second armchair and relaxed, at ease with both women. For some reason the dog stretched out at his feet, as if the presence of a man had shifted its allegiance.

"Bobby likes you." She then spoke to the girl standing a little distance from them. "What can you bring for my new friend, Rachel? Is there any lemonade left?" And then to her visitor said, "Are you a morning coffee man, Mr Brideswell? We have in some good French coffee, or if you like it black and strong I have some from Armenia …?"

The young woman said slowly. "There's a jug of lemonade in the fridge."

He smiled at her. "That'll do fine for me. Thanks."

"What's it like out now, Mr Brideswell – that morning mist was a shock. I found it quite cold, in fact that's why I came in here as soon as the sun came out – to warm me up."

"It's quite hot. I'd like a cold drink. I've walked from Knutsford."

"Really? That is a long way. Not a lot of buses come our way now."

The girl left them. "She's a silent one. Rachel had a bad start in life. It's not easy for her to leave all that behind. She goes to my synagogue in Cheetham Hill and wanted somewhere calmer than Trafford Park. I offered her my spare room. It's a mutual symbiosis." She nodded as if the word pleased her. "She pays no rent and I do no housework – and I'm teaching her Russian. Rachel wants to go there… to Russia. Like many of us her roots go back to 1900 and the exodus to England. I have told her about my sister who also went back there. Have you heard of Nizhny Novgarod? It used to be Gorky. My sister lives there now, but I can't visit. Much too far."

"It is on the Volga?"

"Yes. It has the Regional State Library – a special place. I would almost go there for that – over 4 million books and a wonderful collection of manuscripts going back to the Renaissance. They hold the only large version of the Latukhin Chronicle ... and open every day, including Sundays. You should go there from Smolensk. Apologize to my sister for me. She thinks I am a bit of a wimp not taking the train from Moscow. Well, there are other things holding me back."

"I shall think about it. As you say, rather a long way, and you'd need to know what trains."

"A Moscow express. When I was a girl it used to take 12 hours to do the 300 miles to Gorky – can you believe it ... now it takes less than half of that. Of course, you will have to ask for the right Novgarod, there's two of them and that wouldn't do – you'd end up totally lost."

Rachel came in with a tray, jug and two glasses. She placed it on the floor while straightening the table, tapping the loose pages into an even bundle and taking them over to a windowsill.

"Not there, dear, they'll crinkle in the sun. Bring them back – they can go on the floor, I shall need them later." The girl returned and placed them down with almost a spiritual gesture, her look towards the doctor of music contained layers of reverence. "We must not let this novelist, Rachel, think I exploit you as a home slave ... we'll be appearing in his next book and I shall be a villain. What can we tell him for our protection?"

"The doctor teaches me Russian, Mr Brideswell, and I do things to help. It was very messy before I came."

The older woman laughed and shook her head. "What a secret to give our visitor. Don't tell him any more. What can we give him to eat?"

Brideswell raised his palms in mild protest. "Please ... nothing for me. Just some of your lemonade."

"We make it in the Russian way," said the doctor, "limes, lemons, sugar and ice." He was handed a glass. Rachel left. "So what have you brought me in your folder, Mr Brideswell?"

"Would you call me Michael, please. I'd prefer it."

"Yes. What do you want me to look at?"

"The three chapters my publisher didn't like."

"Are you hoping I will like them?"

"No. Just tell me where the weaknesses are. George Lev – he's the new fiction editor – once lived in Smolensk. He thinks this part of my book is poor and that Russians would laugh at it."

"You don't agree?"

"I do. That's why I'm going out. I leave for Warsaw on Saturday and travel onward the following day."

"There's not much time for me to comment, is there?"

"I could come back later on in the week."

"Look ..." A rapport begun on the train was firming into an understanding and friendship. "I have three letters to post, two of them need weighing. If you would take them along to the post office in the village – it's a bit past the Kodak factory – I'll read the chapters while you're away. But you must have some lunch with me. I can't discuss literature over lemonade. I shall open a bottle of wine."

He lifted his finger – humour and compliance – "You've got me there. How can I say 'no' now, Miss Oman?"

"And don't be so silly. My name is Sasha ... Sarah even ... and I don't like being prefixed with status, 'miss' or 'doctor'. Rachel likes to do it, and I have submitted – but not from you. You must tell me what your novel is about. You can't expect me to comment on three middle chapters if I've no idea what's come before."

He gave her a brief outline. She listened, and when he stopped she was thoughtful.

"Your unfortunate Davidov. It seems to me he could quite easily have been one of Dr Liadev's patients."

"Dr Liadev?"

"I mentioned him on the train. You wrote down his name."

"Oh yes, the doctor who comes to Smolensk. He has a patient there."

"You'll need to know some more if they've arrived before you leave Smolensk. His mother lives above my sister Irina, in Nizhny Novgorod. He was appointed when Gorbachov rose up and the whole Communist edifice was beginning to crumble, to rescue and heal those artists, writers and poets abused and diminished by all that Soviet Stalinist madness. He's a good man, a good son and a fine doctor. My sister phoned me last night. She is heart-broken – the Liadevs are moving to Smolensk – Varvara, Maxim and the niece who lives with them, Natalya." She paused, her mind and heart with her far away sister. "I have told them about you. The doctor came onto the phone himself and explained why they had to move. There is a vacant flat in a church house. That's where you'll find them ... the Church of St Peter and St Paul. Perhaps you've seen it – know it?"

"I have certainly seen it and been in. It is the oldest church in the city."

"They will have a downstairs flat. It seems there is an

upstairs tenant the doctor wants to keep an eye on, his patient, like the one you mentioned. He has become the church's choirmaster – the man like your character Davidov."

"Thank you. I shall remember all that."

"That scar on your neck. Is it all right to travel?"

"Fine. Almost healed." He touched it. "Do you remember that I told my old friend Maria I was going to try and find her daughter Ivana, someone who works in the cathedral? There is also someone else …a composer. A man arrested and taken away to one of the camps. Perhaps the doctor would have heard of him."

"He might. Who is it?"

"Kutsov. Andrei Andreyevich Kutsov."

The woman beside her shook her head and touched his arm. "I'm sorry, I'm afraid you might never find him. They say Composer Kutsov has been dead for years."

*

Afternoon, Monday July 10th

Brideswell was shaken by the information that Kutsov was dead. Coming as it did from Sasha, so close to everything in that world whose origins were Russian, whose sister had chosen to live there. It had to be true. He wrestled with what she had said, disturbed – despairing for Alice and Kenny. Yet a faint light softened the heavy clouds of dark thoughts – they had asked him to make enquiries. There was hope, if only in their hearts, and that of their London guardian, Vladimir Andreanov.

As he walked along the quiet country road surrounded by the drowsy abundance and a continuing heat-wave, he allowed his mind to distance itself from anger, from the wanton destruction of an innocent man. He paused at a gate, leaned on it and surveyed a deep-set, unending field, a sea of green lace-tipped with the flowers of mature potato plants. He made a promise. To himself, his friends, Vladimir in the hospital bed, to Brother Robert, to Maria with a lost daughter, that he would go and find out all there was to know. Everything. A station with four exits, each one pointing its own direction. Each one leading him to Smolensk. And the deep, unknowable mystery of a composer sentenced to dying in a labour camp. There were questions he had to put to Vladimir before leaving; had the man been taken after his release into a hospital? Was that where he died? Only one day left now for his questions – it would mean travelling down then meeting up with Alice and Kenny afterwards for their trip to Dorset to see his father. Then back for the coach from Victoria on Saturday morning, the Polish coach to Warsaw. Events were crowding in on him. He left the gate and peaceful scene with a deep sigh; all life was movement – it required reason and purpose to separate it from madness.

Alice phoned him from her rehearsal, her voice embracing and affectionate.

"Michael ... it's me, Alice. Where are you ... what are you doing?"

"Oh – just thinking, reading a bit ... but I was losing the words. Thinking of you. I was going to ring."

"I was wondering if you'd like to come over and have supper with us? Kenny's been invited to Graham to watch a video afterwards. We can have some time on our own ...?"

"Thanks ... I'd like that." His heart quickened. He took a deep breath.

"What time do you want me there?"

"I'll be home at six. Kenny is going to Graham's at seven and is staying till 8.30pm ... we'll go over and pick him up."

"Alice ... about our trip down to Dorset – d'you think we could go a day earlier so I can talk to Vladimir? I leave for Warsaw on Saturday morning."

"Darling ... Wednesday is impossible. I have these rehearsals. They go on till five."

"I see ... of course. Well, supposing I met you and Kenny at Euston about 8 or 9 pm and booked us all into The Exeter?

Then we could travel down from Waterloo or Paddington in the morning?"

"Let's talk about it tonight, darling. Now ... do you eat shepherd's pie?" She laughed lightly. "Or are you a vegetarian?"

"Not at all. I love shepherd's pie, with a cheesy top ... that's how my mother made it."

He gave himself plenty of time to reach Pitt Street. The address surprised him – on the Manchester side of Altrincham, more in Sale. The district once he had left the main road was tranquil. Brideswell was affected by the trees and gardens in so mature and such a well cared-for area, by the incoming softness of a summer evening. The road he was looking for had a line of neat terraced houses. He easily found theirs, number 74. An excited nervousness entered his hand as he reached for the knocker. The stretching movement stung the scar in his neck. Kenny came, opening the door with hesitation and uncertainty, but when he saw who it was, relaxed.

"Uncle Michael! Alice said you'd be here at six." He shrugged with a mannerism far from Manchester, "I can't talk to you tonight, I have to go to Graham's to see a stupid video."

"It may not be that bad."

The boy shook his head and brought him inside. A faint smile – "Dr Who and the cybermen? It's from last century!"

"You're not impressed with the doctor?"

He sighed and spread his hands. "Graham got it for his birthday, that's why I have to go. His father wants to see it."

"His father ... he's a fan?"

"Yes. I could do without all this."

"So ... you're rather off space and time travel, Kenny?"

He half closed his eyes and peered at Brideswell through the slits. "I'm a trekker," he said firmly and bluntly. "Star Trek, Uncle Michael."

"I see what you mean. Captain Kirk is different."

The smell of cooking reached him. It came from the kitchen at the end of the hall. Alice stood there, an apron over her dress. She kissed him lightly on the lips.

"Welcome to our little home, Michael. You found us all right?"

"I know the area a bit. It's a lovely district on a summer's evening."

He looked around, a small colourful kitchen with a back door into a garden. Through the window he could see some flowerbeds and a silver birch – a very Russian tree. "It smells good ... your cooking."

She pursed her lips with a humour. "Shepherd's pie. Kenny grated the cheese topping for you." A flush came into her cheeks and she touched her son with affection. "Show Michael your room, dear, while I finish off these vegetables." Suddenly she saw Brideswell's neck. "Good Heavens, Michael. Whatever have you done there?" She allowed her fingers to rest on the fading scar.

"Oh, it wasn't much. All shrinking now. I was mugged. It's nothing really."

"Nothing? On your neck? You poor man, how horrible!"

Kenny led him upstairs to a back room lit by the evening sunlight. A bed was placed against the window. Brideswell handed over the package he had brought. To the boy he was already a hero, surviving an attack by robbers who had cut his throat. "What's inside, Michael?"

"Have a look. Maybe you can put them up somewhere."

Kenny opened the large envelope and drew out two enlarged photographs – Mr Spock and the captain of 'Starship Enterprise', Capt. Kirk.

"Wow!" Kenny was stunned. "They're brilliant! Gosh ... how did you get them ... how did you know?"

"There's a shop in Knutsford." Brideswell was moved by the boy's joy.

"They have lots of photos like that, especially Dr Who. I thought you might have the Doctor so I bought these. Pure chance really."

"Let's put them up, Uncle Michael." Kenny passed them back to him to hold while he ran downstairs. In minutes he was back holding a slender hammer, picture hooks and spring clips. "Alice says we're to use these for now and then you're to come down. Dinner's ready."

He tapped in the hooks where the boy said he wanted them and suspended the photos. "It might be best to put some more grips at the bottom to stop them curling up ... but in the long run you're going to need a frame to keep them flat – the sun will soon bend them out of shape. There are some very simple clip-on frames that would do the trick. They don't cost much. Easy-peasy." He laughed, affected by Kenny's delight.

When they reached the bottom of the stairs Alice took them both by the hand into the front room where the table was laid. Kenny was in a happy mood, the boring video with Graham was on another planet. He was still elated when they drove him over – Brideswell with Alice in the front and Kenny in a reverie behind. After dropping him off, she came back to the car, lifted Bridewell's hand and kissed his palm.

"What a difference you've made, Michael – to both of us. It's wonderful ... and for Kenny it's like having his father back, only someone else nearly as special. For me ... I can't begin to tell you."

He laughed. "I'm glad I've passed."

She rubbed her leg against him. "How I've wanted you – it's been almost unbearable ... now we have an hour and a half." She stroked the hair on his forehead. "I am on fire. I can't wait any longer..."

Alice parked the car outside the house. They hurried in. She closed the door behind them and kissed him passionately on the mouth, caressing him with her tongue. She sighed and was breathless.

"Please Michael. I can't wait. Take me here ... now. I'm so ready. I am wearing nothing underneath." She pulled up her dress, leaned back against the wall and spread her legs apart, pulling him in towards her. She undid his belt and pushed his trousers to the floor. She drew him into her, guiding him as before but trembling and already in a passion rising so fast it threatened to overwhelm her before his surge. Then it broke almost instantly. She bit his shoulder, gripped him and raised her legs from the ground. The forces racking her were unbearable and she shouted loudly rocking and riding his movements. Suddenly she arched her back, cried out his name, her voice rising and rising until it became a scream. Then like the storm it was, bending and racking her body, it subsided. He flowed into her, a flood released.

He carried her upstairs to the bed. They made love a second time, slower, more gently. She rolled on top of him, then knelt astride, waiting for her love contractions to return and reoccupy her. As she leaned forward he caressed her breasts.

"I love you, Alice."

She could not speak but lowered her breasts onto his

chest. Tears fell quickly down her face and a deep, exquisite, longer gripping took her down into a joy she had never known before.

When they collected Kenny, he was excited and jubilant. He exclaimed –

"Dr Who was brilliant ... nearly as good a Captain Kirk, Uncle Michael. Please, can you buy me his photo in your shop?"

A neighbour came in while Alice drove Brideswell to Altrincham where he could pick up a train. In the car they were quiet. Brideswell felt her closeness and the resonance of their passion. He left with a sadness, not that of separation and departure, but because he would never be able to tell her that her father was dead.

★

Wednesday July 12th
Noon

At the ward he was told Vladimir Andreanov had been discharged. The sister spoke icily to a foolish man who had discharged himself against medical advice, yet she did look at his scar. She told him she would make a report into his notes, that Mr Michael Brideswell was not dead. Then she smiled and took from a drawer a travelling chess set.

"He left these behind, Mr Brideswell, in his hurry to get away from us. He doesn't live far away – his address is here in the corner. If you are planning to go and see him, take these with you. I am glad you survived. You have a guardian angel."

The weather was still hot but more bearable. The easterly breeze had been sucked into the city, was smothered by it and lost forever. But another wind arrived in its place from the west as if summoned by ancient city guardians to relieve its breathless, sweating and uneasy citizens. He arrived at the gardens behind Unity Court and sat, as he had done with Brother Robert, on a bench in front of the abandoned greenhouse. The gardener's existence clung on in sadness, broken cold frames which now only grew tall Oxford ragwort and clumps of self-sown onions. The cottage once loved by the resident gardener's family was boarded up. It seemed to announce a statement that a more tender age had passed and the care of the old graveyard had been handed over to a commercial world, the time when the spirituality of the cherished garden was lost. Yet not entirely, the space with its timeless trees, diagonal paths, shrubs and memorials blocked into the high surrounding walls was in part out of reach to the cost-cutters and teams on a council franchise. Brideswell left the bench in a pensive mood and entered the block of flats. The double doors he passed through were also marked by time passed. Their glass frames were ornate, curved wrought iron tracery, and delicate. The space they enclosed within was airless, cool, and smelled of polish and lino scrubbed with a disinfecting soap. The whirr of the machine at work cleaning reached him as he climbed a short flight onto the first floor. He met a woman in working clothes and a headscarf. She stopped the polisher. A sudden silence filled the corridor.

"Do you want to get by ... need any help?" A big woman, damp forehead. Her grey hair was pulled back.

"I'm visiting an elderly man, at the end of this corridor?"

"The Russian ... Mr Andreanov, who's just come out of hospital? He's one of my specials."

"Yes, that's him."

"A friend of yours, love, is he?"

"Yes. I've brought him his chess set from the ward – he forgot it when he left. He'll be sad to have left it behind ... he's a good player."

"I can imagine him playin' chess. Really nice man he is. No family, but he never seems lonely. I bought him a few things this morning from the dairy outside."

"He'd appreciate that."

"You'll find he's all right for bread and eggs – and cheese. I got him tea and sugar ... he likes a nice cup of tea. Always asks for Red Label."

"Thanks for that. Did he settle up?"

"Always. I call him Vlad. He's foreign but he do appreciate even the smallest thing. When he hears my polisher outside his door, he comes out smilin' and teases me. He says he always knows it's me because the way I polish."

"He's got a good sense of humour, rather dry."

She moved her hand as if to restart her polisher but held back her finger.

"I'm so glad, love, he's havin' a visitor. It worries me sometimes, him stuck in there day after day on his own, miles from his Russia."

"I shall talk to him today about Russia. What name does he call you ... so I can mention I've seen you and thanked you for what you do for him. For being so nice."

"Just say Florence. I like it better than 'Flo'."

Brideswell took a card from his wallet. "If you ever need me, Florence, my number is on here and my London address."

She studied it for several minutes. "All right. I'm glad he's got a friend ... and you don't live far away. Near St Barts. I've been there many times with my legs. I don't know if this job is killing them or doing them good. I like the work ... Mr Brideswell. Funny isn't it, polishing corridor after corridor ... but you'd be surprised how many friends I have in this block. Some of them never go out. Some days I'm the only face they ever see."

"You're kind person, Florence. They're all lucky to have you. And my Russian friend."

He thanked her again and walked on, along the cream-sided corridor with its shining floor, emptiness and smells. He rang the bell on the last door, a glass door, a smaller version of the ones in front with some of their delicate tracery. A curtain in front of it, for privacy. No reply. Even though the bell had sounded loudly. He tried for a second time and heard a movement from within, an inner door being opened setting a play of brighter light, sunlight, onto the inside of the door-curtain. The door was opened cautiously. An elderly man faced him, surprised to find a man there. He'd expected someone else – perhaps his friend Florence. Disappointment in his face and in his voice.

"Yes?"

They both listened to the retreating polisher. Andreanov didn't appear to know who he was.

"Brideswell. I've brought along your chess set. You remember ... we had a game and talked about Russia. Your friend Kutsov. I leave for Smolensk on Saturday."

Recognition made the face younger. "Ah." He raised a finger on his left hand. "Anya's friend. Yes, you made an excellent opening. Come in. I thought it was my friend from down the corridor ... she calls."

He entered the flat. The man walked carefully as if uncertain of his legs, yet a different man from the restless, ironic surgical ward patient with a head full of dark thoughts and the approach of dying. "Is it still hot outside? This flat keeps cool. I'm glad of it. But I miss the sun sometimes."

They passed through a hallway of sombre colours into a wide, square room lined with oak panels. The windows were open where they could be at the top, half-lights, allowing in a movement of air. The light coming in brought with it a sense of peace, a disconnection from the strong light of day.

From the window he could make out the bench where he had been sitting.

"Yes it is still hot, but not as bad as yesterday. The wind has come round into a cooler direction, but the heat-wave's lasting."

"I'll open the door onto the balcony and let some more air in."

He pushed the balcony door firmly, it moved open reluctantly. Brideswell handed over the chess set and the Russian thanked him, placed it on his desk.

"You drink coffee?"

"Not unless you're having some."

"Sit in a chair."

Brideswell lowered himself into a deep club armchair and marshalled his mind, lining up questions he would need to put to Andreanov – what was there known about Andrei Kutsov, and what he knew about the cathedral where he would be looking for Maria's daughter, also a cleaner. And who might be Dr Liadev who had now stepped onto the stage but remained in the wings. His thoughts were interrupted by his friend coming back holding two mugs.

"Only instant coffee, Michael. I don't ask Florence to look for any other."

"I could buy some for you and bring it back, before I go. I saw the Welsh dairy outside ..."

"There's no need. She wouldn't like it. She doesn't mind doing my bits of shopping." A Russian accent had entered his voice, perhaps his mind was already reaching out in that direction and into his past. He returned to Florence. "It breaks up the tedium for her, pushing that machine up and down all day. She's good to me ... a very thoughtful woman. It is a job for a reflective person, alone for most of the day, and a machine that keeps on circling and whirring – eight floors, eight corridors ... add all that up, my friend. You'll be looking at a quarter of a mile of linoleum. But it's lonely. That's why we're friends ... two lonely people." He surveyed his visitor in a quizzical way. "So ... my chess partner is going to Smolensk, like I said he would. Thank you – you're going to give me an easier death without Kutsov on my conscience."

Brideswell did not know how to reply. The older man nodded. "It's all right, Michael, I doubt if I shall die for a while. Tell me, how are you going to get there?" He leaned forward, easing his chair nearer and holding his friend's gaze with a penetration of unspoken sentences. An intensity had come into his face – a man whose thoughts were being drawn out, extracted from his past, as if his spirit had been clamped onto a medieval rack. A moment of importance for him, a door to open the past, or to close it, lock it firmly and forever. His look was too strong for the man opposite who averted his head and turned his eyes onto a neutral space where his coffee stood. Brideswell picked up the mug and sipped the hot, sweet liquid.

"I go by coach from Victoria ... to Warsaw. Then an overnight break there before pressing on. It's a long bus ride, but a fraction of the air fare. Do you know Warsaw, Mr Andreanov?"

"Vladimir ... please."

"Right. Thanks. I shall be staying near the State Opera House, a hotel called Dom Chlopa."

" No, I never went there. None of that area was safe for a defector."

"I shall be taking a train from the Central Station the next evening. I have a sleeping berth. We get to Smolensk if the border's OK at 11 am."

Andreanov's look softened. "Well, that's one way to go. Certainly cheaper ... though you'll have a hotel bill." He drank his coffee. "How well do you know Anya?"

Brideswell did not answer at once. It was not something that could be measured in time, the dimensions came from another source, from a place like the room he was in, disconnected with time. "She has changed my life."

"Yes. I thought so. Listen ... I shall tell you about her father Andrei Andreyevich."

"I may take some notes?" He felt in a pocket for his diary and a pencil.

"If you want to. Nothing I'm going to tell you needs setting down, no places, no addresses ..." Andreanov returned to the past, a life as painful now as then, perhaps even more. His drawn face became even thinner, almost skull-like. He recalled days he had tried to wash from his mind – a deep sigh, an exhalation of ice-winds that had scoured Russia for half a century.

"His full name was ... is ...Andrei Andreyevich Kutsov. A Smolensk family. His father had a law practice and hoped his son would follow. Not to be. Andrei was quite different, an artist, a thinker and a rebel. Quite the opposite. It must have caused his father pain, and anguish. Plus the bad effect on his family's standing in those conformist Communist ideologies. There was no place for people like Andrei. From an early time at art school his group and friends were known and watched – dissidents, counter-revolutionaries ... they were barely tolerated. Had Smolensk been Moscow or Leningrad, they would have been dispersed and sent out to do factory work or farming in unknown places." He paused and looked at Brideswell. "They were bad and dangerous days for creative people. Many people compromised and toed the party line – for survival. There were some intrepid brave ones. If they were not protected they were in danger of their lives. Many were shot, other exiled to labour camps across Siberia." Andreanov reached for his coffee mug. It was empty and he put it back down.

"Andrei fell in love with a young music student ... what was her name. Something now I forget. Once I forgot nothing. I had the best of memories once. It served me well here in England. Now so much seems out of reach.

Well, you don't need to know. Anya will tell you when she wants to. No ... wait a minute. It has come to me. It's like that, things come out of the fog when you don't bully them. The woman was called Marsha – a very pretty girl, gentle – they were very much in love. She was slim and slight like her daughter, our Anya, and played the violin with her heart, a rare passion and sensitivity – a beautiful violinist. I can see her playing – so slender and vulnerable ... and such music. She was a gift to the world, to Russia – to everyone who listened. A small, frail woman expressing the largest things in the world – love and longing, being and belonging, failing and falling, beauty ... and a world that was disappearing from it. Listen ..."

He rubbed his hand across his upper lip and chin. It was moist. "They only had one child, Anya – and how they loved her. Marsha taught her to play the violin when she was still young, a very small one. This was a little girl growing up to be like her mother, to be able to play in the same way, at first mother and teacher, then pupil until they began to play together. You should have heard that, my friend, you would have wept – like we did. How pleased Marsha would have been to know her much-loved daughter was playing for famous orchestras in England – and had a gifted grand-son."

He broke from his narrative to linger a while in the present, a respite from what he had to lead on to.

"Anya's little boy... what's his name?"

"Kenny."

"Ah yes, so it is. And does he play the violin too?"

"Piano, I think."

"Such a talented family. Does the boy know about his Russian grandfather, Maestro Kutsov – such a fine composer?"

"He knows a little, Vladimir. I don't know how much. I shall try and find his grandfather for him, in Smolensk."

"Ah ... there is always hope."

"He's a serious boy, and he misses his father. He would be devastated if he discovered his grandfather was dead. I've met a woman, someone high up in music whose sister lives in Russia. She says Andrei Kutsov did not survive."

"Many people believe that, but they have no proof. Tell me more about my friend's grandson. I want to know. To picture him."

"He believes there are two forces in the world – the Hand of God ... and the Hand of Dog."

Andreanov gave a dry, amused laugh. "He is a Russian boy, not English. They were a remarkable family, quite fearless. We were also serious in those days – everything so vital, so passionate. We believed in the revolution, but not in Stalin. We knew about the cruelty, the deaths, the starvation of the Kulaks, the misery, the heartbreak and the genocide. What an ignorant pig of a man, and yet so gentle with children and brought up first to be a priest. We were ruled by a Tsar from a Georgian cornfield – the hungrier for power and domination because of that. It takes an elevated corporal to set Europe ablaze, or the impoverished son of an Austrian customs clerk. What malice arises in poverty!"

He stopped, gripped his two hands together until the knuckles blanched and stared out of the window. He then looked at his visitor and shook his head.

"It is not possible for you to know anything about Russia, Michael, anymore than I can understand Henry the Eighth, the reformation, cricket – or the history in some of your words. We are a strange country and have tried to forget our past, invent a new one. In the beginning we were idealists, passionate for change, but not wise enough to know how to use it. We are now remembering – it's a good sign. A man with one eye on the past can step forward, but with no backward look he will fall over. Why is it we Russians admire so much the strong man ruler. It is somewhere in our blood. Is it because we are too close to having been serfs and slaves with no rights, a nation of victims. In England you are centuries distant from your days of rural serfdom, and you've had your Magna Carta enshrined in the English mind as something inviolable. In Russia we change very slowly, freedom has been bought dearly by each and everyone of us. So many brave young people dead in two wars. And look how our Jewish people have suffered. Perhaps now we have a new light in Yeltsin, though he has more the bearing of a Tsar than a parliamentarian like your Cromwell."

He stopped. What he had been speaking about had moved him deeply. The gaunt old man rose from his chair unable to remain seated while all those thoughts twisted up his mind and muscles. He crossed the room to the window. A fine tremor shook his hand, which he stilled by grasping the half-open door to the balcony.

"Great novelists arise in stable times when people have the leisure to read what they've written. Great poetry arises in conflict like a cry of agony. Great music spreads across both because it is as part of the world as sunshine or frost. You are a good listener, Michael, to an old man who spends too much time alone … forgive me, my friend." He returned to his chair. The movement and break from the story had calmed him. He pushed away the wetness on his face with his palms.

"Let me continue about Andrei Andeyevich." He continued, sometimes looking directly into Brideswell's eyes, sometimes to the hospital beyond and to the sky above it.

"We were a small group – call us dissidents if you like. We refused to join the Communist Party, and issued leaflets deploring the tragedy of the collectivisation programme. We were hated by the State, targets for the secret police … enemies of the people. We had in our group brave people – poets, musicians … some academics like myself from the university. Andrei was our leader and inspiration, quite without fear. The music he wrote was all his own, nothing for the Party, and for that he was castigated in Pravda and accused of formalism – of writing Western music that had no relevance for Russian workers, subversive and counter-revolutionary. Everything in those days was for the workers, they were icons – nothing was allowed from the imagination, no place for reflection. Of course, we all knew of the danger we were in but we were young and had a mission to uphold other values than party dogma, traditions going back to Tchaikovsky and Chekhov. It was a heady mixture and heads would be broken but we drew strength from each other. We wanted to stand up and be counted. Kutsov was a married man with a 10 year old daughter at school, our Anya. He had everything to lose. And she was a gifted girl. They loved her at her school and were so encouraging about her music – so proud of her …"

He stopped to rub his eyes with the heel of his palms. "That's how it was, Mikhail ... it all comes back. I am right there now." He moved his position in the chair and continued. "In the way of things, with a different family, Anya would have gone up to one of our great Conservatoires ... in Moscow, and would have had the finest teachers like David Oistrakh, but no – her father was fast becoming a non-person. Criticism was not tolerated – a man, an unproductive composer questioning the leadership and the path the revolution was taking, a man unafraid to shout out that what they were doing had become inhumane, was flawed, and would lead only to misery. As it did." His voice had become taut, raised as he relived those days. Emotion was taking hold of him.

"I shall have to shorten this account, it's distressing me too much." He locked his fingers together, making the pallor of his hands even whiter. Andreanov then thrust his clasped hands between his knees and lowered his head onto them in a kind of supplication – a prayer, or in anguish. He remained in that huddled position like a man beaten by guards, or someone who had received tragic news. At last he straightened with a sigh and inhaled the English summer air reaching him from the open balcony door. "I'm sorry, my dear friend ... it's hard for me to go on."

"Take your time. Let me make you some more coffee."

"No. While it is on me, weighting me down, let me take this through to the end. Listen. I had a tip off. Even now I can't say from whom ... that the KGB were going to make a raid on the Sunday in the early hours – three days ahead. Dawn – their usual time of visiting. Our group discussed it. I went back with Andrei Andreyevich to his flat. Marsha was distraught, weeping, she fell on her knees and begged me to get out and take Anya with me. It was possible – I was part of a delegation leaving for London the next day. They said they would stay put and see it through, carry on the fight, go into hiding, set up an underground press ... all those things. But they were so frightened for Anya." His voice quietened. His eyes were inward though they were directed outside towards the blueness of a sky which had not changed for two weeks and where, from its cloudlessness, a great heat had poured down onto the city.

"I made a fateful decision which haunts me still. I caught an early train next morning with Anya to Leningrad and joined the Soviet party for London. We were guests of the London University Slavonic school. No one commented about Anya. I said she was going to her aunt who worked at TASS. Our news agency. The KGB came for the Kutsovs not on the Sunday as we thought when they would have found the flat bare and empty, but on the very next night. They found Andrei and Marsha packed and ready to go in that very morning – such is the fickleness of chance and fate. Marsha was outraged, she screamed at them to get out of her house. Marsha was shot dead. Kutsov was taken away and shipped out to the worst camp – 323 – where Siberia meets the Urals. They beat him and kicked him. His brains were beaten out. They left him naked in a cell in the depths of winter, he was burned with cigarette ends and made to stand out in the snow. Then I heard no more. Maybe he died out there after all that. No man can endure such cruelty and violence for long. It is beyond human endurance." Andreanov's body shook, his hands trembled. Tears spilled from his eyes and pooled in the hollows of his face. Brideswell stood up and put his arms across the old man's shoulders.

"But you brought the child out. A young and gifted life was

saved." He left Andreanov and went through to the kitchen, switched on the kettle and made two fresh mugs of coffee. When he returned the older man had calmed. Brideswell eased the empty cup from his grip and set his hands around the hot one.

"Yes. That was the only good thing. I brought out Anya."

Brideswell touched his arm and sat back down in the deep, embracing leather armchair. There was more to ask him. "This prison camp. Where was it?"

"They are nowhere and never exact. In Siberia ... they all were."

"How could I find it?"

"The camp will have been destroyed by now, and all the evidence burned, as if it had never been."

"Could Kutsov still be alive? My friend the musician – her sister lives in Russia – she says he died a long time ago."

Andreanov seemed numb after his reactions and weeping – he shrugged. "Who knows what any man can endure and survive. There is a will to live; if it's there and burns whatever happens ... who can say?"

"When the camp was liberated, say in 1987 during the Gorbachov reforms ... where would the survivors been taken?"

"To a hospital."

"But which one? Would the records have gone with them for the doctor in charge?"

"Perhaps. If they still existed. Some of the poor wretches wouldn't know, would have no idea who they were. Leaves left after a gale through a rubbish heap. There were some good hospitals, some good doctors ... and there were the others."

Brideswell leaned forward, his voice sharper. "Vladimir … have you ever heard the name Dr Liadev?"

"No. Who is he?"

"A doctor set up by the Gorbachov *perestroika* to find and rescue lost artists from those dreadful labour camps, from the psychiatric hospital prisons. He would know Camp 323. If there were any survivors."

"I've never heard of such a doctor. Is it possible – are they so humane all of a sudden? How come you know about this doctor who believes in the resurrection of lost souls?"

"My music friend. Her sister has the flat beneath the doctor's mother in Nizhny Novgorod."

"Well, I am amazed there is such a ministering angel."

"The whole family, mother, cousin and doctor are moving to Smolensk. I shall meet them. And ask about Kutsov."

His friend sighed and sipped from the second mug. "You are an unusual and remarkable man, Mikhail. But I knew that from your chess."

"How old would Andrei Andreyevich be if he were still alive?"

"About my age … seventy something." And with that, his mind moved away from his haunting past. "Anya's marriage … what a pity about all that. How the little boy must have suffered. What was the father's name, remind me."

"Williamson. Frank."

"He wasn't the right man, was he? Too cold, too English … no love of music. I'm glad she has found you, Mikhail." Lighter thoughts had come to him. It showed as a half-smile in his eyes. "And how do you find their little boy, Kenny?"

"He also is gifted with a rare imagination and insights. Not surprising with Anya as his mother, Kutsov the grandfather, and Marsha his grandmother, the violinist who should have gone to the Conservatoire."

"Yes. You're right. You don't seem to think Frank added much."

"I don't know. The marriage worked in the beginning but they drifted apart and he looked elsewhere and found a woman. Kenny hates her. She is small-minded. The boy won't be as tall as his father. We get on well; I'm teaching him chess."

"Really? So young? You're more the father he needs. Tell me about yourself. Have you a brother and sister?"

"My sister died. Some people thought it was an accident."

"Ah ... and you're not sure. You have sorrows of your own, my friend. But you're moving on – not like me, not moving anywhere. I shall hold on until you come back. Russia is a sad country; she is like the sky at night which is obscured by mists. I believe in the sunrise to come. I am hopeful. We should play chess now." He rose from the chair, set a low table between them and opened the chess set Brideswell had returned. Andreanov arranged the pieces precisely as they had been.

"You have a wonderful memory, Vladimir."

His friend smiled and raised his fingers. "Sometimes. With chess, perhaps. I believe it was my move?"

Brideswell nodded. "Just one thing more. In Smolensk I shall be looking for a woman – Ivana Petrovna Madiewska ... would that name mean anything to you?"

"No. A common enough name around there – Polish or Russian or both. Why should I know your friend?"

"A Smolensk family."

"That doesn't say much."

"She works in the cathedral as a cleaner."

"So?"

"I have just been to her father's funeral."

"Well, I'm glad it wasn't mine. You were seeing off a dead man and now ...playing chess with a dying one. You're a strange man, Michael. And judging by your neck, that scar, those weren't the only things you did."

*

Next day, after morning rain

"Why's this station got such a funny name, Uncle Michael?"

The train had come to a halt at a small country station. Milk churns were being rolled up into the guard's van with the penetrating clanking of metal. Through the window came the faint smell of stale milk. Two families boarded as well, the children excited, summer holidays beginning – they were loaded down with beach equipment, bound for Weymouth. They made more noise than the milk churns. Michael smiled at the boy who drew his head in from the open window.

"I suppose it is a funny name." He felt the urgency in Kenny's gaze, trusting him to explain. "It's an old Latin name. Marston would be the settlement perhaps in honour of Mars, some Roman victory here, and the word 'Magna' just means large. Like in the word magnify ... making things look bigger."

"I thought magna came out of volcanoes." The boy's gaze and attention left him as he watched the two groups coming on board with their shouts and laughter. Nothing came to his eyes of a battle. The god Mars was the Roman

God of War, that he knew already – the two Gods who batted his life between them, were not interfering today – God or Dog.

"That was all two thousand years ago, Kenny. The only signs of burning are along the edges of the roof overhang. That's been caused by steam engines blowing up smoke. This used to be a busy line once. The Channel Islands Express direct from the ferry at Weymouth to London ... Paddington." The guard acknowledged the stationmaster's wave and they moved away. Kenny was pleased they had been through a battlefield.

"How many Romans lived in England, Uncle Michael?"

Alice intervened. "Don't pester Michael so much, darling. You've been asking him questions all the way down and we're getting off soon. Michael won't have any voice left for his father."

Brideswell touched the boy's hand. "I won't forget the question, Kenny. We'll talk about the Romans on our way home. They were remarkable people and we still drive along the roads they made. Some of their houses had central heating and we're only now just catching up with that ..."

The train stopped longer at Yeovil Pen Mill station. Brideswell was glad to get out into fresh country air, out of a hot train. He felt a nervousness invade him – meeting up with his father after so long and wondering what this invitation was all about. They had never liked each other. Josie was the one, the apple of his eye. But he could never tell him that his beloved daughter had killed herself. He turned to Alice and Kenny – he needed to warn them.

"My father can be a bit sharp. Don't worry or even think about it ... he lives on his own. It's not easy – no one with him since my mother died. And he's very sad about my sister, too. But he loves chess. You might ask him, Kenny, if he'd like to play a game with you …"

They left the station and entered the forecourt beyond. Brideswell did not recognise the waiting car.

The doctor had seen them emerge from the station entrance. The sun was hot but filtered where he was by tall overarching limes. The sight of his son filled him with irritation – he hadn't asked him to come down with a married woman and her son. He felt a pricking around his eyes and a tightening feeling around his heart … if only he still had Josie. And his son's wave angered him – the unfairness of life. He moved towards them with a sigh.

"Hallo." He shook hands with the woman. The greeting he gave Michael had much of the past in it, more of departure than welcome. He looked back to the woman and her son and said to him, "You've brought your friends down for some country air?"

Brideswell accepted his father's indifference. "Yes, father – they're from Manchester. This is Alice … and her son Kenny."

With the boy his father was gentler. He touched Kenny's head lightly. "When I was a boy we had a dog called Kenny – a very gentle creature. He had once belonged to an old school mistress who couldn't look after him any more. I think he was very wary of men, but he did love children. He loved playing and he loved his walks."

Kenny was surprised he bore a dog's name. He felt the warmth in the old man's voice and decided that this dog was too nice to be part of the Hand of Dog. "I'm not named after a dog."

"No. And I don't know anyone who is. Why don't you

travel in the front seat with me, Kenny. It's a new car ... well, almost new. Do you mind coming into a Japanese one?"

They walked to the car and Kenny to the front seat beside Dr Brideswell who helped him fasten the safety strap. He then closed Alice's door for her. In his mirror he saw a glance pass between his son and the woman, Alice. There was some humour in it. It was pleasing glance. He found the boy unusual, as was the question put to him.

"What's your name, please?"

"Dr Brideswell."

"Alice drives a French car."

"Really? Alice?"

"That's Alice." He turned and pointed to his mother.

"Hmm. Right. And who's that with her?"

Kenny was astonished at that – a father not knowing who his son was.

"Don't you know?"

It was the doctor's turn to be startled. Had this child of eight divined he did not know his son? His voice lost all coldness and irritation. "Sorry – I was just wondering what you called my son. But you are a bit right, I don't think we know each other that well. Who's your best friend?" He started the car.

"Graham. But he's a show off. He sends me postcards then asks for them back."

Dr Brideswell backed the car out of the parking space. "But you don't mind his funny ways?" Kenny did not reply. He was still thinking about what the old man had said before, that he didn't know his son. It occurred to him that as he grew up, Frank wouldn't know him very well either. They moved slowly around a parked bus. "What sort of French car does Alice drive, Kenny?"

"A Renault Four. You change gear up here." He moved his hand to the dashboard and made some in and out movements. Alice leaned forward.

"Kenny, Dr Brideswell doesn't need lessons on how to drive my car."

The doctor shook his head. "Not at all, Alice. I'm very interested in all things mechanical."

The atmosphere between them had changed. Brideswell felt his heart slow as he relaxed into the accelerating car. His father half-turned his head. "I don't need to be called 'Dr Brideswell', Alice, by your son. I've retired from all that. Harold will do – that's what my chess partner calls me … I'm used to it. Names are funny things but they're not so important to me, but I like to get them right. It's bad to call someone the wrong name."

"Uncle Michael is teaching me chess, Harold."

"Really?" The doctor smiled as he heard his name from the lips of this highly unusual boy. They turned into the main road after a wait – a long line of cars had built up behind an army lorry. "So – perhaps then, Kenny, you'd give me a game?"

"I only know the opening moves."

"Then we'll be all right. The opening is the most important part of the battle."

"That's what Michael says, Harold."

Harold Brideswell shook his head with amusement. He could become friends with this eccentric young man. He turned slightly. "Is that what you say, Michael?"

They laughed. The joke was lost on Kenny. Grown-up jokes were always mysterious. The words had hidden meanings he didn't understand, hidden from him – like the unknown message upon their tablecloth at home. No one in the world knew that secret except the person who put the message there, in code. He was amazed at the narrowness of the lane they had turned into from the main road. He watched the A 30 disappear from the side of them as it snaked its way up a steep hill. Never before had he seen such high hedges and deep cuttings. Everything so narrow.

"Supposing we meet another car along here, Harold?"

"There are pull-in places to pass, but I wouldn't like to meet a milk tanker. We're all used to these roads, living here all the time. Your roads in Manchester are much bigger."

"Of course we have bigger roads in Manchester."

The elderly doctor changed the subject. "My house is in the next village. We'll have to turn off this road into my drive … I hope you'll like it. It's a nice day – we could have our lunch outside on my patio?"

"What's a patio?"

"A sort of concrete lawn. Close to the house."

Kenny smiled. Graham would never, not ever have had his lunch on a concrete lawn. "Did Uncle Michael live here when he was a boy?"

"That's a long story, Kenny. Have you been asking Michael any questions on the way down?"

Brideswell answered. "He has a thirst for knowledge, father." Easier to say 'father' now. But never Harold. Something had changed. Kenny – the healing effect of a questioning boy. Nor had he ever heard his father speak with such benevolence. Kenny had charmed him.

"Ah, a thirst for knowledge is a good thirst. You hold onto that, Kenny, never let it go. My two children were the same, though Michael hid it from us … he was a dreamer."

"He writes books, Harold. You have to dream them up."

"Yes, how right you are. I think you already know Michael better than I do."

"Books are dreams, aren't they?"

"Yes. I suppose they must be." Dr Brideswell was informed. He murmured a faint laugh. "Well, there you are then." He had not laughed for a long time.

They slowed to enter a small village, the kind of place Kenny had seen on postcards from Graham – a church, a shop with a red post-office sign and a monument. The boy pointed.

"What's that? Is it for a famous person?"

"Not famous, Kenny – but not forgotten. It's our war memorial."

As they rounded it, he could see names. "We'll take a closer look when we take Rupert out. He's the dog I have now."

"Why is he called Rupert?"

"Ah ... he came to us as a puppy. Josie named him."

He was aware the name Josie inserted a sadness, just like the war memorial. Kenny had heard Alice and Uncle Michael speaking on the train when they thought he was asleep. Josie's memorial was in London and was being looked after by a man called Lewis. The car swung off the road. The boy was astonished, the track they were on was so narrow and overhung by branches that they were plunged into deep shade. Beyond, he could see a house, large and low, wide and sad. The wheels made a grinding sound on the gravel in front, crunching like a beach he had once gone to with Frank, before Dog. Before Carol.

"Is that your house?"

"Yes. What do you think of it?"

"It seems forgotten."

"Hmm ... you have a very unusual way of seeing things, Kenny. I think there's something of the poet in you." The elderly doctor stopped the car and looked at his child passenger for some moments before releasing the safety belt. His question to the boy was tentative, as if unsure how to frame it. "Do you have another grandfather?"

The moment held an importance. All three waited for Kenny's answer. But the boy was puzzled. He had not realised that Harold with his sad house and Japanese car might be or become a grandfather of his. He frowned, turned away and opened the door for himself.

"I do have a grandfather in Russia. Uncle Michael is going to find him for us. No one knows where he is."

"Well, that explains it ... you have all those thoughtful Russian feelings from him. What did you grandfather do ... was he an artist, or like Michael – a writer of books?"

"He is a composer," said Kenny, changing the tense.

Alice said she would cook omelettes for them in the Polish style with onion and ham. It had been the intention of Dr Brideswell to speak to his son somewhere and to apologize for the way he had neglected him as a boy, for giving all his love to his sister – but these thoughts had gone. He had become enchanted by a small boy with odd insights, who treated adults as children, who was at ease with their first names, whose grandfather was a Russian composer and whose mother was going to cook his favourite meal, omelette, and who had sent him out to shop.

A topsy-turvy world was drawing him in – willingly and with pleasure. Already two things had entered his mind – the house needed brightening up, the outside painted and his drive, a mess of overhanging branches needed drastic pruning to let in some sunlight. And one thing more; his world in the space of half an hour had lost its greyness. He went out with Kenny and the dog Rupert for the village shop.

The boy held the lead. The dog sensed a different hand but did not pull ahead.

"It's better to have him on the lead, Kenny, in our village. You never know who is going to roar through – idiots on motorbikes. They come from Yeovil and shatter the peace. This is a narrow road with a dangerous bend at the bottom down there ... we're not a motorway."

The word motorway struck a remembrance in the boy's mind. "Who was Josie who died on a motorway?"

Harold Brideswell was shocked at the starkness of the question. "What an unusual fellow you are. You know then about Michael's sister and where she died."

They stopped. The dog looked up at Kenny with a question in its eyes. Why had they stopped – when would they go on. His new master who held the lead softly was embraced by different matters but also to do with time and movement. "Only that she stepped out in front of a car, the car Lewis was driving."

A fine tremor shook the doctor's fingers. He touched his new young friend on the shoulder. "Yes, something like that. Is there something about it, Kenny, which bothers you?" He found himself speaking to the boy as if he were a person closer to his own age.

"She smiled, Harold, and waved at Lewis as he hit her. Why did she do that?"

The doctor felt the grasping of a fist in his chest, an angina he had begun to notice now when he was upset or trying to rush. His mouth had become dry but his eyes wet. "Here ... let me tie up Rupert. He's not allowed in the shop." His hands were shaking. He took the lead. This boy was taking him into all the thoughts that had haunted him since the accident, thoughts which when invading him at night brought on a cold sweat and a hurry of heart beats. The boy's next question was logical and from that pre-dawn chill.

"Why didn't Josie want to live, Harold?"

They didn't enter the village shop. A sound came from the post office sign as a sudden breeze reached and pushed against it. Dr Brideswell felt the cool wind move across his face. He heard the rustle of leaves in the tall limes on the edge of the green. How unknowable – its advent out of a morning so still. He untied the dog. Not the moment to go inside.

"Let's go over there for a minute ... you were asking about the war memorial." He passed the lead over to Kenny. In the centre of the green was a pillar, the names upon it weathered on the south-western side where gales drove in gusting winter rains. On the opposite side, the names were half covered in a yellow-green lichen, able to flourish there out of the storms. All around was a small garden, weeded, watered and loved by the post-mistress Miss Hinton.

"These names are of young men, Kenny – most of them no older than Josie. Their lives were cut short by cruelty and chance. They fought in battles because they had to, when they should have been on their father's farms, sons from old families who knew and loved the land, then they died for it. They died to rid the world of Hitler, and before that many died in Flanders, on the Somme, and all for no good reason. We are still suffering when we think of all that. I didn't know until today that Josie wanted to die. She must have been very sad about something."

The dog sat at the boy's feet and raised its head. Kenny stroked the soft hair around its ears. "Lewis looks after the grave. I think the garden around it is flowery like this one.

Graham's front garden hasn't got any flowers. It's all concrete so his father can put his new car on it."

Dr Brideswell smiled. The darkness around them had passed over. They walked back to the shop, tied up the dog and bought ham for Alice.

In the train home, Kenny slept. Alice leaned him against her and quietly opened her handbag. She passed Brideswell a photo.

"This was me at ten, Michael. I thought you should take it with you."

He looked, studied the sad-faced child placed before a departure at a photographer's studio. The man's name was written in small gold lettering. 'Israel Levich. Smolensk.' He turned the photo over – some words in Cyrillic script… 'Anya, Smolensk, 1967.'

"This was taken just before you left?"

"Yes. We each had a copy – one for me and one for my father and mother."

Brideswell was moved. He placed it carefully into his jacket pocket. "Would your father still have his copy, Alice?"

She touched his lips with her fingers. A touch of great tenderness. Alice made no answer.

★

Saturday, July 15th 1995
Northward ...

The weather, a two-week heat wave, broke on the day after the visit to his father. The temperature fell from the 80's to a normal heat for mid-July. An easterly wind blew in a relieving freshness across the capital. Finally, in its turn, it gave way to a maritime breeze from the west – an airstream to end a summer's desiccation with relieving rain.

Brideswell said his good-byes. His farewell from Alice had moved them both. She wept – he held her for a long time. No return date; an open ticket and an open brief. He promised to ring often and to send Kenny lots of postcards from Russia that he would have to give away to no one. And on that valedictory evening, he played Kenny a full and proper game of chess. Before he left for home, late, he and Alice made love downstairs – tenderly. She held him tightly into her, unwilling to release him. Her contraction passions were long, her cries soft and in his ear, her back arched finally as she was overwhelmed.

On the Saturday morning, the London train left Stockport early, arriving at Euston on time – 9.50 am. Brideswell reached the terminal for the Polish coaches in Victoria fifty minutes later to find he had over an hour to wait before his coach left.

Grey London, muggy – a fine drizzle had wet the pavements of Pimlico. In the precinct, a marbled piazza with a unique fountain, he found an Italian café and was glad to put down his luggage at an outside table – small white suitcase, shoulder bag with notepads and maps, three rolls of toilet paper and a large bar of bath soap. In his jacket pocket pressed in behind the back cover of his paperback was a photo, the one given to him by Alice in the train, of herself aged 10 and about to leave everything she had ever known finally and forever behind.

From his table he could see the Warsaw coach – a double decked modern vehicle surrounded by a throng of people, the air washed by their excited voices, their movements and gestures like some film with sound added, a cavernous luggage hatch presided over by a large, unhurried Polish driver.

He listened and watched, sipped the hot sweet coffee before unzipping his travel belt to check his passport, money and ticket. His detachment was surreal, an observer not a participant, an actor thrust into an unknown film with a quest and endless journey in front of him, a cast of players unknown a month earlier when his drab life had been overturned – love with a new woman, love for and from her son, a disappearing gash mark on his neck, a name in his diary … Dr Liadev. And a cemetery where a film director set an opening scene, an elderly driver attending the grave of a young woman who had stepped out calmly in front of him, smiling, from a motorway hard shoulder. Enter Brideswell – unscripted. That morning of departure he was having an out-of body experience, only the smells were absence to signal the incoming of a fit. The terror it struck into him.

He found he was not reading the open book on his knees – different, unwritten words were coursing through his mind like a sky changing in variations of the light, or curtained and then opening above clouds hurried through on an equinoctial wind. Chance was like a season yet to come or one past and quickly forgotten; he did not hold the simple two-fold grasp of spiritual guidance embraced by Kenny – the Hand of God, the Hand of Dog. He smiled as he thought of the boy – his directness, his enquiring and seeing mind thirsty for knowledge, and smiled more at the eccentric way Kenny had addressed his own father with a familiarity he himself had never achieved, not as a boy, not as an adult. Remarkably a cold mist had been lifted because of a boy's sympathy for an old man who lived alone in a sad house with a dog called Rupert.

The coach was not full. He was glad. As he boarded, a young man in a front seat looked up and asked a question in Polish. Brideswell shook his head. He took a window seat upstairs half way down, but not so far as to be disturbed by people going down a smaller flight of rear stairs to the toilet. Movements day and night. He was wise to that. And he wished, prayed, that the films would be quiet ones, but he knew deep down it was a vain hope – they never were. A young woman, small and slight, thin and with no make-up leaned towards him over the empty aisle seat beside him. He was pleased with her neat body – a large heavy man would not have been a welcome companion for a coach journey of 30 hours. She addressed him in English.

"I think this must be my seat."

"Sorry … yes, I'm sure it is." He moved away his shoulder

bag and the carrier with his bottles of mineral water and sandwiches. She gave him a faint smile and lifted her backpack up onto the luggage rack over his head. She made the seat and space beside him her own, much as dog would circling a basket before crouching. She took a packet of American cigarettes from her anorak pocket, stood and left him. Outside he could watch her more closely, a woman in her early twenties perhaps, might have been more. She smoked her cigarette restlessly with deep inhalations and sudden expulsions of smoke upwards. Without her pack she seemed even more slight, almost frail. Suddenly she sat on the kerb and put her head between her knees as if in prayer or meditation. Or upset. No one was seeing her off. She threw away the cigarette and came back to her seat.

"What a silly fool!"

"I'm sorry?"

She swung towards him with angry tears in her eyes. "For God's sake, it's not that much to ask – to get here on time!"

He nodded and pursed his lips. "It's easy to get held up – the tubes are always stopping in tunnels. It gets worse and worse."

"Held up from Smith Square? A 15 minute walk!"

"Ah ... I see. It's often the way, the one who lives nearest arrives last."

"I'm going away for six months for Christ's sake ... this isn't some day trip to Clacton!" Her voice was sharp, bitter in disappointment.

"Sorry. That's bad luck." The coach moved off. Outside, a pavement full of friends and relations surged into the road behind them waving and blowing kisses. "Of course he might have gone to the main coach station – not everyone knows some of the Polish coaches leave at this Green Line terminus. Easily done ... a mistake like that."

She looked away and remained silent, lips firmly shut. Then she began to cry. Brideswell looked away, out of the window. They were moving slowly in a line of traffic over Westminster Bridge, the beginning of a voyage to Warsaw, a city he knew and liked – its trams and bendy-buses, the park and summer palace where you could listen to Chopin recitals, and the modern art museum looking down from a ridge at the far end ... the Arts Club café ...

He allowed his gaze to descend towards the wide unhurried Thames halted by a tide full up and not yet turned. The Dnepr at Smolensk was not so majestic – but this English river was at its mouth not yet opening into the great estuary and deeps in the seaward approaches. The Dnepr had yet to run a further thousand miles before it might release itself into the sea. Sadness in both though – the Thames for its loss of shipping, quays and docks, the other whose banks were sown with the spirits of wasted lives – soldiers, wives, children, Jewish families and Russian ones and the invaders ashes, many of them just as innocent. The coach had found a space in a bus lane and suddenly accelerated. The woman beside him had stopped crying. He was glad. They rounded The Elephant and Castle and moved easily along the Old Kent Road.

A voice...

"I'm sorry about that display of nonsense." She extended her hand. "My name is Grace. You don't need to worry about me, I won't invade your space."

He nodded and smiled with his eyes. "Brideswell ... Michael." No more was said. He watched New Cross Station fall away and felt her lean against him as the coach swerved sharply onto the Dover Road. He moved and took off his jacket. "Are you going all the way to Warsaw?"

"Yes." A restraint had entered her. He took his glasses and book from his jacket pocket then folded it, placing in on top of his carrier. She watched him. "How can you read with all this jerking about?"

"We'll be on the motorway soon. It's easier then."

After a while she stood up surveying the upper deck of the coach, the passengers, the rear steps to the toilet, the disappearing concrete dual carriage-way then peered forward into the broad ribbon of the Kent motorway. The coach gave a surge of power pitching her back into the seat and knocking Brideswell's book from his hand.

"Sorry. Bloody driver thinks he's on a runway." She reached down, gathered the book and glanced at the cover. " 'Easter Table' ... I've read that."

"Really?"

"By who ... Bracewell?"

"Brideswell."

She paused at the name and looked more closely at him. She raised a finger on her left hand. "Your name? A relation?"

"I wrote it."

"Yes? That's cool. Reading your own book?"

"Some corrections. They're running a reprint."

"It's doing well then?"

"Not bad."

"I thought it was OK ... nothing much wrong."

"Only small things. People notice ... they love to write in and correct me."

"Really? Yes, I know people like that."

She settled herself back into the folds of her seat and closed her eyes. She was not a chatterer; for that he was thankful.

*

Wedding of a medical man

It had been arranged at very short notice, a civil ceremony at the Bureau of Marriages, Births and Deaths – each held in their own room, each with a different potted plant. The office was an annexe, attached to the State Library where all the records were housed – except those offensive to the USSR which had not yet all been found and returned. Some never.

Both women – Dr Liadev's mother and his bride – insisted that he must have his work-suit dry-cleaned. Each polished his shoes, uncertain if the other had done them. A new silk tie was obtained from the market alongside the steamer and ferry landing. Both Natalya and Vavara Davidovna wore long dresses, new ones, reaching down well below the knee. They had been bought from a Jewish tailor who gave them discount for buying two and charged nothing for the alterations. The colours in each dress were different as befitted their age gap – the younger woman's was of a bright lemon yellow, that of her aunt a much deeper and quieter shade, more like the Siberian wallflower. Each costume was also chosen to match the amber gifts Dr Liadev had given them – a pendant for his wife-to-be and a brooch for his mother. In addition both ladies wore wide traditional scarves across the shoulder – Natalya's being white but with a blue-green embroidered hem to let it be seen that she was not a first-time bride. The shawl chosen by her husband's mother was a shade of beige, a light Armenian muslin with blue birds woven in on a village handloom. Both were pleased with their choices, which everyone said showed them at their best – handsome women a man would be proud of. Neither bought new shoes, old ones for a second marriage. Natalya was in love with her husband. She knew that shoes were the closest part of the wedding outfit to the ground, and as every village bride knew, a marriage succeeds from the earth upwards.

The day was a joyful one, hot by 8 am. Because he perspired so freely, Vavara Davidovna saw to it that her son had three soft white handkerchiefs in the pockets of the wedding suit – her last loving gesture to Maxim whose care was now passing to his wife, a woman she felt she had chosen for him, but a choice finally made in heaven. She lit a candle of thanksgiving in the Cathedral of the Assumption when the bond had been declared, and also asked Irina to offer up prayers for them in her synagogue.

Irina Bloch came looking neat and excited; she was the witness, signed herself 'Madame' and wept, partly because she was remembering her own marriage, partly because the husband she loved had died so suddenly and left her alone. The music in the Office of Marriages was gentle, sensitive and romantic – Tchaikovsky. The many summer flowers Vavara had insisted on having gave out a strong scent and a feeling of countryside, of shaded summer days. Despite being a former Soviet Office, the room and its ambience surrounded them all in charm and kindness. The Presiding Officer was young and as yet without a marriage ring, she smiled, touched them and was happy to be there in the presence of love at a more mature age. It moved her.

And afterwards – a reception. Dr Liadev asked the young woman registrar to come too – she accepted and said she would be delighted ... 'Just for a little while'. The place he chose was the Station Restaurant under the watchful and humorous eyes of the patron Grigori, helped by his wife and three daughters. The food was plentiful – Armenian and Georgian dishes, traditionally baked fish from the Volga, Russian champagne, wines from the Caspian Sea, vodka for the balalaika band. Natalya had invited many friends from the GAZ Motor Works. They brought with them small gifts, much laughter, a deep thirst, and a love of dancing. The Weddings Officer was swept off her feet by a tall, strong welder. She did not leave as she had thought ...'Just for a little while'.

The melodies played by the band became more wistful, more Hebrew. When a wedding reaches the stages of wistfulness and the fingers of melancholy beckon the heart, everyone is at their happiest. The ladies admired Natalya's ring – broad banded and in a rare pale gold. Liadev had bought it at Kaliningrad in a small jewellers by the dock entrance. It had a story. He was told that the ring had belonged to an English sailor, a man from a noble family who had abandoned his inheritance and chosen instead to go to sea, taking with him only one thing from his family, his mother's wedding ring. It was said she was almost a Tsarina and the gold ring was a token of her love for him always, gold from beach sands in a Welsh bay – gold of that colour was always chosen by the kings and queens of England. The women wept at the story and asked why the sailor had sold so precious a ring. Liadev did not tell them.

Vavara Davidovna also had wept, on and off all day long – her son leaving her for another woman's tenderness. But when she danced with Grigori she felt better, and when the dance ended she remembered that the future care of her only son was in the hands of a good woman. She knew that Natalya, her niece, would make a sensible and good wife, a woman who had coped with a big Swedish man and had made him happy. She knew that Natalya loved Maxim and understood big men, how to please him with her cooking, how to help him in the marriage bed and to overcome his shyness. Irina Bloch had said that her husband had been shy and timid for weeks after their marriage, then he became as fierce as a reindeer and filled her with their child. Together they wept at the music. Irina said that the bandleader Jakob was playing for her grandparents who died in a death camp. And more – that the Hebrew melodies reminded her of songs her mother sang in England when she had bad dreams and woke up crying.

*

Novgarod to Smolensk, via Moscow

A week after the wedding they left Novgarod taking with them Irina Bloch. She had said she would help them to move in and couldn't bear the thought of suddenly not having her friend living above her. After Smolensk she would leave them to go to Vitebsk to visit her grandparents' synagogue and see the rabbi. But she would come back to them afterwards to get over all the sadness.

They set off like a school party on an outing, three women and a doctor, weighed down with cartons, cases, large square laundry bags, shoulder bags and handbags. When they reached Moscow, Dr Liadev had told them what they must expect, what they would all have to do – to go down into the underground, the Metro from Kazan station to Kiev Station, both on the circle line, the Koltsevaya. The first leg of their trek would take 6-8 hours depending on what was happening down the line. They bought three tickets – the doctor was able to use his government pass.

Moscow shocked the women. They were quite unused to so many people pushing and pressing into them, not in the least polite or respectful, scowling and throwing at them angry, fierce looks whenever a case or carton touched them. In the Metro they were shouted at and treated with contempt, as if they were Kazak gypsies. The ladies were deeply shocked – by the bad language, the curses, the rudeness and the withering stares, but their leader the doctor merely shrugged. He was a big man used to being sworn at on the Metro. They found seats though, and he did his best to reassure them.

"A move like this is only done once in a lifetime. We don't have to change lines down here, and there's only a few more stops to go. So nothing to worry about. In Moscow they are all in a tearing hurry. It does them no good. We shall leave them all behind soon, once and for all. We have each other, don't need them – now or ever." Then he raised his voice so that everyone could hear him. "If you want to see good manners you have to go to St Petersburg."

They got out safely and intact at Kievskaya Station but were swamped by hurrying crowds elbowing past them. They were so distracted they had no time to pause and appreciate the marble elegance of the artistic murals. The surge compressed them towards an exit. Irina Bloch stayed close to her friend Vavara.

"These people, Vavara – they're a disgrace! No wonder our husbands died before their time… can you imagine the big Swede of Natalya's trying to service their buses? I would rather live in Tashkent!" And in one heavy crush she reached for her friend's hand clasping it tightly, as if they both were lost and bewildered children. Their luggage and bags, cartons and boxes bumped and rebounded between them like jewellers' stones in a polishing mill.

"Thank God for daylight!" exclaimed Liadev's mother. "Never shall I get into a Moscow Metro again – it's only fit for worms, moles and rats!" With Irina they had fallen behind the others. "Wait for us, Maximoushka ... don't lose us – for goodness sake, slow down!"

Only Natalya was confident and at ease. She had worked all her life in the city and was used to it – but she was upset for the others who were frightened and struggling ... she had her husband's arm through hers. A wife in every way. She paused and turned. "Do come on you two. Aunty, stay close to us, please."

"We are trying to, Natoushka, but we get pushed back by all these rude men!"

"And the women are just as bad," called Irina, glad to stop for a moment and set down her bags – the handles were cutting into her fingers. "They're worse – they should know better. Men never behave in a crowd!"

"Moscow is Moscow, Aunty," said her daughter-in-law as they drew up alongside. Names are hard for a new wife who has always been a niece. An aunty does not easily become anything else. The older woman shook her head, looked scornfully towards Irina and raised both hands in an eloquent but indefinable gesture at whose centre was outrage.

"Maxim, you must take us for some tea or coffee – we ladies are not used to all this ignorance. We don't have it in Gorky and don't expect it in the capital city of Russia." She slipped back into the old name because she was upset, flustered and cross. Her downstairs neighbour and best friend who shared her heart added in her own judgment.

"Muscovites have never known how to behave. I'm just thankful that my Ivan wasn't good enough to play for Dynamo ... can you imagine what might have happened to him living here? He wouldn't have lasted two minutes. They'd have stolen the shirt from his back and the boots from his feet. Such a place it is!"

"Even the very laces, my dear."

"Everything, Vavara."

Vavara Davidovna sighed. "Ivan is much better off, Irina, in telephones. He'll be more mobile in phones than ever he was at football."

They peered into a café packed with people. The air was blue with cigarette smoke – the air emerging through the open door was a blue pungent haze. The women considered that the people inside were undesirables and were afraid of being robbed.

"Not 'undesirables', mother," said her son patiently, "just ordinary Moscow people on their way home after a long day at work. They're only tired and thirsty like we are."

"Well, it's a funny place to be in, Maxim, when you're supposed to be on your way home. You are far too generous – it will do you no good. Most of them are probably criminals with nothing better to do!"

The Warsaw express did not leave until 10.35 pm. Liadev had used the overnight express many times and booked sleeping berths for them all. Though the train was in, they were not allowed to board it. At last they could.

The women were revived and rejuvenated by the sleeping car – wide-eyed and childlike in their delight. Vavara Davidovna was at last calmed down.

"Just look at this little bedroom, Irina." She pulled a curtain across to show her friend how to obtain privacy. A small ladder led to the upper berth. The attendant came towards them from his cabin. He introduced himself with a slight, old-fashioned bow, as pre-revolutionary as the carriage itself.

"Good evening. I am Ilya Malkovich your sleeping car attendant."

He shook hands with Dr Liadev who explained where they were all going. He introduced his mother, his wife and then Irina, in that order, as befitting a married man who had lived with his mother until he was fifty. The introductions made him perspire. Perhaps it was a delayed sweating, relief at being clear of the Moscow Metro and safely aboard their train and he spoke with the authority not of a new husband but that of a married man with three women in his care.

"We should like some tea now please, Ilya. Tomorrow morning we shall take our breakfast at 7 am and will require a call an hour before that." He passed the attendant their tickets, reservations and wedged between them a generous tip – a sheaf of roubles.

"Thank you, Dr Liadev." The tickets were returned. "You may depend on me. My cabin is at the end of the car," The man indicated with the whole of his hand, his fingers spread, "and my door is never closed, just on the long hook to stop it banging. I do not sleep till after Smolensk when day has come. I never sleep during the night." He spoke in a curious old-fashioned way, which laid an unexpected grace upon a passing communist era. Vavara Davidovna had no such niceties. She jabbed her finger and shook it.

"Ilya," she said sternly, "you certainly must stay awake. We do not want our things stolen. We've all heard about the goings-on on these trains."

"Madame Liadeva, you may have every confidence in me. My sleeping cars are safer than Mr Yeltsin's rooms in the Kremlin."

The doctor smiled. "That doesn't reassure us, Ilya. Mr Yeltsin is far from safe."

The attendant hesitated as he was about to leave; on his mind were his mother's little cakes. For people he liked or for those he thought would notice, he would lay up his tray with a clean white serviette and place on a plate some of his sleeping-car cakes, small sweet cakes, lemon-flavoured, made freshly for him each journey by his mother's own hands. He gave her all the profit from them and the money supplemented the wreckage of her pension. The price he charged was on a sliding scale, perhaps means-tested ... the greatest surcharge was to Americans.

"Will you have some Bolshoi cakes with your tea, Doctor?"

Liadev looked to his wife. "Would you like cakes, Natalya?"

She shook her head and assumed a precedence in the matter over her aunt.

"We have our own food, Maxim. Is there an extra charge?"

Ilya bowed slightly towards her. "Yes, madame – but only a modest one. I recommend them. They are home-made by my mother."

It is never easy to assume superiority with a doctor's mother. "You may bring us your cakes, Ilya," said Vavara Davidovna. She looked at her daughter-in-law without smiling. "I shall treat us to them, Natalya. We must have something with our tea. Tell me, Ilya, why do you call them your Bolshoi cakes?"

"Because they are light, Madame ... like the ballet."

"Does your mother use fresh eggs?"

"Of course, Madame Liadeva, the freshest of eggs. My uncle keeps hens. We can vouch for them."

"You're not being clever with me, Ilya, are you?"

"No, madame, not at all. All my uncle's hens have their own names."

"Then bring us four to try. If we like them we'll buy four

more in case we need tea during the night. Now, tell me ... how do I get up to that high bed?" She pointed to the upper bunk in a suspicious manner.

"The ladder is very sturdy, madame. I check them after each trip. You may feel quite safe on that ladder."

Vavara Davidovna placed her hand gently but certainly on her friend's shoulder. "Irina, my dear, you had better take the upper bunk, you're lighter than me."

Irina looked at her in astonishment. "No one could be lighter than you, Vavara, except a bird."

"But you are also much younger ... so mobile and ..." she raised her finger like a teacher might, "...much more nimble – just like your son and his football. Maxim must have a lower one with Natalya above him – she's used to climbing about over motor cars."

Ilya left them to prepare tea, to place beneath the glasses his whitest napkin, to select the best sugar bowl and the most even, unmarked sugar lumps from the packet, not from the tin of re-collected ones. For him, the doctor's mother, Madame Liadeva, might have been a Romanoff.

No one objected to the allocation of berths – the situation had required someone to take firm control – but Vavara Davidovna was conscious she had overruled her niece, her husband's wife. She touched her cheek.

"My darling Natalya, when we get to your house in Smolensk, we will do exactly what you tell us, won't we Irina?"

"Of course. A wife must come first in any household. And you, Vavara, must remember that!"

Before entering Smolensk, the railway follows the northern bank of the great Dnepr River but in this early part of its course it was smaller even than the Oka, and a minor waterway compared with the magnificent Volga. Both Vavara Davidovna and Irina watched the river's movements from the window of train as it slowed towards their journey's end, both wondering why that had to travel such an enormous distance to see a river so small. The older woman watching remember the steamer voyage to Lyskovo with Maxim and Natalya, seeing in her mind Yakob and his balalaika band. She pictured the waiters bowing solemnly to her at the Azov café. Vavara Davidovna shed some tears and felt Irina's arm on her shoulder. "Such a little river, Irinoushka – why have we come?"

"I shall always be back home for you Vavara. My Ivan will never find such a good woman to marry. He is only in love with his telephones. You can come and stay with me in the spring and we'll take the boat again down our beautiful Volga – all the way to Lyskovo. Now remember … Natalya won't want her mother-in-law to be under her feet all the time, and contradicting."

That brightened Vavara up. She retorted with some asperity, "Since when do I contradict people, Irina? Whatever are you saying now." She felt for her friend's hand and squeezed it. Tears for three rivers – the Volga, the Dnepr and from her heart.

From Smolensk station there are four exits – all leading to the city. Laden with their boxes, bags and cases, they left the forecourt, pausing at the exit arch – an arch which had escaped destruction in the war but suffered, now restored and gracious. Smolensk itself was a city surviving on reconstruction, a phoenix amongst towns, each new brick contained a dead soul. Dr Liadev left them there to search for a licensed taxi, one with an official number on the roof, knowing from long experience they would be held to ransom if they risked anything else. He found one. The driver was an old, weathered man with a white beard. To the doctor he looked like a saint sent to save them.

"To the church of St Paul and St Peter, please. I know it's not far but we are four and have a lot of luggage – some big cases and boxes."

The driver sighed and spat something from his mouth. He motioned the big man to get in beside him. They drove slowly up to the exit arch, threading their way between departing buses and trams. The driver pointed to a dark tower, white tipped.

"That's your church."

"I know, but we're too tired to manage that distance on our own. I have three women. They are exhausted."

"All Russia is tired, my friend."

The driver said no more. He eased himself out and surveyed the boxes and luggage as a phlegmatic Baltic fisherman might examine a poor catch. He stowed the cases and bags in the void of a vast boot. The cartons he lifted to feel their weight and then decided that the ladies could hold them. He passed them back. Two large laundry bags he heaped upon the expansive doctor until he was almost buried by them. He gave a satisfied nod. Within his eye was a glint of triumph, a stare of suspicion. They drove slowly the short distance to the twin facetted church – brown brick and white. Which colour was for St Peter and which embraced St Paul was anybody's guess. The church itself was a mystery, a double building for two saints, one part of its structure echoing the ancient east, the other western Christendom. Perhaps, the doctor thought, St Paul had the darker church for he had preached in the Near-east and had been blinded on the way there. The priest's rooms were set in the white part. Liadev paid their ancient driver generously. The man seemed moved, though what had passed through his mind in the course of a drive as slow as Christ's entry to Jerusalem was as deep and hidden from view as his lips were by his bearded face. He shook his head. "I don't need so much, sir. Are you the new priest?" The first words he had spoken since pointing out the church.

Liadev closed the man's fingers around the money. "Take it all. You have helped us to arrive. No, I'm not the new priest ... my name is Dr Liadev – this is my mother, next to her is my wife, then over here is Irina, my mother's friend. I have rented the priest's rooms for myself and my family."

"Ah." The cab driver crossed himself, relieved this was not a priest arriving with three women in tow. "Thanks be to God. May He bless and keep you. He loves all his children. Welcome doctor. We are a sad city, but try not to show it."

A man almost as old as the driver left his piano and came to the front windows of his upstairs flat. He watched the arrival of the doctor with much interest – the doctor who had brought him out of a distant hospital to begin again a life – a life in music.

*

Sister Katrina

The Convent of St Barbara and St Chrysostom was a twin house in some ways like the adjacent church but different. Though the church looked in two parts, it served one community – in the Convent there were only nuns but across the world, an order of brothers. For both it was a working Order. In the brothers' case, they were looked upon with favour, respect and much kindness by the great Carthusian Monastery near Grenoble. In London the tiny monastic community – a very distant arm – was held in the same regard by another monastery, Charterhouse. In all 11 brothers – six were enclosed by working from their London base, the remaining five lived and worked in the North of England, Cheshire. And one of those, Brother Robert, suffered from hay fever, asthma and a chronic shortness of breath, still fortunately relieved and controlled by his two inhalers but made worse by summer train journeys, and a case too heavy for him.

The convent was so close to the church that it shared a high dividing wall. The heavy door inserted in it was kept oiled and easy by the sacristan, but rarely ever opened. The

Mother Superior on the convent side of the door, Sister Katrina, had no cause to visit the church priest. But now she felt a guidance to do so and prayed that what she was about to do would please God, that she would be safe and that none of her nuns would be exposed to temptations of any kind. A feeling had entered her heart. She prayed that it was a spiritual one and not one of curiosity, to visit the elderly man who had come to live in an upstairs room and studio in the priest's house, and who was by repute a composer. The upper rooms were not unknown to her – once they had belonged to a verger, the church's sexton and an assistant priest. They had, one by one, all left. Rooms empty for seven years. She wanted to meet the old musician, introduce herself and place before him a special request.

The well-oiled lock had not rusted in seven winters or in the rains of seven springs. It opened under the pressure of a large key held in a large hand – Sister Katrina was a firm, tall woman from a northern province, the Murmansk Oblast. She suffered not from her height but from her weight which did not diminish in spite of rigorous and frequent fasting, plus a minimal diet on Fridays. She was unfortunate twice over – an abruptness of speech and manner, both failings she was ashamed of. It gave the wrong impression because she was a kind person, a caring and devout woman, a mother to her nuns and novices – and they all loved her. They accepted her way of speaking, recognised her natural authority and were grateful for her kind encouraging words. Sister Katrina was visiting the composer not just to introduce herself but to ask for a some music that her nuns might sing when the Metropolitan Bishop visited at Easter, and also they would be receiving Brothers and nuns from many outlying houses.

She climbed the iron staircase to an upper balcony and walked carefully along it, somewhat nervously. The walkway was shaded from the hot sun by a sloping overhang, which had been constructed to allow the incumbent priest some shelter from rain, snow and sun while he walked up and down in quiet reflection. She knocked firmly, touching her white shawl in a moment of prayer, and easing back the blue cowl with her fingers. A man answered her knock, as she knew he would. Her heart beat quickly.

"Yes?"

Unaccustomed to men, she tried hard to soften her voice, but the tension of the moment sharpened her words. "I am Sister Katrina from the convent ..." she pointed to the building over the wall, "... the Convent of St Barbara. I wanted to welcome you here and say ..." she prayed silently that God and His Angels would supply her with the right words, "we are your neighbours."

The man opened the door wider. The woman's loud voice jarred his ears. He took a step back. "Would you like to come in, Sister Katrina?"

She noticed his backward step and made a supreme effort to speak more kindly, less forcefully. "Please excuse my manner, I'm not used to men."

"Of course. I understand." He closed the door gently behind her.

"It's kind of you to come over." He brought her into a spacious room with a piano beside a wide window. A room sparsely furnished, no carpet – it had in a corner a low bed and by a second window a table with a manuscript on it. His attention was away from her; she was glad of that. His gaze was through the window, outward. "I'm not the only new arrival, Sister Katrina. There is a doctor and his family now downstairs. I hope you'll call on them too when they're settled in."

"Yes," she said sharply – but the movement of her person to the window was that of a gentle sensitive woman. "I have heard about them from the seminary – Father Adrian. He told me a doctor was coming with his wife and his mother."

"They seem to be four – another woman … and a lot of luggage. I shall leave them to it – I would be a hindrance." He spoke in a quiet way as if his mind were not fully engaged with any of the happenings – perhaps only in his music. "Dr Liadev is an old friend of mine. We first met many years ago, a long way from here. He's the kindest of men." He drew a chair from the table and with his hand invited his visitor to sit down. But Sister Katrina could not be at ease sitting with a man in his bedroom. After looking down on the new arrivals she retreated to a more defensive position near the door. He understood. A breeze from the window lifted the edges of his manuscript and he placed upon it a paperweight.

"I'm sorry not to have given you my name at once, Sister – the fact is … I don't know what it is."

The big woman put her hands to her white shawl in a gesture from deep in her past, from when she was a girl and her appearance mattered. "I don't understand – surely everyone knows their name. Even an old lady knows who she was before she got married. Our names don't blow away." The comment had begun gently but her voice rose as she went on. He made no answer. She moved closer to the door. She had not expected someone so strange.

"That is true, Sister Katrina. Names are as much part of us as how we look – and when a name is shed, blown away if you like, we may not be able to recognise ourselves, or be known to others any more. There is a great mystery in names, they carry our spirit. You are right to say our spirit remains with us for ever, but I'm sorry to correct you, a name can be lost. Mine has." He looked down as the last boxes were being carried in. "It hovers somewhere looking for me in the ice and snows of Siberia. I was named by the director of the hospital they took me to from the camp – 'Yuri Perm'. Short, not offensive and I have grown into it, though I know it is borrowed from someone else."

The Mother Suprior was moved. She addressed him now as a woman, a woman to an injured man. "I'm sorry ... you have suffered. What should my nuns and I call you, please? Not by a borrowed name that isn't close to your spirit."

"I was given a photo once by Dr Liadev ... he said it was found when my camp was demolished – of course, it might have been anyone's photo."

She came a step nearer, drawn in by his words and manner. "What kind of photo. Of a place you once knew – and remembered?"

"No. A photo of a girl. On the back it said 'Anya. Smolensk. 1967.'"

"Do you remember knowing this child? This Anya?"

"Perhaps. I can't be sure. There is something."

Sister Katrina crossed herself – a silent prayer of thanks, that the Lord, The Lamb and Saviour has sent this sad old man a sign. "What was that something?"

"Oh ..." He turned away embarrassed. "Another name."

"What was it?"

"Just something that came into my head from the child's face, from her lips."

A shiver passed through Sister Katrina. "What did the small voice say?" She trembled. The voice of Christ had never touched her like that. Only His love.

"Andrei. It was offering me back my name."

She sighed with relief. Had there been any more words, she would have dropped to her knees before a man who had received holy words spoken by God and His Son to a prophet out of the wilderness, a man received into the inn of the Samaritan.. Her voice slipped back into the sharpness that roamed her speech like an unchained dog.

"So there you are then, that is the name we shall all call you by. We shall know you as Brother Andrei. My nuns will feel easy with that."

"Of course." From the window he watched a large black taxi drive slowly down the narrow drive to the gates and the road beyond. Such a lethargic pace, he smiled and nodded – a former funeral car and undertaker's man? "I am happy with Brother Andrei, but I make no claim to a life of prayer or devotion."

Sister Katrina remained where she had moved forward, nearer to him. The edge in her words was tempered by the hesitancy of the request it contained.

"I have also come, Brother Andrei, to ask you if you would compose some music for us. We have a choir … some of my nuns have excellent voices."

"Really? A composition? You have heard I am a composer? I could try – what sort of piece had you in mind, Sister Katrina?"

"Something sacred and not too difficult for us. Perhaps a setting for vespers, or psalm settings…" she raised the fingers of both hands towards him, "but not too long, something we could manage." He looked at her in an enquiring manner, eyes wider, inviting her to continue. "Next year at Easter we have a special celebration … it comes around every ten years. We build a tower to our patron saint, St Barbara and people come to us, brothers and nuns from all over Russia and beyond. I had in mind perhaps some thanksgiving canticles…" Her voice tailed away, a flush had spread up into her cheeks.

The man nodded. "It sounds a very special day indeed. But will your chapel be large enough for so many people? Should you come here for this thanksgiving service? I can mention it to Father Volodya. Oh … just one thing – do you anticipate some male voices?"

Sister Katrina put her hands to her cheeks. "Oh no. My nuns are not at ease with a mixed choir like that. Please write for women's voices only … and we must be in our own chapel."

"Just as you wish. But before I can say what I might or might not do, I shall have to listen to your choir, think about the sound they make and how it comes through in the acoustic of your chapel. How many singers do you have, Sister Katrina?"

She sighed. It was all so difficult. "Our choir is twelve. We keep it that way. I have found it is good for my nuns to have something to strive for… there is competition to become part of the chapel choir," she reached for the door handle, "but we are a united house and live in God's presence, His mercy and the love of His Son. I shall tell everyone what you have said, that you must hear them sing. They are going to be very nervous when I tell them that – a man sitting in our chapel listening and watching. But … if you must."

"Yes. I must."

As he came to the door with her, Sister Katrina saw that an absence had entered his eyes. The sadness within them cast over them both a sadness. She felt that she was not the one leaving, something in the man they would know from now on as 'Brother Andrei' had already left.

*

Phone call from a ferry

The coach swayed and shook. It negotiated the angled steel ramp to the vehicle deck of the ferry, and they entered a darker world. A seaman in a luminous jacket waved the driver forward with a baton.

The coach stopped with a jerk and hiss of air brakes. The engine was switched off. The noise and vibrations they had come used to suddenly ebbed away into a stillness. No one spoke or moved, as if the silence had entered each one of them like a stillness after a roll of thunder and the wait for rain. The restless woman beside him stood up. Her movement was a release for others – voices, people standing and stretching. A space, momentarily a vacuum, became filled with purpose. A resumption of life. But the disappearing day to be replaced by an echoing darkness had a bad effect on Brideswell. He experienced a tunnelling of his vision and a removing from his mind the clothes of normality. The awareness of hovering nightmares signalled to him a threat, that his recovery was far from complete.

The woman looked down at him. "Let's go ... you don't

want to stay in here, do you?" She eased herself further into the aisle. "I need to phone."

He stood up and pushed his book down into his jacket pocket. "Can one phone out from a ship?"

"Of course. But it costs a bomb."

The telephones were placed in wall booths near the purser's office. Two some distance from each other were free. He was glad they could be apart. Not that he had anything so private, just that his mind in its present state would find it hard to hold on to any conversation with Grace's voice in his ear. He put in a pound coin and dialled. Kenny answered.

"Hallo?"

"Is that you, Kenny? Michael here."

The boy did not say anything as if surprised, stunned. When he did speak his voice was firmer, louder. "Where are you, Uncle Michael? Have you gone to Russia?"

"Not yet, but well on my way. I'm ringing from my ship, the ferry to take me over to France. The coach we're in is parked in the bottom of the ship, on the car deck."

"Oh ...?" The information was not what Kenny expected.

"It's a French ferry and everyone is speaking French except us. How's things with you – who are Altrincham playing today?"

"The season's over. It's cricket now."

"Does Cheshire have a cricket team?"

"They're a minor county."

"Ah ... well what other news is there?"

"Alice says my hair is getting longer."

"That's good."

"I've been playing with Graham. He says he wants all your postcards."

"Really? What did you say, Kenny?"

"No."

Brideswell drew in his breath in a half-laugh, half-smile. "Good. That's the way. Don't be told what to do with my postcards. How is Alice?"

"She's been at a rehearsal. That's why I had to go to Graham."

"Perhaps one day she'll take you with her. Give you a break from him."

"He's all right. Just a show-off."

"Is Alice there?"

"She's standing beside me, Uncle Michael, and wants to take the phone away." A pause followed. Brideswell heard him say – 'Uncle Michael is on a ship and his coach is in the bottom of it.' And Alice's reply 'Yes, dear.'

"Hallo, Michael?" Her voice entered into and through him.

"I've missed you, Alice ... so much."

"I miss you, darling. Don't stay away from us too long."

"I won't ... I promise. I have your photo safely in my book. As soon as I arrive I'll make contact with Dr Liadev, and send off some postcards."

"Please ... phone me from Poland tonight. I can't wait for a postcard."

"Sure. Of course. It might be late though ... the border and everything."

"Whatever the time."

"Any news of Vladimir?"

"He phoned. They want him to have an operation. He has great faith in you, darling ... we all have."

"Alice ... I love you so much."

The phone went dead. Cut off. The money had run out. He replaced the receiver slowly – he knew she had heard him say it, that he loved her.

*

Smolensk, Saturday

Hot, thundery but as yet, no rain. Dr Liadev left the women to unpack. A big man, he would only get in their way, besides, three women together do not want to be disturbed by a man. The afternoon was advancing and the heat from midday had brought over dark clouds. A storm threatened. How curious was it all, a new home, a new life with a new wife – though she was his cousin and they had known each other since childhood. A different sort of love bound them together now. He walked slowly through the cloister and wiped his brow with a soft absorbent handkerchief washed and carefully ironed by Natalya, not his mother. His mood was calm; he was happy.

The doctor felt the drop in temperature as he entered the cooler air trapped in the veranda, now also freshened by the cold airs which travel in front of a storm. He walked out beside the lawns and turned the corner of the church to enter a narrow strip of lawn with a border against a high wall, the wall that separated the church from the convent. He paused at the iron steps leading up to the rooms where Andrei now lived.

A large religious woman was coming down – a nun in a light brown habit, shawl and blue cowl. Not a young woman. He waited some distance back from the foot of the stairs. At first she did not seem to see him, lost in her own thoughts. Liadev spoke softly so as not to alarm her.

"Good afternoon, Sister."

She stopped abruptly three steps from the ground, held the iron rail and looked up towards the voice. The woman answered shyly, shocked at being addressed by a man standing between her and the gate to the convent.

"Good afternoon. Are you the new doctor?"

"Yes, Dr Liadev … I'm sorry to have startled you. I was thinking of going up also."

She descended to the bottom of the steps and felt in her bag for the gate key, as if by holding it she was safer. "I am Sister Katrina, the Mother Superior of the Convent on the other side of that wall.." Her voice contained a harshness, which surprised Liadev as her movements and face were quiet. He assumed it was a tone she adopted towards her nuns in the name of discipline. And he wondered what had drawn her upstairs to visit a man with no memory. As if reading his thoughts and embarrassed coming down from seeing a man on his own, she added with a warmth and flush rising to her cheeks. "Brother Andrei speaks very highly of you, Dr Liadev. We have a convent choir… I had things about our music to discuss with him."

"Of course. We are both lucky having him so close. He is a fine composer."

She felt calmer with a doctor so at ease with her. "We have a special occasion next Easter and I'm hoping Brother Andrei will write a small sacred piece for my choir to sing on the day. Some of my nuns have beautiful voices but they're shy.

It is something they'll have to learn how to cope with, to be able to sing in a gathering of men as well as women."

"Perhaps they'll feel comfortable in these surroundings, this church – somewhere welcoming, and not too public."

"Thank you, Doctor. Brother Andrei has said he will need to listen to our choir before he composes music for them."

"Well there you are – a good first step."

Her words, which had become softer as she was explaining about her choir and her visit, suddenly became taut. "I believe you have brought the women of your family here with you."

Liadev smiled and raised his fingers in a gesture of agreement and to reassure. "My wife Natalya, my mother Vavara Davidovna and her friend who is like a sister to her – Madame Irina Bloch."

She moved into the space opened by the doctor moving to one side. "They'll be very welcome to visit us on a Saturday afternoon – we permit visitors and guests then. Of course … only ladies. We have to make an exception for Brother Andrei, but he has to come for the choir."

"Thank you. I shall tell them."

"The public entrance is in Ulitsa Portovaya. We have a vesper service at 6 pm, but they will hear the bell."

"I shall pass that on, Sister."

She looked down. The man's gaze was embarrassing her. "But if I may, I shall call on them before then, when you've settled in a bit." Her way to the gate was now a simple matter and she felt her confidence rising, she was liking this large sensitive doctor. "For we are neighbours now, aren't we."

"They will be delighted to meet you, Sister Katrina. We are on the telephone; you might just check first that we're not all out – there are so many things we have to do, and my wife Natalya is starting work at the cathedral on Monday."

"So you'll be with us for some time, Doctor?"

"Yes, for a long time – we've come here to live ... from Nizhny Novgorod."

She half turned away, a gesture revealing her need to go. "I'm afraid that's a city I don't know. I am from the north ... Kola ... Murmansk. I'm glad you've taken our priest's flat with your family, Dr Liadev. I have always thought it sad and wasteful for those beautiful rooms to lie empty for the want of a suitable tenant."

He noted the compliment, smiled and gave to the mother Superior the slightest of bows. "We shall do our best to be the right tenants.

Unfortunately, though I enjoy my work, I do have to travel a lot. My family will value your friendship, Sister Katrina."

"Thank you, Doctor, and I theirs. We are so cloistered, it is good for a Mother Superior to have friends outside ... to keep the balance. As you may know, the brothers of our orders all work in the outside world. I should like to move my nuns in that direction, but such a big change can only be done slowly. I'm glad your wife Natalya is to work in our cathedral, perhaps that would be a good starting point for some of my sisters, too."

In those moments the hard vowels left her voice and Liadev saw a caring woman that the nuns and novices must respect and love. She left.

He climbed the stairs slowly, looking around as he did so – shading his eyes from the dazzling whiteness of the church walls. In the sheltered shade, distanced from a world's noise and confrontation, he could hear the faint ringing of a telephone.

The two men embraced. A contrast – the composer

grey-haired, gaunt with a face engraved by Siberian winters, and the doctor who had found him – a friend, large, forehead studded with droplets of sweat, suffused with all the benevolence of the newly married. They sat – Kutsov on the bed, Liadev at the table.

"A lot has happened to us, Andrei in eight years. I met Sister Katrina on the steps – she's enrolled you as a brother … I shall have to get used to that."

The old man lifted his shoulders, widened his eyes; it was a gesture of irony that Liadev had often seen before. "I am not spiritual in that way, Doctor, but she thinks if I'm Brother Andrei it will be easier for her nuns … because I have to go in and listen to their choir. They want me to write a piece for them."

In his eyes was a question that Liadev could not read, as if asking for the past to speak louder. A whisper had returned his name, but nothing else, and not even that completely – a man with half a name. A man in effect not unlike a mirror in which most is hidden from view, nothing behind the glass, no place for a spirit captured and ashed, a man with no shadow. A captive where a release has been signed, but not accomplished.

"Does the name Kutsov mean anything to you, Andrei?"

"No." But his friend was disturbed by the question and looked sharply away. "Should it? Who was this Kutsov?"

"A composer."

"I don't remember names."

"Composer Kutsov was from Smolensk. There was a child … Anya."

"There are many Anyas; why do you ask me this. I have never heard of Kutsov – when was he born?"

"1932."

"Then he was born from my generation. My memory for those people has gone. If there was a child there must have been a wife."

"She was killed – murdered by the KGB."

Liadev's words were harsh. The old man was silent. Tears had come into his eyes. "What are you doing to me, Dr Liadev – Anya is the name on my photo, the face that gave me my name back. I know nothing about Kutsov."

He brushed his eyes with his fingers. "… But you are a married man now. We watched you arriving. It is good to have you all living underneath me – and I can compose again … not just small pieces for a choir, but real music, like before."

"Like before, Andrei? Do you remember pieces you wrote before the arrest, before the camp? Tell me. I shall find them and bring them. Your name will be there for you to see."

"Did I say that? I don't know what I meant, Maxim." He used the doctor's first name, something he had never done before. "I must have remembered something."

"Perhaps a concerto … or a symphony?"

"Who knows. Never ask an old man how it was when he was a warrior. Never ask a woman if she was once beautiful."

When the doctor returned downstairs, already the rooms looked as if a family lived there. Irina came to him with a tray on which she had placed a glass of tea, a bowl of sugar lumps and wide plate for his supper – dark bread, chopped tomatoes in olive oil and garlic and a broad slice of cheese.

"Maximoushka, you must be so hungry. We've had to eat something, forgive us for not waiting for you." He took it gratefully and smiled with his eyes. Nothing to forgive. "Did you hear the telephone. How wonderful to have had a call already. It was from my son ...in Gorky, from my flat." She used the old name. It fell from her tongue – she was excited. "Ivan has had a phone call from England, from my sister. Sasha!"

He reached forward and touched her hand. "Well, isn't that amazing? Even in England they want to know where you are – you have a fine family. I remember Sasha when she came over ... she took us all to the Kirov. What a day that was. She's a professor now?"

"Almost. She teaches in university, in their Music School." She was proud of her sister and her music.

"And did she ring for a reason? Did she know about this vast journey her sister was taking just to help her best friend start a new life among strangers?"

"Not just that, Maxim. There's an Englishman coming who wants to meet you."

Liadev was astonished. "What? There must be some mistake ... whatever have I done that an Englishman should want to see me about!"

Natalya and Vavara Davidovna had come in from the kitchen. They were not in the least surprised – Maxim was a famous doctor ... of course an Englishman would want to meet and speak to him. They listened with the wide eyes and belief of children. Irina Bloch looked at them both and shook her head in a wry smile as if she knew exactly what they were imagining.

"Well, I'm sure that's true, but he's a friend of Sasha's. A writer. A writer of novels!"

"Ah!" He waved his fingers at all three. "A writer of novels ... then that explains nothing." He gave a soft laugh.

"Listen to her, Maxim, this isn't a joke."

"But I'm in the dark, Mama. Who do I know in England apart from Sasha?"

Irina drew in her friends closer. "Sasha's friend is a famous novelist."

"Like Dickens?" asked Natalya.

Liadev shook his head, his eyes alight in amusement. "No, Natoushka, no one in England is that famous."

Irina Bloch ignored the interruption to her moment. "He lives near Manchester, close to Sasha and he's coming to Smolensk!"

Liadev put his arm around his wife's shoulders. "What are we to make of this, Natoushka – a mysterious writer from England coming to interview me?

When does he arrive?"

"On Tuesday." All three answered his question.

"So soon? Is he in a hurry. What's all this about, can someone tell me?"

Irina Bloch delivered her final words. "He leaves Warsaw by the night train and arrives here in Smolensk on Tuesday morning, Maxim."

"But I don't know this man – do I really have to meet him? Why hasn't he written to me instead of working it all out through Sasha and Ivan?"

"You don't have to meet the train, Maxim. They have suggested a meeting at the cathedral after the midday Mass."

"But why me, Irinoushka? Did Ivan say?"

She studied the scribbled notes she had made from her son. "His name is Mr Michael Brideswell." She pronounced the name perfectly. Not all her English was forgotten. "He's coming to Russia to find out about a dead composer."

"Ah. So that's it! Now we know. And how would I know anything about that. Even a famous writer from England won't be able to find a composer who is dead. But you're right, Mama, this is not a joke. I shall meet the train and bring him here. We will show him how much we Russians love the English, and beat them in Crimea. They are brave." He paused and moved a step closer to Irina Bloch. "What is the name of this mysterious dead composer, Irinoushka, and what is it to him?"

"Kutsov, Maxim ... Andrei Andreyevich Kutsov.

★

On deck

The voice of his travelling companion penetrated the bandage of silence which was winding itself around him.

"Do you want me to go somewhere else?" She had lighted a cigarette from the butt of another. "You've become far away. Lost in thought?"

An ominous thought had entered Brideswell's head, like the point of a rapier. A fit – an idea taking hold of him, and it filled him with dread. Two years fit-free, but now something deep within him, unknowable and ill-defined, was whispering ... perhaps it arose from the flickering sea-dazzle. He had never liked lights, especial bright ones – restless, irregular and shimmering.

He raised his shoulders to press into the back of his neck where a coldness had entered. "What do you want to do?"

"I'm OK if you are. Is my smoke a problem?"

"No." He took his sunglasses from their case and put them on. She made no comment. The ship picked up a curious mid-channel movement. A side-to-side sway as she dipped her bow into a cross swell.

"What are you hoping to do in Warsaw, Mr Brideswell?"

With the dimming of the sea mirror he felt better. The whispering in his ears and around his lips disappeared.

"Michael ... it's easier. Please." She drew on the new cigarette, waiting for an answer to her question. "I'm breaking the journey. I travel on the next night to Smolensk."

"Is it for a new novel?"

"In some ways."

"What's it called?"

"House at Spissikoye." The Dover cliffs were losing their whiteness, diminishing into a thin pale line. The slow corkscrew movement of the ferry soothed him – a calm sea and a cooling breeze, partly – some of it from their forward motion. He felt better and was glad to have someone to talk to. Her next question inserted his name.

"So, when can we buy it, Michael?"

"I don't know. It depends on my publisher – he wants to bring it out in time for the Christmas market, but it needs work on it. In the middle." He was now while aware standing close and talking, that she was older than he first imaged. Her curiosity about him and his long day's night into Russia continued.

"Do you know Warsaw?"

"A bit."

"I don't know it at all."

He remembered the bitterness and tears she had shed at not being seen off by her friend. She had a story. As a novelist, that in itself had set him thinking.

"And yourself? You said you'd be away for some time."

"I have a Polish Government scholarship to study at the Chopin Academy. In Warsaw."

"Really? I know it ... it's just off one of the main central roads. Nowy Swiat."

"Should be able to find it?" A tentative tone had entered her voice.

"Yes. The road leads down towards the Royal Mile and the Opera House."

"What does it look like – the Academy ... as old as Chopin?"

"Not what I've seen – quite newish, but then most of Warsaw was rebuilt after the war. I've been to recitals there ... I think you'll like it – spacious, with a lot of wooden panelling."

She seemed reassured by that. "I am a pianist. I shall be studying with Professor Razimowska." She flicked the cigarette into the sea. "She came to a concert I gave at Princeton and sorted me out a scholarship. She wants me to study Szymanowski ... she says I have the right style and feeling for his music."

"That's good, to be helped liked that. The academy is not all that far from the Holiday Inn where our coach stops. I'll walk down with you, if you like. Where are you staying?"

"Jolly Bush?"

He smiled at the way she said it. "Good – that's a nice district. Plenty of buses and trams into the city. It's an inner district – quite old and gracious. It wasn't flattened like the centre."

She made no reply. A woman not given to chattering; which is what she had said when she arrived at his seat. A bonus for him. He watched the movements of the sea and the trail of foam behind in their wake, glad to have the glare cut out by the sunglasses. After some time he asked her a question.

"Have you ever heard of a Russian composer called Kutsov? Andrei Andreyevich Kutsov?"

"Of course. Any professional pianist would know that name. Few still play him, except the piano suite 'Six pieces for a wedding.'"

"Ah ... and do you like them?"

"They're happy, song-like pieces. Yes. I do like them ... I should play them again. They are dedicated to his wife and daughter."

"What are their names?"

"Why? How could I know that?"

"You read it and might remember."

"I learn the music not the dedication. Was it to a Martha, or Masha ... something like that."

"Marsha. That sounds right." Brideswell fell back into himself. The silence this time between them was separating, distancing. The young woman must have sensed it and felt the need to bring him back.

"There's also a two movement piece for piano and orchestra. I've never played it – never seen it ... in fact you can't get it. Out of print. Maybe it was only ever published in Russia, by the Underground."

"The Underground?"

"Kutsov was a non person. Still, it's possible you can get a copy now, times have changed so much. Perhaps when you're in Smolensk you could ask around, please. I'd like to see it ... post it on to me at the academy. I am Grace Lubkowska."

He was aware of a sharper tone in her voice, a touch of iron. A determined woman – and also he felt her warmth and concern for him. "Yes. I'll ask and deliver it on my way back." Brideswell left her to be alone. No escaping the whispering; it had to come. The rest of his journey would be a retreat to find strength. It was Kenny's Dog. A black Dog which ate into his brain.

She rejoined him on the coach. "Are you all right, Michael? Something wrong?"

"Something I get. It'll pass. I'm best on my own when I see it coming."

"I'm here ... but I can shut up."

From Calais the coach headed north into Flanders, past Dunkirk and Ostend before angling east for Brussels and Cologne. He did not sleep. The fits came at night. Always in the dark. Brideswell gazed out of the window into a day ending, a world in a spectrum coloured by a sunset. Villages entered his eye and left quicker than they had arrived – small shops, a baker's, a restaurant. The flatness of the land was the flatness of his spirits – doubt, realities, time and movement ... and the vagaries of chance. Yet none of it had the meaning of past years – now he was loved. The visitation, the convulsions were no more significant than Brother Robert's asthma, except it entered into a black hole, left – and returned when it wanted to.

From Poznan they threaded their way, mile after mile, through pine and birch forests. Sparse, sombre and leggy, not like a forest in England. A coolness of dawn forced its way in, a new day for a bus overcrowded with sounds unrelated to life, mechanical – the endless throbbing of the engine, the sounds of thick tyres on empty uneven roads, the body noises from sleeping people. His eyes closed. Sleep now was free of harm and invasion. He woke up near Warsaw feeling better.

When he left Grace at the academy, she shook his hand with a firm grip and reminded him to look out for the music she wanted – thanking him for his company and kindness. She was worried, and asked if his dark mood had lifted. He made no reply and felt her eyes on him until he turned a corner.

At the hotel he entered the lift to the 5th floor. Room 502 and stepped out, confused, disorientated and full of foreboding. Lack of sleep, exhaustion, a hovering presence in his ears and a sweet smell surrounded and reached out for him. The lift attendant saw his confusion and came out, speaking to him in Polish overlaid with a languid Russian accent.

"I will show you your room." He went back, immobilised his lift with a key and returned touching his passenger on the arm. Brideswell thanked him in Russian and explained he was English, just arrived from the London coach.

"I speak English. Give me bags." A smile came into the man's face. "London – long way. I watch Arsenal when they play Legia. They too much good for us." He took Brideswell's arm as if he were an injured mid-field player and in his free hand he took the white case. "You sleep – you better." He unlocked the room and turned on the light. The shutters were across the windows. He released them but eased them apart only marginally then put down the case and pointed at the bed. "You sleep good." He closed the door quietly behind him not asking for or wanting a tip – a proud, sensitive man who drove lifts now he could no longer repair masonry on high buildings. The heights he faced now were safer, within a lift he had come to like.

Brideswell looked about him – a dim room with the afternoon light kept at bay by shutters, both for sun and snow. He found the bathroom and turned on the light. It had had no window and smelled stale, airless. He placed the chair against the door's outside to keep it open and let in a cleaner air, and to stop it falling on him. He undressed to his underpants, laying down his trousers carefully on the bed. Back in the bathroom he spread two bath-towels on the floor and stuffed a hand-towel between his legs to soak up the urine.

The smell in his nose was stronger. He lay flat on the towels, placing himself on his side, the recovery position he had learned when he was six. He was now ready for the invader, thanking God it was arriving here, not in the coach, not in the street, nor when he was with Alice and Kenny. It came at midnight – a smell so sweet in his nose that it was sickly like a gas. Twitching – on his lips, rippling down his arms, contractions pulling at his legs – then spread, pulsing, each time with greater force, quicker and quicker, faster still. Slowly his back arched and a cramping vice-like grip expelled all the air from his lungs. He hovered in those moments between life and death.

A woman in her bath next door heard thrashing sounds, sharp cries and the deep-throated sob which followed. She felt like weeping. Her husband never roused her like that. Not even on her marriage night.

Late in the following morning Grace Lubowska entered his room, let in by an anxious lift attendant. Dark, a staleness, and the smell of vomit. Her friend was lying angled across the bed. Between them turned him and sat him up.

"Your train leaves at eight, you should be getting up and getting ready, Michael. Reception rang me. Our friend here was worried. He opened the door." She turned to her helper. "Thank you, Boris... he needed us."

Boris, the lift man, opened the shutters wide and the inner windows, pushed an outer pane and let in fresh air. "Will you be needing me any more, Madame Lubkowska?"

"No ... but thanks so much. He's not well, but I can see to it all now."

She opened her purse to give some zloties, but he shook his head.

"Not wanted. He suffer – and support Arsenal."

At Warsaw Central she located the sleeping car on the night train to Moscow, his reservation, but there was plenty of time. Grace took him to a café at the side of the booking hall, bought coffee, black and sweet, and told him to eat the chocolate she was handing him. In her hands he was obedient like a child, and mute. Back on the train she found the car attendant and pressed into his hand a ten dollar note.

"My friend, Mr Brideswell is ill. He needs to be kept an eye on during the night, please, and helped off at Smolensk. I shall not be coming on with him. There is a Dr Liadev at Smolensk ... if you wouldn't mind."

"I am Ilya Malkovich, madame. Dr Liadev is a good man. I know him. Your friend will be safe with me. You have my word on it. I never sleep at night." And he returned the American money. "Excuse me, but it is not right for me to have this." They helped him into a berth. Grace kissed Brideswell on his cheek, each side, despite the rough stubble. He seemed bemused and in a daze.

"Mr Brideswell is a famous English novelist, Ilya. We must take good care of him."

"I shall see he reaches the doctor, Madame Lubkowska. I shall also make him some tea and give him some of my mother's Bolshoi cakes."

★

Meeting the Warsaw train

The express from Warsaw was 30 minutes late – a slower than usual change over onto the wider gauge of Russian railways. Dr Liadev waited on the platform watching the train come to a halt – very few people getting out. Smolensk was not the destination. Then a few more came off, not clearly identifiable – some tourists, city people returning, flax traders, business men and some for the Baltic states connection. At once he recognised the sleeping car attendant hurrying towards him.

"Dr Liadev ... Doctor ... I have your patient. He needs your help."

"Ilya? It's good to see you again – what patient is this? I'm waiting for an Englishman, not someone needing medical help."

"Oh no ... he's yours, Doctor. His friend in Warsaw put me in charge of him – your Englishman. I've helped him to get ready but he doesn't seem to know if he's coming or going. All over the place in his head..."

"How very odd."

"Would you come this way please, Dr Liadev."

"Lead on, my friend. He must have been taken ill on his way here."

In the exit space at the end of the sleeping car stood a dishevelled man, unshaven and surrounded by an air of dismay and confusion. His clothes were crumpled and not straight, despite the best efforts of Ilya Malkovich. The attendant spoke in a low voice.

"He's a famous English novelist!"

"So I've heard. You're a good man, Ilya – thank you. And he is a very fortunate one to have had such good care. If we had more people like you in Russia, we would be a better place."

The railwayman flushed at the compliment. They helped the Englishman from the train. The door was slammed shut and the express continued on its way north.

"I am Dr Liadev. My English is not very good, please to excuse. We had a message from your friend Sasha in England, that we should expect you this morning. Mr Brideswell …?"

The unkempt man looked up at him with uncomprehending eyes, then shrugged. "Thank you, Doctor."

They walked slowly down the platform, the man swaying, bumping the case he was carrying into his legs and stumbling.

"Here, let me hold for you." The doctor took the case from him and took the shoulder bag strap, easing in deep into his shoulder. "You're not well. I'm glad I came here and not waited till we met at the cathedral. There's plenty of time to tell me. I shall look after you. You're quite safe – as safe with us at Smolensk as in … say … Durham?" He gave a quiet laugh.

"A bit further, you might say."

The air of complete mystification shrouded the man like a sleeper not yet fully awake. The doctor touched his arm.

"In my house, Mr Brideswell, you'll feel very comfortable. My mother's best friend Irina, Irina Bloch, speaks perfect English though she rarely uses it except when her sister phones ... your friend Sasha. Irina was born in England but chance and destiny brought her to a state flat underneath my mother in Gorky." He smiled. "The old name, now replaced by a much older one."

Dr Liadev was mystified. A man in a daze, yet no outward signs of a stroke, or alcohol, or fever, or any obvious diseases. He waited. He knew that in medicine a diagnosis often had to come through in its own good time.

In his hand the English visitor held a small book; from it jutted a card. A photograph in danger of slipping out. As it happened a hurrying woman with a case bumped into the Englishman spilling his book. Dr Liadev stooped and picked it up, a Russian classic, Turgenev. The photo had fallen face up a few feet away. He picked it up carefully – a young face he knew so well. His heart quickened. The doctor turned it over, but he knew what he would see:

Anya. Smolensk 1967

Shocked, stunned by disbelief, he slid the photo back as a bookmark. His questions would have to wait. He addressed his companion slowly, in Russian.

"You are not well, my friend."

"No."

"We will look after you." The man looked at him for some moments then nodded. "What has happened to you?"

"I am recovering from a bad convulsion."

The warm morning air outside the station seemed to make the Englishman stronger. He swayed less, but remained silent. They walked to the church. The sun was strong but not yet full of heat – the air fresh after the storm of the day before. Across the river stood the cathedral, shining green and white until the glare of noon would bleach its colours. The wide Dnepr, its bridge nearly rebuilt, flowed with a summer's timelessness. It was in no hurry to complete its long journey south where it would grow, expand, slow through the margins of the Pripet Marshes, flow in solemnity under the morning bells of Kiev, onwards and down, now a great river embracing lakes, and on to the sea. It had become a river almost as great, almost as wide as its sister, which coursed through the blood and veins of Russia, the Volga. Rivers the doctor knew well – one of them, the Volga, brought a moisture into his eyes – part of their lives once, now beyond reach. Lives shaped in sharpness, smoothed out by the river, always flowing, always changing, never in the same mood; for his mother it was like losing a child, for him a friend, one faithful and always there when the time should come for him to return. One day. It was true as the Greek philosopher said, no man may step into flowing water the same way twice, for the waters of the first immersion have moved on. The two women he had uprooted were blessed by a bridge, the strength and enduring friendship of Irina Bloch, who would never leave the flat where she could see the great Volga from the windows on the top floor of the unchanged block. His mother would go back, he knew that deep down; there are jewels from the past which cannot be pawned.

Above the doctor's family in the church house, now lived a composer with no memory, who each morning would study the photograph of a ten year old girl. After gazing, he would turn it over and read the words engraved on the back, words he was linked to in ways closed down, inaccessible, and each morning he would say those words aloud, like a prayer.

    Anya, Smolensk 1967

*

Cathedral

Mid July; it became very hot. After three days Brideswell was able to leave his room to walk out into a world restored to normality, with light which did not dazzle or blind, with aromas of cooking and coffee – not the nauseous sweet smells, the winged messengers of epilepsy. The doctor had to leave them – he was needed in St Petersburg, and at the beginning of August he must travel on, a recall to Moscow.

The women in the household anointed the Englishman with kindness, sat with him at night when strange dreams made him cry out – they calmed the night terrors, bathed his forehead and held his hand when he shook. They brought meals to him on trays and read aloud the Russian version of one of his novels. When he became calmer, Irina Bloch sat in his room in an easy chair by the window. She wanted to know everything about her sister Sasha, about the English village she lived in – every detail. His descriptions entranced her. With a novelist's gift of observation, bit by bit he laid out before her a picture of her sister's life, described the house, her helper Rachel from the synagogue – how Sasha was teaching her Russian in exchange for sharing household chores. He explained how thin Rachel had been at first, coming from a poor home on an inner city council estate. How she moved about the house silently as if on tiptoe in soft shoes, and then how she emerged into confidence and companionship under her sister's affection, into a stronger person. He told her about Sasha's work teaching music at Huddersfield, and she laughed when he described the dog – a mongrel with a face too sharp for a terrier, legs too short for a greyhound.

Natalya also would sit with him after finishing her work at the cathedral. She spoke only in Russian but slowly so that he could gather it in – her marriage to a Swedish mechanic, a big man with a gift for repairing buses. He was told how despite his great strength and size, one day he suddenly died and she was left alone, no children – only her aunt Vavara Davidovna so far away in Gorky on the banks of the most wonderful river in the world, the Volga. She confided that she had always admired Maxim, her cousin. She decided her only future lay in her aunt's city – and there she went one day on impulse when the old man she was working for said he didn't need her any more, he was going to live outside Moscow with his brother. Her aunt had been astonished when she knocked on her door, but from the first they loved each other. And she had been blessed, a loving home at last and a job at GAZ, the motor works. And then that special day when all three of them had such an outing, sailing down the Volga in the steamer 'Aksakov' all the way to Lyskovo, and how there, in the funniest way, in a little Georgian restaurant, Maxim had asked her to marry him.

She talked easily to Brideswell, finding in him a quiet and sensitive listener.

All four women were agreed – he should not go up and see Andrei Andreyevich yet. The composer was an old man who had suffered so much – the news that his daughter was alive, that he had a grandson, must be given to him slowly when Brideswell – Mikhail- was stronger. Gently, and with the photograph.

In the late afternoon when much of the heat had been taken from the day by a cooling wind from the north-west, from the Baltic, he went out. Walking back through to the station, over the bridge, he found a side turning towards the river. There he discovered a promenade, raised up and with benches at intervals. He sat down and lifted his book from his pocket. His mood was curious, overlaid with déja-vu, a heightened awareness of colours so intense they seemed to be taken from paintings. Voices – those from passing walkers echoed in his head as if arriving from a time past, having no firm existence in the present. All around him was an embrace of benevolence. He watched a drake swim towards him on the slack water, with lighter-coloured females on either side, and behind them six small ducklings in a line. The storms in his head had passed. He had never had them before so violent or to create such havoc. The rapid thaw and clearance of confusion was like that of a late spring upon an enduring frost. A woman passed in front of him with a small dog let off its lead. She was aware of him.

"Good afternoon, madame."

She slowed and paused. "Good day."

The dog came up, part poodle, part some other breed – an inquisitive and friendly creature. He patted it and smoothed down the soft hair behind its ears. "A fine dog, madame."

"Thank you, but he's very ordinary. His name is Gaga."

"Really? A dog from the moon? Gagarin when in company?"

She smiled and pursed her lips in a humorous way. "We always come this way ... he likes to meet his friends."

"Is it easy to cross to the city centre from here, please? I need to go over."

She shrugged, a minimal gesture and lifted her hands. "From here?"

"Yes. I need to buy a chess set?"

"You'll need the craft market ... I've seen them there. Russian, of course, but they do have some others from Poland, from the Tatra mountains." She pointed. "Do you see our cathedral ... just a bit past there. Anyone will show you, just ask for the craft market. I go there sometimes; my husband doesn't like it – too many tourists ... and he doesn't play chess."

He nodded, smiling with his eyes. "Thank you, that's a great help. I'll call in on the cathedral at the same time."

"Of course. All visitors to Smolensk want to see our beautiful cathedral.

It is called the Cathedral of the Assumption."

"I'm not calling as a visitor. I need to see someone who works there."

"Really? Are you a priest then? The services are through out the day. There are intervals, of course, for you to make your enquiries." She took a small watch from her pocket and looked at it carefully for some time, as a nurse might checking a pulse. "By the time you get there I'm afraid a service will be going on; no one can enter unless they wish to worship."

He felt uneasy about detaining her for so long, even the

dog wanted to move on, but the woman seemed in no hurry. Perhaps she couldn't make him out, a stranger and yet with a friend who worked in the cathedral – and his accent?

"I go there myself sometimes to the evening prayers, on Sundays. It is a very special place. But each Sunday is different. I never tire of it. And I do love the bells." She smiled, but it was directed at her dog. "Come on, Gaga, we must leave this gentleman to his reading and not trouble him any more." She moved away, then stopped. "Excuse me ... but are you English?"

"Yes. How do you know ... is it my accent?"

She gave a laugh a girl might make. "No – it's your book. It is a favourite with us, but the title is in English."

He returned her smile. "Of course."

The woman and the small white dog walked away. At some distance she looked back and gave him a wave. Such a friendly gesture and done with charm. He would have liked to talk to her some more.

The service was over. At the cathedral entrance he looked around for Natalya – she wasn't there. Nor after passing through the inner doors into the dimly lit interior could he see her. A large, older woman was carefully wiping fingermarks from an icon. It had been prayed to during the day, touched with reverence and hope by many supplicants, by prayerful women. He noted the grey hair showing beneath her head covering; he saw how respectful and delicate she was with her cloth. He asked a question.

"Please, I'm looking for someone who works in the cathedral ... Ivana Petrovna Madiewska?"

The woman continued to wipe the gilt frame and the protecting glass it held in place. "Are you the Englishman

Natalya has been telling me about, who speaks Russian like a Pole?"

"Yes."

"And you want to speak to me about my father?"

"Yes."

With her left hand she pushed at the loose hair, which had freed itself from the binding head-cloth. A gesture of uncertainty. With the other hand she tucked her cleaning cloth under her waistband, movements unhurried and painted by the timelessness of the cathedral. They sat on a wall bench.

"Thank you for coming to find me. Natalya has told me how ill you've been."

"Yes. But they've all been very kind – I'm better now."

"How is my father?"

He instinctively touched her arm. "He died suddenly. There was no pain."

"I knew. Why else would you have come." She was not shocked or distressed. In her response was a stoicism of all Russian women, which marks their hands, lies as a burden across their shoulders, is tugged by many winds of sorrow, women whose eyes see the present but cannot forget the past. "He died in England?"

"Yes ... in London. It was a moving funeral. I was there."

"You went to my father's funeral?"

"Some of his friends – workers and traders from the market – carried the coffin. We were all moved; the music was beautiful ... the organist was my friend – and so is your step-mother. His friends were of every nationality ... a Pole, a Russian, a Lithuanian and an Englishman. I think Boris would have liked that."

"Yes, he would." Her eyes were on the icon but her thoughts

were somewhere in the past, perhaps in her childhood before her father left the glassworks with a fume and furnace asthma. And left also his wife and their daughter.

"The music was from the Mozart Requiem."

"I should have been there." She gripped her hands, the first sign of her emotion. "How can a daughter not be at her father's funeral? It wasn't right."

"Maria had no address for you."

"No address." She repeated his words as if expressing to herself a deeper truth. "We are a family with no address."

"I was with Maria. Your father was a much loved man."

A silence fell between them. Ivana stood up, went to the icon, touched it, crossed herself and intoned a prayer too quiet for Brideswell to understand, half spoken, half inward – she lit a candle and placed it on a rack with others. When she came back to sit down she was closer.

"I must write to Maria. My father was not loved by everyone, not by Maria's family – not by her daughter. They never forgave her for marrying again, and to a Russian who wasn't even a Catholic."

He had no answer for her. Instead he said, "His marriage to Maria brought him love, affection and a home – they were good friends as well as man and wife. She misses him."

"Did they come to the funeral – her daughter and the son?"

"No ... only the nephew. Her own children have abandoned her."

For the first time the woman was overcome; she placed her fingers against her eyes. Tears washed across her pitted nails. He touched her arm.

"I'm sorry."

"Her children are cruel."

"I think so. Maria and your father were happy together ... the guest- house and the market. I have the hotel card ..." He took from his wallet a small rectangular card, green edged and embossed in thin gold writing. She studied it.

"How strange to see this in print for the first time ... when it's too late."

"Maria wants you to go and stay with her ... she feels you are her daughter now."

Ivana Madiewska wiped her face with the loose sleeve of her gown. "How can I thank you; you are a very kind man."

"Can she ring you? Do you have a telephone number?"

"Natalya will take a message. I have no telephone."

She took his hand in hers and rubbed her thumb across his knuckle with all the tenderness of a large woman. She then crossed herself. "They say your name is Mikhail Brideswell?"

"Yes."

"That is a good name. I must get on with my work. Please come and talk to me again, I'm always here, this is my home. God has sent you; we are both blessed."

From an office in St Petersburg, Dr Liadev telephoned England, a Manchester number. Though his English was passable, he hoped to speak to his caller in Russian. A child answered.

"Hallo?"

"This is Dr Liadev. I am ringing from Russia."

"Russia! You are phoning from Russia? Where is my Uncle Michael?"

The doctor heard the telephone fall to the floor in a clatter. A woman's voice took it up, anxious as if expecting bad news.

"Hallo? Can I help you ... is it about Michael?"

"Can we speak in Russian?"

"If you want to." Alice dragged back into her mind a life and language she thought was dead forever. "Spassiba ... slowly please. I haven't spoken in Russian for such a long time."

"Good. Very good. Is there someone called Anya there?"

"I was Anya ..."

The telephone became silent as if the caller was in shock – unbelieving. "I am Dr Liadev."

"Yes. I have heard about you, Doctor."

"Are you Anya Marshievna Kutsova?"

"I was." Her heart began to beat hard in her throat.

"You father ... Andrei Andreyevich Kutsov?"

"Yes." Her mouth was so dry. An old language – words were sticking, reluctant to be rediscovered.

"Then he is alive."

Tears flowed down her cheeks – like a Russian river coming from a thawing source, welling from a ground in a land she had left and was for the first time reclaiming. Softly. "My father is alive?"

"Yes. He lives here in Smolensk in rooms above us. He is well, but old."

"My father is well ...?"

"Your friend Mikhail is here also with us. He has been ill but is better now. Today he went out for the first time. I'm afraid I took your number from his diary. Please excuse me. It is not something I would normally do. I needed it ... just in case ..."

"I understand. Thank you, Dr Liadev ... for my father ... for Michael ... for everything." Her speech was erratic and jumping, invaded by breathing catching in her voice. "My father is alive?"

"He lives in rooms in our church house. He has no memory. I shall leave the telling about you to Mikhail – it's better that way. He has your photo. They both do. Your father's photo of you was found when they pulled down his prison camp. He looks at it every day. Soon he will know who it is, and where you are." A deep silence now. Alice was too stunned, too upset to utter anything. The doctor continued. "Would you mind ringing his friend Sasha Oman for us please, Anya. She is Irina Bloch's sister, and she lives near you."

"We will never be able to thank you Dr Liadev for finding and caring for my father …"

"Your friend Mikhail – we like him so much, he is part of our family now – he took a very bad convulsion in Warsaw. Thankfully a friend of his sent him on to me. He has a guardian angel, and great gifts."

"Thank you. Thank you. I will phone Sasha Oman." She put down the phone. Her whole body was shaking violently.

Half an hour later, calmer, Alice did ring out, a London number.

An old man's voice, unsteady as if woken up, or so deep in the past a phone's ringing had dazed him. "Yes?"

"Vladimir … Kutsov is alive. He has been found. My father is alive."

Nothing. Then a sobbing, like the sighing of a wind through the new leaves of birch trees in a Russian spring, like the east wind that had entered London and cooled it during the first heat-wave. She set down the phone and placed her arms around Kenny who had come to stand next to her.

"Darling, you have a Russian grandfather. He was lost and is now found."

But the boy was aware of an absence, not a finding.
"Alice ... do we still have an Uncle Michael ... please ..."

*

Glinka Street

Brideswell found the craft market behind the Museum of Art in Glinka Street. From a stall he bought a chess board and a box of matching chessmen. The woman told him the pieces had been carved high in the Carpathians – the Tatra mountains.

In the long twilight after he had eaten with the family he went out again, through the white-stoned cloister, then took a path which wound around the darker brick of an earlier church. Beneath his arm he held the chessboard and in his hand the engraved and inlaid box of pieces. Slowly he climbed the iron steps to the upper flat. A feeling hovered, like the time he had climbed the steps in Bedford Square after leaving the hospital ward – not the dark wings of a fit but simply tiredness within a body still unready for a long day. He tapped on the veranda door, and again, for a second time – more loudly. The door was opened. Standing there looking at him was a thin old man with the sharpness of eye he already knew – the eyes of the man's grandson.

"Yes?" He spoke with a soft intonation to his Russian. "Did you want me?"

For that instant Brideswell was embarrassed – the board and chessmen felt heavy and intrusive, awkward in his hands. "I'm Brideswell ... from London. I'm sorry if I am disturbing you ... I've brought up a chess set ... I wondered if you'd like a game?"

An ironic, friendly look entered the man's eyes. "Come in – you're very welcome. Maxim told me you'd be calling." Kutsov opened the door wider to allow his visitor to step inside. "You're feeling better now?"

"Yes, thank you – it always passes. I'm lucky in that way – and they hit me very rarely." The room he entered was the width of the entire upper floor – cool, despite the heat of the day past. A room hard to exist in during winter – no signs of a wood stove or radiators. The man he had come to must have read his thoughts.

"I don't suppose I shall spend too much time in here when winter comes. It was once a meeting hall and prayer-room. The icons have gone, but it has a clean acoustic and suits me well. My piano ..." he pointed to an upright piano against a wall, beside it a music stand and a violin case. A large white table had been placed against a window; on it lay music manuscript paper. Two chairs. Brideswell nodded.

"You're working on a piece?"

"Yes ... in rough – a first draft. The sister at the convent wants some music for her choir. A few ideas – there's a long way to go."

They sat at the table. Brideswell placed down the chess board. The older man watched with interest. "That's a game I haven't played for many years – strange you should bring it up. I might not be able to remember all the moves." He touched the board with his fingertips as if feeling the texture of a sculpture or a piece for fine linen. "I like your board. It looks Polish ... from the Tatras?"

"I believe so." Brideswell opened the box. "You'd like a game then?"

Kutsov picked up a piece and looked at it, but his eyes travelled beyond – fingering a curtain across his memory, searching for a gap where they were not fully drawn. "Let's start the game and see how we go. I don't have the concentration I had as a young man." He gave the same curious half-smile as before but the irony left it quickly, a simple smile remained. "How are you getting on downstairs?"

"They're a wonderful family – so kind to me. I feel they've saved my life."

"Yes. Dr Liadev saved mine as well. He's a rare man – exceptional ... many artists and writers owe their sanity to him."

Brideswell held two pieces behind his back. "Which hand?"

"Your left." He pointed. "I am thought to be Andrei. I believe it. Seems right." He pursed his lips and raised his chin. "Sister Katrina from the convent insists I'm to be known as 'Brother Andrei' ... but I have no spiritual gifts. Easier for her nuns when I go there to hear them sing. They'll be very shy – a man choirmaster. She's right ... I need to be 'Brother Andrei'."

Brideswell agreed. "I have a friend in London from the same Order. He's known as Brother Robert. I'm used to the term."

"But not on me, please." He had chosen a black pawn. "So ... I'm to defend. I'm used to that also."

Each laid out their pieces. "I'm surprised, Lyovotchka, I remember which way they go."

For some inexplicable reason he named Brideswell with a familial diminutive. It came as a complete surprise – perhaps, he thought, someone from his past he resembled – a Leo? Not an English Pope ... Adrian ... he brought his mind back to the moment. A very warm and friendly gesture – he took the name with pleasure, and some amusement. He opened like he always did with his King's pawn, two spaces. The old composer did the same. Brideswell brought out his bishop on the Queen's side.

"Ah ... a bishop out already. I think ... I must have had a friend who opened like that." He moved out his knight to threaten it. His opponent moved up a covering pawn. "This is taking me back to something, Lyovotchka. Do you remember the fable of the little tailor who caught a small bird in his hand, in a mist? You see, I'm doing the same, coming out of a mist, remembering how to play this game you've challenged me to. Do you mind if I speak while we play?"

"Of course not. I have a friend Vladimir who does the same."

"A Russian friend. Perhaps it was he who taught you to speak Russian like a Pole?" He laughed for the first time. "But then he would have been a Pawel, not a Vladimir. Maxim tells me you're from the part of England close to Irina's sister – a professor of music?"

"She's English, but teaches Russian to a girl who comes to her to help with the house. I've been to Sasha's house. The north of England. We are friends."

"There's so much you have to tell me, my dear friend Lyovotchka." He moved up his other knight. "Do you have children?"

"No. I have a dear friend who has a son. He thinks of me as his uncle – and treats me as an equal. He's eight."

"Good. Then he likes you."

"Since I've arrived I've only sent Kenny one card. He'll be sad – he loves to show them to his friend Graham, a boy with a bad habit of taking them off him. Tonight I must get off another one. He'll be very upset if one doesn't come soon."

The old man left the table. The years which had shrouded and confused him, seemed to be falling away. He brought a photo in a frame from the top of his piano. "You see, I too have a little friend. She keeps an eye on me and reminds me about my name."

Bridewell's heart quickened. A chill reached up into his scalp. Instinctively he touched the scar on his neck as if the sensation had spread up from there. Slowly he placed the frame down on the table and reached inside his jacket for an inner pocket. He drew out his photo and passed it to Kutsov. The man was watching him closely. "You see, Andrei, I know her already. I know the little girl who watches over you."

"Ah ..." The old man breathed a long sigh, an expression which had its origins in a childhood a long time before, a separate lifetime. He shook his head, tears springing into his eyes. "You are also carrying in your heart my child. God has sent you to me, Lyovotchka. I knew it when I saw you. You are one of His messengers." He slowly turned over the copy of the photograph he had been passed and read the inscriptions on the back. He read them out, voice loud and full of emotion, as if addressing the ghosts and demons of his past.

"Anya ... Smolensk ... 1967."

He set it down beside his own. "Who is she, Lyovotchka ... you must tell me."

"She was Anya Marshievna Kutsova."

"Is she dead?"

"No. Married to an Englishman – though that's finished now. Her name now is Alice, except to Vladimir – Anya ... he brought her to England. "

"She was Kutsova ..." He wiped tears from his eyes with the flat of his hand. "Kutsova... that's a strange name, my friend. Is it Russian? How do we both have the same photo? Is she my daughter, Lyovotchka?"

"Yes."

"I knew she must be."

"I love her, Andrei. She is a wonderful woman. The boy Kenny is your grandson."

Kutsov could speak no more. From his pocket he pulled out a handkerchief and pressed it into his face, into his eyes, covering himself to shield the world from his sobbing. Brideswell reached out and covered Kutsov's hand with his own. The coughing and shaking subsided. Passed. Kutsov took the handkerchief from his face and with both hands set it down on the table, his fingertips resting within the folds of the material.

"So, my dear friend, now I know. You have come all this way to find me for her – to tell me who I am."

"Andrei Andreyevich Kutsov, the Russian composer, whose music is played all over the world."

A trace of a smile passed his lips. "With a daughter, a grandson, Dr Liadev's family beneath me ... and you, Lyovotchka ..."

★

House at Spissikoye

On an evening in August, Brideswell sat at a table against the window of a small study at the far end of the upstairs rooms, a floor he shared with a man who had become his friend, composer Kutsov. Spread out on the table in the full clear light of early morning was his novel 'House at Spissikoye'. It was pushed to one side; he had extracted three chapters and was writing quickly, reworking the opening to a flawed passage. Words came rapidly into his head, he wrote fast to pull them down lest they might escape ...

'Davidov had come to the monastery to calm his soul, to repent, to confess and to seek forgiveness from the Elder for a crime that was festering in his heart. A time to emerge from a net that was choking him to death ...'.

He paused, looked for a long time out of the window then continued, more slowly. The scene was there to be read; the events always followed – it was how he wrote. He put himself into the heart and mind of this man, haunted and distraught, a man who had strangled a young soldier, a guard who had barely begun his life, a boy who had raised his rifle to shoot him but the shot never came, fingers cramped, paralysed on the trigger of the Kalashnikov. A mother somewhere in a village weeping; two lives destroyed.

'Davidov smelled his fingers; the soap from the young soldier's neck clung to them – soap, death, after-shave. He could now eat nothing which he had to hold in his fingers, no bread, no fruit, neither the Holy Wafer nor cupped water from the snow-melt stream. A smell that could never be washed away. Everything from his hands tasted of death. Better he should have died in the camp than to have extinguished a life so young and innocent ...'

He put down his pen. What he was describing had shaken him. His door opened quietly. Andrei was standing there.

"Excuse me, Lyovotchka ... I've brought you some coffee." He entered with two mugs and drew up a high-backed wicker chair. "Did you hear me? I've had to stop playing that sad song from my prison days. The day is full of new light ... why relive the past. Can you leave your writing for a moment, and drink the coffee? I want you to tell me more about Anya and my little grandson Kenny – such an English name for a Russian boy. Show me the postcard you're sending him today."

Brideswell nodded and smiled. He lifted the card down from a shelf and read it aloud – translating for the grandfather beside him.

Smolensk. August 15th 1995. Russia.

Dear Kenny,

I'm living upstairs in a beautiful church with your grandfather Andrei and a wonderful family underneath us, the family of Dr Liadev. He is a very special person. My room is a bit like yours only bigger and I look out across a famous river called the Dnepr which flows on for a thousand miles into the Black Sea. I hope you're not letting Graham borrow these cards – you know what he's like with your postcards. I'm afraid I can't come home just yet but it won't be too long, in time for the football season. I bought a new chess set. Grandfather and I are playing some hard games but he's much better and usually wins. When I come home I'll bring you some things he wants you to have and some piano pieces he's written for you. He is so happy to have an Alice and a Kenny now. Please give all my love to Alice and say I'll phone her in a few days. Your grandfather sends you love, kisses and hugs, and so do I.

Uncle Michael

Andrei Andreyevich placed his hand warmly on Brideswell's shoulder.

"Let's go out and post it together."

"I think it needs an envelope."

"Come into the music room. I have one in my desk already addressed to him with the stamps on. I didn't know what to say ... you'll have to teach me English. And tell me everything.

"I will."

Andrei Andreyevich went to the piano and played a melody Brideswell hadn't heard before. He asked him about it.

"Would that be something of yours? Could it be from your piano suite – 'Six pieces from a wedding'?"

The old composer said nothing but played the same melody once more. The second time it was no longer distant and ethereal but firm, outward and reaching far beyond a curtained memory, as if several windows onto his mind were being cracked open.

*

The Dnepr

Brideswell sat on his own, on the same bench where he had sat four weeks before and talked with a woman walking her dog. He was moved by the great river, its eternal movement, eddies and swirls, ripples and reflections. The sky shining in it and on it. He was thinking about the endless journey each block of water had to make after leaving his gaze – skirting vast marshes and wetlands, receiving flocks of geese and mallard, past banks of willow and birch until it reached the great city of Kiev. It was there he had first met it – younger and less troubled.

He remembered how he lived in the city for a year with the family Dubowski. It was they who had taught him to speak Russian like a Pole. In Kiev the river was wide and reflective, a mirror for cupolas and a sounding board for bells. It had become wise, a river whose time was not measured but remembered, unaffected by fame or fall, passed over by long and graceful bridges. It was to Kiev what the Volga bestowed on another city with an old, new name – Nizhny Novgarod.

The same ducks were swimming towards him – their fledglings larger and no longer struggling to catch up with the adults. He made a promise to himself – one day he would take Alice and Kenny to that city and they would board the steamer 'Aksakov', listen to Yakob's balalaika band as they sailed down the mighty Volga to Lyskovo. And there, as once before Dr Liadev, Natalya and Vavara Davidovna had done on such a memorable day when the doctor chose his cousin for his wife, they would take a Georgian meal in the Café Azov. In the ancient market he would buy them presents, and, like the doctor, would ask his love to join him as his wife.

There beside the river another idea entered his head, Where it came from he didn't know. Perhaps, as Andrei had said he was a messenger, but not of God now – a vehicle for the Muses, a channel for a book already formed but not yet written down. A novel. A new novel about a journey to begin on the banks of the Volga ... a young librarian ... Ivan Fyodorov, an unworldly man familiar only with books, unaccustomed to the emotions of people. He is a poet, brought up by an aunt in a country house where he is taught to ride, to row, and is given unlimited access to his grandfather's library. He falls in love ... not with a woman, not then, not yet – but with a river ...

★

Post scriptum

London, Dollis Hill Lane NW2,
May 2000, January 2003, June 2010–March 2015

This book has been spread, one way and another, over the course of fifteen years. During that time it has undergone changes and I have been changed by it. It is hard to pinpoint where it came from, its origins and influences. I would like to draw from the circle of creation three forces of guidance, some special books, one piece of music and a thousand hours spent as a child beside rivers.

I thank from my heart my whole family for their endless support, encouragement, enthusiasm, belief in this work – and to Tom and Andrea for the mammoth task of typing out the second draft – and especially to my wife, Ann. This last and final draft has taken me six months; and I have enjoyed it. More than that, my thanks to Hill Slavid, a good friend, who read the opening aloud on successive weeks at his Stanmore poetry group, and parts of the new draft too – with ideas for changes. I thank Professor Robin Hull in Scotland for his rich supply of information and photographs from both Smolensk and Nizhny Novgarod.

Three books and one composer have been inspirational:

    Vladimir Soloukhin: A time to gather stones.

    Ivan Sergeyevich Turgenev: First love and other stories.

    Sergei Timofeevich Aksakov: A Russian gentleman.

The composer – Beethoven; within whose music this story was first conceived.

I am reluctant to leave Brideswell in Smolensk but he has no further need of me, and he has another book to write after completing the three rejected chapters in 'House at Spissikoye'. And though his last convulsion was severe and dangerous, it was the first in nearly three years. His travelling from now on will be by bus, train, ferry and river steamers – he will not be able to drive.

    I wish him luck, happiness ... and say goodbye.
    To a friend.

*